TEMPLE
OF
CONQUEST

MARK BROE

TEMPLE OF CONQUEST

A NOVEL

CamCat
Books

CamCat Publishing, LLC
Brentwood, Tennessee 37027
camcatpublishing.com

Hardcover ISBN 9780744301311
Paperback ISBN 9780744300987
Large-Print Paperback ISBN 9780744300451
eBook ISBN 9780744300994

Library of Congress Control Number: 2020937877

Cover design by Maryann Appel

53124

Thank you to

*Eleanor Broe, Timothy Broe, Joshua Koenke,
Andrew Steiner, Christopher Broe,
Alexander Fawcett, Bridget McFadden, Helga Schier,
Cassandra Farrin, and Jazmine Kuyayki Broe.*

Chapter 1

Telep had two hands. One gripped the jagged stone and pulled him higher on the rock face while the other held a wooden cup filled with tea. He held it steady near his chest as he climbed, the steam licking the side of his face. A brown leather satchel hung from his shoulder and swung back and forth as he ascended. It was not a difficult or long climb, though doing it with one arm did increase the challenge. He had climbed it many times, always trying to find a new path to the top. This time he chose the easiest steps and holds, as balancing the beverage surpassed any natural desire to test himself. Even holding the tea, he moved up the rock face with a swift grace that he had been honing for as long as he could remember.

The brightness of the full moon cast hard shadows across the rock face, though he did not rely on the light. He could find the holds in pitch dark, so on this climb his focus stayed on the brim of the wooden cup and not letting any more tea spill over.

He had spent his childhood practicing on this rock face. It was one of the only ascents in the mountain hills of Eveloce that had large bushes at its base, which proved very valuable on more than one occasion. The tall greenery's long supple branches, sticky with sap, hid small brown thorns, which contributed to the array of light scars on Telep's back.

Telep almost never climbed a face the same way twice. He often sought out new paths and new techniques and new maneuvers. By the time he was thirteen solars in age, Telep could ascend the wall faster than anyone in Eveloce. Even the most accomplished climbers marveled at his skill, and he began to draw the attention of the elders.

When Telep reached the top of the face, he rested the tea on the ledge and pulled himself up. He looked far and away—to the edge of land where white water shone amid the jagged rocks littering the surrounding sea, all the way to the horizon. People referred to the rocky formations surrounding the island of the Mainland as "jagged rocks," though they more closely resembled clustered mountaintops poking through the sea—large immovable barriers making outward seafaring impossible. The tide was high, so only the tops of them were visible, but when the tide was low, Telep would gaze far out at the rocky maelstrom and imagine himself climbing from one to the next, all the way to the horizon.

He sat with his back to a rock, out of sight of anyone coming down the trail, and covered the cup with his hand. He waited. His chest rose and fell. The faint sound of trickling water created a sense of serenity. Keeping one eye closed, he looked to the moon and relished in its immense brightness. The full moon was nearly as large as a fist held at arm's length. He gazed at it—its pure white surface, the slight red luminescence around it, its dark gray pools that moved across it during the night.

Familiar footsteps pattered from up the trail—bouncy yet soft, more a skip than a walk. He stayed behind the rock until the footsteps passed by. He then saw her from behind. Her tattered woolens cut off above the ankle, her short but sleek legs hurrying to keep up, the wet handprints on the ass of her pants that waved to him as she bounced along, the way she held a book to her chest with both arms—it all gave Telep an auspicious excitement as he crept to his feet. He slunk up behind her until she was close enough to touch.

"Excuse m——" he began.

She spun around in such terror that he stopped mid-sentence.

"Hey, hey, it's me," he said holding up a calming hand.

She put a hand to her chest. "Telep!"

He laughed and tried not to spill the tea when she slugged him in the shoulder.

"I'm sorry, Root. I didn't mean to make you scream."

She looked to the sky, still breathing heavily.

"This is for you, for your voice." He held out the cup of simmering tea. "I'm sorry, Ell." She looked at him with playful grumpiness, followed by a smile.

"Aw, how did you get this up here? It's still hot," she said, tucking her book under her arm and taking the cup.

"I have my ways." He put his hand on her shoulder and thumbed the side of her neck.

She glanced down at the creamy liquid and brought it up to her face. The fresh, soothing aroma overwhelmed her senses.

"You came to meet me?" she murmured, nudging him with her shoulder.

"Of course. I gotta take care of you." He pulled her close, and they continued down the path.

She smiled with pinched lips in a way he found endearing.

———

Gripping her hand, he pulled her up the grassy slope until they stood on top of the ridge overlooking the Temple of the Moon, an enormous land basin of light soil carved out of the ground. It stretched at least four stone throws across. Telep pulled a dark wool blanket out of his satchel and spread it out for he and Ell. They sat with their legs hanging over the edge of the basin while gazing into the distance. The bright soil glowing in the moon's light made all else seem darker, like the edges of a dream. Cool, soft light reflected on Ell's face giving her an angelic glow.

Telep undid the clasp on his sandals and set them aside. Putting his hand on Ell's thigh and sliding it down past her knee, he grabbed her woolens and raised her foot to remove her sandals as well. Then he lay back, gazing at the points of light in the sky.

His eyes drifted to Ell's long dark hair nearly touching the ground as she sat upright. He reached out and touched her, gently sliding his fingers over her back.

"Ell."

"Um-hum?" She set the cup down, making sure the steaming liquid wouldn't spill.

"What's on your mind?"

She paused before answering.

"Do you think we're going to make top tier?"

"What?" He pinched her shirt and pulled her back on the blanket. Rolling onto his side and pressing his body into hers, he looked at her. "Of course we are."

"Okay." A wind whisking through the grass calmed, and their ears rang with silence. "Sometimes I worry. The elders let so few people up there. Sometimes I just can't see it happening for us." Ell's gaze remained fixed in the sky.

"Come on, Root. Your father and I are a great team. Since the collapse of the North Rim, he and I have delivered twice the supplies as the next most efficient team." He nuzzled his face into the side of her neck.

"I know. Sometimes the elders just seem . . ." She was lost for a moment, unable to finish her thought, or perhaps unwilling. The thoughts weighing on her mind dispelled with the tickle of Telep's tongue on her neck. She took a breath, seized his shirt, and rolled on top of him.

In so doing, her foot knocked over the cup. Tea spilled over the edge and ran down the light sand of the basin.

Chapter 2

Hot, white slits of sunlight drifted up Telep's cheek as he lay in bed. The blinding light squeezed through the gaps in the wooden shutters covering his bedroom window. When the light finally reached his fluttering eyelids, he stirred and recoiled. Purpose and routine dragged his feet to the floor where he pulled on his climbing attire: thin woolens to increase maneuverability, a knit shirt that hugged his body tighter than the shapeless tunics that could snag a rock, and a pair of firm sandals that were closed at the toes and had extra straps extending up his calf. He'd had the same climbing garments for several solars now, and they had become worn and tight on his growing frame. His wool trousers barely extended past the calf. His toes had blisters from being forced into outgrown sandals, though he always seemed to stretch the leather a little bit more every time. His knit wool shirt had started off white, but solars of grazing rock faces had stained it a reddish brown. Every time he put it on, he pulled the fabric away from his chest to stretch it out a bit.

Out of the saltbox, he pulled two chops of lamb and put them on a thick slice of hard bread. Grabbing his large lumber satchel, he was almost out the door when he heard his parents descending the stairs. Both stood a head shorter than Telep, though his father sounded much larger the way he stomped down the steps. Both of them wore robes, his mother cinching hers, and his father making no such effort.

"What's the cargo this sun?" his father asked.

"More dark wood," Telep said.

"Alright. So, when will it be done?"

"The Temple of the Sky?" Telep asked the question even though he knew what his father meant.

"Yeah. You've taken so much lumber up there, can't it reach the sky yet?" His father crossed the kitchen and leaned on the saltbox to stretch his back. His mother followed behind impatiently.

"Did you get enough breakfast?" she asked, trying to lift the wooden hatch of the saltbox, which her husband's lean made impossible.

"Yes, Ma. I'm fine."

"When are you back?" his father groaned amid a deep stretch.

"Should be back tonight."

"Neil, would you move?" his mother pressed.

"No classes this sun?" his father asked, and then turned to his wife. "He said he ate, hun."

"Can you just stretch on the floor?" she shot, still pulling on the saltbox lid.

After a moment of silence, Neil laughed and grabbed his wife around the waist.

"You want to put me on the floor?"

She giggled.

"Yeah, I'll be back tonight," said Telep, turning out the door. The laughing got louder as he closed the door behind him.

Blue skies radiated overhead as he walked the main path to the wood stockade, which had been moved after the collapse of the North Rim. The collapse had slowed the transportation of raw materials on Eveloce, and Telep found himself busier than ever. He and Ell's father, Caleb, were among the select few who were able to scale the South Rim with a decent payload of cargo.

Construction of the Temple of the Sky had slowed considerably with the supply of materials dropping off after the North Rim's collapse. Though most of Eveloce's habitants were skilled climbers, only the best were able to traverse the jagged vertical faces leading to the top tier crescent. This was where the highest elders and mountain elite resided. It was also where many of the most sacred temples were built.

Telep looked up to the top tier with admiration. To him it was something to strive for, something to idolize, a place embodying the pinnacle of human endeavor.

Even in his earliest memories, height had enthralled him. His mother liked to speak of his infancy when he would sit at the bottom of the stairs as if in a trance, his eyes fixed on the top step.

Telep couldn't deny that he found much of his identity in climbing. It made him valuable in Eveloce. It gave him a chance to advance his societal rank to top tier. And it was through climbing that he had met Ell, his love, the girl he wanted to hold until his last breath. Climbing put it all within his reach.

Looking up the path to the wood stockade, Telep saw the brawny silhouette of Caleb. This surprised him as he almost always reached the stockade first; something he did to show Caleb how responsible he was. He felt a kinship with Caleb because he was the only climber in Eveloce whose ability and zeal matched his own. They had been climbing partners for three solars and had grown very close. Looking at the sun's position over the mountain, he took a breath, confirming he was not late.

When he reached the stockade, he saw an inordinate amount of lumber behind Caleb, who waved him over with a smile. Usually there was just enough lumber for three or four stacks, an amount that he and Caleb could move in two sun's time, but he counted twenty-four stacks. Only two were dark wood, he observed, one already loaded into Caleb's lumber satchel.

"Morning," Telep said.

"Hey." Caleb slapped him hard on the shoulder, and they walked over to the other stack of dark wood. "I learned something about you, Telep."

"Yeah?"

Caleb knelt next to his fully bundled satchel and started examining the straps. "Do you need silver? Does your family need silver?"

All flippancy faded from Telep's face. He always tried to present himself to Caleb as well-off and capable. After all, he was Ell's father.

"No, we are fine. Well, I mean we need it; we all work, but—"

"I mean are you struggling? Does your family have debts?" Caleb looked at him with concern.

Telep bit the inside of his lip hard. "No, we are fine. We're more than fine."

Caleb jiggled one of the straps on his satchel and started tightening it.

"Why do you ask?"

"I spoke with Elder Anaea," Caleb said, standing up. Though he was a hand shorter than Telep, the power he asserted could intimidate a bear. "He tells me you have been bartering the price of the wood."

Telep looked down at the pile of dark wood, slung the leather satchel off his shoulder and knelt to start loading it. "We are fine."

"Okay." Taking a breath, Caleb knelt down to help load the satchel. "Listen, I know you can take care of yourself. I know you contribute to your family. And I don't doubt you could take care of Ell."

Telep stopped, a log mid-air in his hand, and looked up at Caleb as he continued.

"You know this landslide has been hard on everyone, the elders too. They are cut off. They used to get their supplies very cheap from the North Rim—"

"Anybody with a wheelbarrow could deliver on the North Rim."

Caleb grinned. He secured the last strap of his satchel, and they departed.

———

The South Rim had several sections of vertical rock face, and each one needed precise planning and execution. If a climber didn't know where the next hold was, there would not be much time to find it considering the weight of the load was enough to peel even the strongest climbers off the wall. Relative to his weight, Telep had the strongest hands in Eveloce but with a full load, there were times when they burned with exhaustion.

Caleb and Telep climbed slowly and steadily, resting after each section of vertical rock.

The sky darkened. Black clouds enveloped the horizon. The dark wood grew heavier as they made their way up the South Rim. Calling it the "South Rim" made Caleb and Telep laugh because prior to the landslide, it was known as the "Southern Cliffs." It was scarcely travelled because of its extreme climbing difficulty.

Halfway up the third vertical face, they looked to the next landing. They named it "The Precipice of Perdition" because it came before the largest and most strenuous section of the climb.

Telep looked up at Caleb, about ten holds ahead of him. He stopped and took a deep breath. The strong aromatic scent of wood from his satchel permeated the air. He felt honored to be carrying dark wood to the top tier. It was a very rare wood used in the most sacred temples. While the other supplies could be lifted up the cliffs using hoists, the elders required dark wood to be carried by climbers so it remained connected to the people harnessing its power. It had a smooth texture but was dense and heavy. The bark was black; the wood, dark gray. It proved very difficult to burn, but when dark wood did ignite, it released an intoxicating fragrance so palpable that people spoke of tasting it rather than smelling it. A dark wood fire sent thick dark smoke high into the sky. It was said that, if set on the top tier's burning pyre, the smoke could be seen anywhere, from the seawall of the south to the lakes of the West Isles. Everyone in the world would be seeing the same thing.

Telep noticed the humidity rising. The rock face felt moist to his touch.

POP! The sound pierced the air.

"TELEP!"

His eyes shot up. Logs of dark wood plunged toward him. He leapt from the wall and grabbed for the safety line, kicking sideways at the rock, trying to evade the falling logs. He gripped it. A barrage of dark wood whipped past him. A strong *WHACK* from the descending lumber rang in his ears. His left hand jolted off the hemp rope which began burning through his right hand, unable to support the weight. He forced his hand back on the rope, trying to stop himself from sliding, but the weight of the cargo dragged him down. Tiny pieces of calloused skin clung to the rope as it passed through his hands. With a pained yell, he cocked his hands in different directions and ground to a halt.

Again, his gaze shot up. Caleb was falling, his outstretched hands searching for the safety line just out of reach. Telep froze in terror. He stuck out his left foot, hoping it could help in some way, but all he felt was a whoosh of air as Caleb flew past him. His eyes shivered in horror as they followed his mentor, his friend, Ell's father plunging toward the rocky ledge below. An image of Ell shot in his mind—she was smiling so big as she always did upon their return from a climb.

Caleb kicked at a rock jutting out from the face. It pushed him forward just enough to wrap his extended fingers around the safety line. He gripped hard. The rope shuddered with tension. His feet swung under him violently. One leg wedged itself between two rocks, jolting him to a stop an arm's length above the jagged ledge. Caleb's bloodcurdling scream seemed to silence all else. He hung upside down from his jammed leg, bucking like a snared animal, desperately grabbing for anything to ease the strain. Between screams, each breath surged from his throat as a tortured wheeze.

Telep was still, just for a moment before panic seized his body like a muscle in spasm. The dark wood on his back became a suffocating weight; the purpose of the climb, instantly worthless. He wanted to tear the strap off his shoulder, but Caleb had swung directly underneath Telep's safety line. Jettisoning it could crush him. Stings of acid prodded Telep's chest. Something needed to happen *now*, but he couldn't do anything *now*, nothing that would quell the screams from below that were churning the blood in his veins.

"I'm coming!"

Needles spread through his hands as he released the rope and grabbed a hold barely large enough to support two fingers. He jammed his fingers into the rock and began to move across the rock face, away from the safety line.

"Oh God, oh God, oh God," he whispered. "Just hang on!"

His heart throbbed. His lungs churned to the beat. He continuously looked down to see his progress. Caleb finally found the safety line and pulled the weight off his trapped leg in spurts, his screams turning into low roars of agony.

When Telep was a couple body lengths to the side, he slid the satchel off his shoulder, and the bundle shrank peacefully along the cliff before erupting on the rocky ledge. The worn leather popped, spewing dark wood in all directions. One log bounced much farther than the rest, striking Caleb in the chest. A pained cry shot up the cliff, consuming Telep's ears.

"Fuck! Fuck! Fuck!" gritted Telep, grinding his forehead into the rock. For an instant, thoughts of disbelief invaded his mind —This was a dream. This wasn't the sun he climbed second; he was first as usual. His parents playfully arguing in the kitchen. He was just at home. How did he get here? Ell's smitten smile. *Fuck. Everything was perfect!*

He shook his head, then struck it against the rock.

"I'm coming!" his voice cracked. Looking down, he saw Caleb's safety line wedged between the two rocks along with his leg, and he wouldn't dare climb down his own safety line that Caleb was using for each excruciating breath. He found a lower hold, grabbed it, and began his descent. He moved fast. His speed, usually accompanied by a sleek elegance, was replaced with fear and panic. He jammed his fingers into holds and kicked his feet into steps almost with malice.

Once low enough, he dropped to the ledge and leapt from rock to rock until he reached Caleb.

"I'm here, I'm here."

Caleb's face was blood red.

"Telep, you gotta unwedge it!" Caleb sputtered between breaths. Telep put both arms under Caleb's back, trying to ease the strain, but Caleb pushed him away.

"No. The leg. Get it out!"

Telep gaped at the leg. A yellowish bone stuck out just above the snared knee. Large lacerations tore through the discolored calf, dark purple and red. Telep reached for the ankle but then pulled away.

"Do it!"

Telep squirmed his hand behind the trapped foot, gripping the heel. Caleb made a pained cry through his clenched jaw that made Telep take a single breath before ripping the leg free from the rocks. A pop, a tear, a scream, and Caleb passed out. Telep held his weight by his limp and mangled extremity and lowered him to the rock below. He could not reach far enough to lay his whole body down. When he let go, the body fell like a sack of damp wool. Telep looked at the converging rocks dripping red, then down at Caleb whose blood was amassing under the shredded limb.

Chapter 3

The medical tent had a tangy odor, like a barrel of lime peels had been left there. Telep sat hunched at Caleb's bedside. A low fire crackled in the corner as a small piece of fuzz floating over the sedated body kept him mesmerized.

The medic burst through the leather flaps and Telep jerked to attention.

Ell followed on the medic's heels, her face frozen in distress.

"Any change?" asked the medic as he slapped his fingers on Caleb's jugular.

"No," Telep said, receiving Ell, who gripped his shirt in her fists, never taking her eyes off her father.

"Papa, can you hear me?"

"He's had five drops of hondrekk milk; he won't be hearing anything for a while," said the medic as he threw the blanket off Caleb's leg.

Telep's shirt stretched in Ell's hands. She let out a pained gasp at the sight of what was underneath the blanket. The leg was black and swollen to nearly twice the size of its counterpart. A rope tied tightly just above the knee contained the discoloration. The tips of his toes were black as soot. Dark purple streaks surrounded every gash in his calf, the biggest one spewing a dark yellow puss. Telep clenched his jaw and swallowed the lump in his throat. Never had he seen such a thing. It sickened him.

The disgusting and grotesque limb was useless. The weight of it sank in like death, staining the symbol Caleb embodied, robbing its purity. The man he had known was different and he would always be different. Looking at him now, his body seemed smaller, weaker, dependent—the antithesis of what he'd been.

The sight of it brought tears to Telep's eyes. Instinctively, he looked to the ceiling and tightened his arms around Ell, pressing her head to his chest.

"The leg has to go." The medic's stoic gaze didn't flinch.

Ell shuddered. "No! You can't. He will heal. I know he will, even if it takes four seasons. He will heal!"

"The bone in your father's leg is shattered.. This isn't a choice." His voice was cold.

Ell released Telep's shirt and faced the medic. "There is *always* a choice!" she screamed.

The silence that followed her outburst was palpable.

The medic let out a breath, his mouth in rigid restraint, just waiting.

Streams ran down Ell's cheeks. She softened, both in body and voice.

"But he's a climber," she pleaded with an expression that made Telep want to hold her tighter.

The medic walked past and began stoking the fire. "All I can do for him is take the limb."

Ell's body shuddered. Telep struggled to keep his arms around her.

"All you can *do* for him?!" she shrieked, lunging toward the medic who stepped back, surprisingly composed. Telep held Ell back, and soon her body softened again. She buried her face in his chest. He felt the fury heating her breath as she sobbed. Telep rested his cheek on top of her head and turned to the medic, who stared at a host of tools hanging on the wall. Among them was a hacksaw as long as his arm and a large file meant for smoothing bone.

The medic exchanged a glance with him and leaned in close, whispering, "She can't be here for this. I may need another pair of hands. Stay close so I can call you, but make sure she stays outside."

Telep's heart pounded. The medic pulled back, catching his eye to make sure he understood.

"What would you need me for?"

The medic took a breath and leaned back in. "Hondrekk milk is a strong sedative. It can keep a patient under through a lot, but if he does wake, I will need you to restrain him." The medic checked for a pulse behind the knee of the wounded limb.

"I don't know what else I could have done. I washed—"

"Listen, son. You did what you could. It wasn't enough. The damage was already done. His knee was crushed. In two suns' time his urine will turn dark brown, and he will die. The limb has to go."

Telep looked away.

"You're the climber, right?"

Telep's eyes narrowed, unsure how to respond. He opened his mouth, but no words came to his defense.

"So maybe you can appreciate this . . . *I'm* the best at what *I* do." The medic held his gaze for a moment before nodding toward the exit and turning to his patient.

As Telep ushered Ell out, he glanced back to the medic reaching for his saw.

———

Ell rested her head on Telep's shoulder while they sat with their backs against the stone wall outside the medical tent. The sun had fallen out of view making the light tepid and uniform. On the horizon, the sky glowed red, fading into orange, the farthest clouds lined with gold. They watched the luminous aura of color slowly dissipate into a shadowed scale of gray.

Telep replayed the incident over and over in his mind.

Climbing for Eveloce was Caleb's whole life, aside from Ell. It was his lifelong pursuit to elevate them in the social hierarchy. He worked to be the best, worked toward the highest ideal, transformed himself into a symbol of that ideal.

Telep imagined what the high elders would think—that being a symbol required the presentation of an image, and Caleb's image was now reduced to nothing more than a cautionary tale of possibility lost . . . that he was disfigured, his image destroyed. The loss of a limb, the loss of a dream.

Rising to tier five was Caleb's dream, and the plane of the dream had been pushed so close to the plane of reality that it felt tangible, physical, like it was meant to be. Now there it would stay, one hold away, filling the view of those who believed in it and worked for it, taunting them, living in their minds so they would always know what was never to be.

Shame needed no sound, but the sliding of metal across metal from inside the tent gave it one. Shame needed no touch, but the warm tears falling from Ell's cheeks provided one. Things would never be the same.

Telep pulled Ell closer.

"Everything's going to be all right." The warm tears falling to his chest cooled his skin in the twilight air. "Do you believe me?"

Silence.

"No."

Silence.

"Why?"

Silence.

"I don't know how to believe you."

A rhythmic gnawing sound emanated from inside, their dream of reaching top tier slipping farther away with every slice of bone. They held each other and wept, pretending not to hear.

16

Hosts of thoughts bludgeoned Telep like battle-axes landing blows, each delivering a demoralizing realization, each harboring a stinging, undeniable truth: He would never climb with Caleb again—Ell would never be the same—the elders would advance neither Caleb nor Ell to the fifth tier.

The more he thought about it, the more he tried to cultivate hope for Caleb and Ell's future on Eveloce. *Caleb is not a broken symbol. Losing his leg does not change what he has done. How could such a man be denied after a life of devotion?* Though when he thought of Caleb's unsightly body, he couldn't help but feel detached from him.

Distant. Separate. The thoughts circled in his mind like hungry scavenger birds.

Telep looked to the darkening horizon. The clouds were no longer lined with gold. The red and orange had become a soft yellow and pale gray.

Every tear that Ell shed on his chest made his own eyes well up. He smeared them across his face. When the tears continued, he leaned his head back and let them roll to his ears. A lump formed in the back of his throat, and he knew he would not be able to speak without his voice cracking. Pursing his lips, he swallowed it back; letting out each breath slowly, careful not to make a sound.

He thought back to the last time he allowed himself to sob openly. It was when he was nine solars aged and his older brother Areto died. When the finality of death struck him, Telep lay in his bed and sobbed for the loss of his father's son, his mother's firstborn, his friend, his teacher, his tormenter, his rival, his blood, his brother. He sobbed loudly, screaming into his cotton-wool pillow until it was lumpy with tears. He sobbed his throat raw. And when he was done, a stillness settled in the air, and he made a conscious decision to never cry like that again.

Tears will fill my eyes, but they will drip silently from my face. Never again will I sob like a child.

Every time tears filled his eyes, he pressed his chin into his throat, and let no sound through. His brother had gotten his last sob, and it would remain that way.

Placing his finger on Ell's forehead, he swept the hair from her eyes. She stirred, sliding her hand over his stomach and holding his side. Silence came from the tent behind them.

He looked back to the horizon. The yellow sky was gone.

Chapter 4

Caleb stared down where his leg used to be, his gaze full of loathing. He lay in his bed, crippled by the feeling of impossibility surrounding his most learned desires. The feeling clung to him. A hundred and eighty seasons he had worked, climbed, and innovated for Eveloce—carried supplies, ran safety lines, carved trails, escorted elders, invented climbing tools, and trained young climbers. Now a hearing of the elders had been called to decide the future status and habitation of Ell and himself. In a few suns' time, they would be subjected to their collective verdict.

Thick shades blocked the bright dawn light, keeping the room in preferred darkness. His sheets were damp, and his body was limp with despair. He knew the ideology and credo of Eveloce and what it meant for someone in his condition. But deep down he held on to a glimmer of hope that maybe things would work out, maybe he would be surprised, and his lifetime of devoted service would be recognized in the way he had always dreamed, though he kept more hope for Ell than for himself.

Ell entered his room with a pail of water and a washcloth for him to wipe himself down. When he finished, Ell brought him a bowl of oats and orange berries and a cup of fresh milk. She sat at his bedside while he stared at his food.

"Ell . . . I want you to stay if you can."

Ell lowered her head as if this was a sadness she knew was coming, but then peered up at him with her readied response.

"And I want to stay with you."

Caleb swallowed. "My whole life has been about ascending these mountains—"

"I know, Papa, but—"

"It's not just about you and me."

Ell looked into her father's eyes, now moist, a sight she'd seen only once before.

"It means something, Ell. Being top tier means something. The cultivation of knowledge. Real knowledge. Proven wisdom and insight. The best artisans, the best smiths, the best masons and carpenters, the best thinkers and reasoners, the greatest minds and hands . . ." He stopped. Staring down at his deformed body, a tear rolled down his bruised cheek.

Seeing tears spill from her father's eyes instantly brought them to Ell's.

"You have so much left to give, Papa."

Caleb drew a slow breath.

"I cannot divorce my body. Everything I am will remain encased in this deformity . . . bound to a visible failure. My knowledge, in practice, allowed this to happen. On the mountain hills of Eveloce, everything my mind can give will be tainted."

Ell grabbed her father's hand, his skin as hard and calloused as the pad of a bear's paw.

"Don't say that. When I look at you, I don't see failure . . . No one has ever made it from tier one to tier five as a laborer. You are the closest there ever was. And I am so proud of you."

She kissed his hand and looked into his eyes, seeing something deep inside him . . . a comfort. It was him telling her that he understood how hard this was for her and not to worry . . .

that he was not broken . . . that he would find a way to continue on.

"I want you to stay."

She spun away with a sniff, squeezing his hand, then slowly letting it go.

"Ell."

"Eat your fruit." Her voice cracked.

———

Glaring anxiously at the shortness of his shadow, Telep stomped up the dark dirt trail toward the iron gates of the Temple of Law, his parents struggling to keep up.

As he walked, Telep heard a distant buzzing. He ignored it, though he felt an innate interest to see what it was, as he had never heard a buzzing quite like it before. As he continued on his way, it grew louder and louder until the sound was right next to his ear. With a quick hand, he grabbed at the air behind his head and the buzzing ceased. Something delicate and sharp was in his grasp. When he opened his palm, he saw an insect unlike any he'd seen before. It had a black head, a rich brown body, and a long, dark stinger with a green stripe running down to the sharp black tip which poked into his skin. Two large wings extended from a body spanning the width of Telep's hand; they were translucent with a yellowish tinge and the sun passing through them made golden spots of light dance on his palm. He threw it to the dirt.

The Temple of Law was a long, gray stone building with a flat roof, which slanted down very sharply in two strips, one on either side of the doorway. Water would flow down these slants into two knee-high flowerbeds extending into the courtyard. This was something that Telep would usually admire, but now it didn't merit a second glance. Everything of consequence lay inside.

He had gone to Caleb and Ell's home that morning, thinking

he could assist Caleb to the top of the fourth tier where the Temple of Law stood but found nobody there. Upon entering the temple, he saw them seated in the front, recognizing the cleverness of Caleb making the climb by himself. Three elders sat atop carved stones on the platform in front of Ell and Caleb.

The one on the left wore a gray robe and matching sash from which he pulled fruit. He threw the remaining peels and cores out an open window with surprising accuracy. The other two elders had maroon robes with ivory sashes and stroked long pointy salt-and-pepper beards as they whispered back and forth.

Telep sat behind Ell and Caleb, and when his parents caught up, they sat next to him. Caleb covered his lap with a blanket. There were a few other people in the temple, mostly friends in support of Caleb.

There was a hole in the temple floor centered in front of the elder's platform and a corresponding hole in the ceiling almost directly above it. When the spot of light shining from the ceiling disappeared into the hole below, the center elder leaned forward to speak.

"We are here this sun to acknowledge the contributions of Caleb of tier four and to determine his future status and that of his supported kin." His voice sounded drab and hollow.

The elder on the right with the slightly more peppered beard stepped in, almost out of embarrassment over his colleague's lack of enthusiasm.

"Are all those directly affected by this hearing present?"

Apprehension filled Telep for he knew the answer the elders were looking for would be "yes" even if he was not there.

Caleb sat up straight.

"Yes, Elder. I, Caleb of tier four, and my daughter, Ell, my only direct kin, are present."

Telep was not used to hearing Caleb speak so formally; it sounded unnatural.

"All right, let us begin. I am Elder Roh, this is Elder Edwin, and this is Elder Monix," he continued, gesturing progressively to his right.

Edwin stroked his beard and Monix made no acknowledgement of being introduced, though it did coincide with a well-aimed shooku core thrown out the window.

"We will be presiding over this hearing, and our decision will be in the interest of the communal whole. It will be final. Is that understood?"

"Yes, Elder." Caleb nodded.

Telep suddenly realized a strange sensation in his hand. He looked down at his palm where the insect's stinger had pierced him. The sensation had been there since entering the temple, but he'd paid it no mind. Now he could feel it growing. It was a kind of numbness, but different . . .

"Excellent. Now, what was your title upon birth?" Elder Roh asked.

"Caleb of tier one."

"And how long ago was that?"

Telep could hardly feel his hand. He flicked his palm, and a tingling tremor emanated out to his fingertips and back to his palm like a wave.

"Two hundred and sixteen seasons. Fifty-four solars."

"And how long have you lived on tier four?"

"Forty-five seasons, this leaf fall."

"And you are applying for residence on tier five, is that right?"

Caleb raised his chin. "That is right."

"Well, this certainly is unprecedented. No man or woman in history has worked their way up more than two tiers and you wish to ascend four," Roh acknowledged with admiration.

The strange numbness spread to Telep's wrist. He turned his forearm back and forth trying to stop his hand from flopping about.

"So, tell us what you've done for our community and its

evolution since moving to tier four, and what do you see yourself doing on tier five?"

Caleb took a breath. "I have transported material and supplies, thousands of loads between the tiers. Many were valuable loads, too valuable for the main road or in need of expedition requiring a more specialized route. I carried supplies to the workers of the North Rim during its construction. I have invented several climbing aids including the pulley platform you all used to get here. I have escorted many elders between the tiers . . ." Elder Edwin fidgeted in his seat. ". . . I secured safety lines and built climbing paths, most of them between the fourth and fifth tiers since the collapse of the North Rim." Caleb paused and wet his lips.

Telep bit the inside of his lip trying to keep his attention on the hearing and off the pulsating numbness now halfway up his forearm.

"But what I have really enjoyed," Caleb continued, "is teaching young climbers, getting them to realize their potential. And that is what I see myself doing on tier five. Having helped provide the fuel to the tier of the burning pyre for many solars, that is where I'd like to pass on all that I know."

Telep pictured the burning pyre near the very top of tier five, the symbol exhibiting Eveloce's constant pursuit of progress and the passion it requires. He let out a breath.

"As a mountain people, climbing is a necessary and invaluable skill for all of us," Elder Roh affirmed. "As events have shown us, the broad paths we've built cannot be relied on solely. And, through such hardships, your efforts and skills have proven vital to our community." Elder Roh paused a moment. "But as you know, Eveloce is a community of progress, ideals, the cultivation of our species' capacity."

Elder Edwin nodded his agreement while Elder Monix stared out the window, taking a break from his fruit. Elder Roh's eyes narrowed as he stared at Caleb.

"So, I must inform you, Caleb, that you no longer symbolize the apex of human capacity."

A lump formed in Telep's throat. He looked at the side of Caleb's face, hard as stone.

"If I may, Elder," Caleb said. "A man in my position may be able to more effectively instill teachings of failure prevention."

Elder Roh stroked his beard in contemplation. Then a new voice spoke out. It was Elder Monix, still gazing out the window.

"Let me ask you a question, Caleb of four," he began, his voice young, confident, and precise. "Do you like fruit?"

A moment of stillness.

"Yes."

"Of course. We all like fruit. It's delicious. It sustains us and gives us energy. Here, take a look at this." Elder Monix pulled a fruit from his sash and tossed it to Caleb.

Telep leaned forward to see. It was a ripe green and yellow pongo.

Elder Monix continued: "Tell me, is this a good representation of what fruit is?"

Caleb turned the pongo over, revealing a dark black spot where a worm had burrowed. Caleb stared at it, placing a calming hand on Ell's knee when she started fidgeting in anger.

"It is not damaged product I wish to provide, Elder, but knowledge and technique, of which no one has more than me."

Elder Monix furrowed his brow as if he'd been misunderstood.

"No one is disputing your skills or experience. *You* are the product, and you symbolize collapse. How can you inspire by the burning pyre if you represent a limit to what can be accomplished? You are the visual embodiment of failure."

A cold silence accompanied Monix's stare as if waiting for Caleb to accept what he had said. Finally, he leaned back, crossed his legs, and returned his gaze out the window.

Caleb's eyes fell to the stone floor. Elder Roh spoke next.

"This is the position of the Elder Council, and consequently it is our diktat that you, Caleb of tier four, be expelled from Eveloce with our utmost respect and gratitude for any and all human progress stemming from your hand." His tone gave the decree a feeling of inevitability that pushed the air from the hall. "Now—"

"I have a request," Caleb interrupted.

Edwin scoffed.

"Yes, the council will hear a request," Roh said.

Caleb drew a breath. His hand on Ell's knee tightened.

"I would ask that my daughter, Ell of tier four, remain in Eveloce. Neil and Adel of tier three have already agreed to accept her into their residence."

Roh and Edwin exchanged a glance.

The hair on Telep's arms stood on end. He gripped the back of Ell's pew, staring into the elder's eyes. He didn't notice the numbness in his arm creep past his elbow. Elder Edwin leaned toward Elder Roh and whispered. Telep placed his good hand on Ell's shoulder. Elder Roh nodded.

"Tell us, Ell, what is it that you do?" Roh asked.

Ell's body stiffened.

"I attend school. I am interested in science."

Telep could feel the anger behind her words.

Before Elder Roh could respond, Elder Edwin leaned forward, stroking his beard with his gaunt fingers.

"What do you do for the community?" he huffed.

"I work at the river of four, regulating the amount of water root."

"And how do you do that?"

Ell pressed her knees together.

"Well, there are markers on the riverside of where the water root should be, but water root reproduces very quickly, so it often moves beyond the markers and I remove the excess growth."

"I see. So, you do away with excess water root from the river on tier four."

"Well, I also have to rotate—"

"So, would it be accurate to say that any able-bodied man or woman could perform the tasks that you do for the community?"

Telep's chest tightened. His gaze burned contempt into the elder's forehead.

"Well, I—I don't think—"

"Would the statement be fair that with minor training—swimming lessons perhaps—someone else could carry out your communal contributions?"

Silence loomed as all focus shifted to Ell. Hatred of Edwin burned in Telep's chest. Hatred and dread.

"Yes," Ell agreed reluctantly.

A feeling of damning finality swept through the temple. Telep gritted his teeth; every breath he took fed a growing swell in his chest. He looked to Caleb, who had his head bowed and his eyes closed.

Edwin continued: "You have resided in the top tiers dependent on your father's contributions, not your own . . . and with no other binding attachments—"

"She does have other attachments," Telep blurted, standing to his feet. The eyes of the temple converged on him. The assertion was not a conscious choice so much as an impulse.

Elder Monix broke the silence.

"Are you married?"

Telep looked down at Ell who stared at him with wide eyes.

"I would marry her. I want to marry her." His mind raced.

"Are you self-sufficient?" asked Monix, as if checking requirements off an invisible list.

Telep stared at Monix's bored expression.

He doesn't want an explanation. All he wants is—

"Then sit down, son." Monix turned his gaze back out the window.

Hollowness swallowed Telep's chest as he slumped back in his seat.

"As I was saying," Edwin resumed, "without any binding attachments, it is the judgment of this council that you leave

Eveloce with your father, though you are more than welcome, once you are self-sufficient, to apply for residence on tier one. This hearing is concluded."

The three elders rose and exited. Caleb gripped Ell's hand. Neil put a hand on Caleb's shoulder and whispered into his ear. Telep stepped in front of Ell, who looked at him for a long moment before embracing him, neither of them wanting to speak first. He hugged her tightly but only one arm wrapped around her; the other one hung from his shoulder like that of a corpse. As her tears fell to his chest, the hollowness inside him filled with anger. It was a while before his mind cleared enough to feel the gentle pulsations of pleasure, pain, and numbness rippling through his arm.

Chapter 5

Though the cuts, bruises, and strained joints that Telep sustained on the South Rim with Caleb had been healing for nearly a full moon, he still felt their lingering soreness as he paced back and forth across his parents' small kitchen. With his long strides, he hardly took three steps before having to turn around. His father looked on from the corner.

"How could they do this? Under what moon and sky could they do this?" Telep fumed. A slight numbness lingered in his left arm, though he regained most of its feeling and control since leaving the Temple of Law.

"They don't think she's good enough? She's a genius. They didn't even give her a chance. She would do more for this community than they could dream. What have those elders done for the community? Zero. Less than zero because they force valuable people to leave!"

Trying to remain silent, Neil bit down hard on his bottom lip.

"He spends his whole life climbing the tiers. Literally climbing the tiers . . ." Telep shook his head. He couldn't keep up with his thoughts.

"She doesn't contribute enough? Horseshit! How dare they talk to her like that? She is Ell of four, not Ell of the Mainland. She doesn't belong there. What the fuck does the Mainland do anyway?"

"Hey!" Neil's voice cut through the room. He stepped forward with a finger pointed at his son. "You think you're better than somebody? You're not. You think Nexus and the rest of the Mainland is for lesser people? It isn't. We have given our lives to Eveloce and its ideals, but don't think for an instant that makes you better than anyone or entitles you to anything."

He was now a pace away from Telep.

"I know, Pop. I know. I'm just . . . venting."

"Alright, son." He pulled Telep into an embrace.

Telep gripped the wool of his father's shirt. Resting his clenched jaw on his father's shoulder, he looked around; the house seemed smaller, a dwarfed replica of where he'd grown up.

"Do you really wish to marry her?"

Telep closed his eyes. She was there.

"I would die for her."

———

Thick fog and cold morning dew determined Telep's pace as he climbed the trail from tier three to tier four. He was not accustomed to walking on the trail; he usually preferred the shorter, more vertical route, but the thickness of the fog and slickness of the rock made him think better of it. He had not made a decent climb since the incident on the South Rim, making this by far his longest drought. The elders had permitted his absence but were now growing restless. With the North Rim still incapacitated, and few climbers to transport goods to the fifth tier, needs were going unfulfilled.

Telep ignored the issue. Fulfilling the climbing needs of Eveloce had consumed his life for a long time, but now it seemed secondary. His focus switched to Ell. He wanted to see her every chance he could in the time she had left. It had been two nights since the hearing at the Temple of Law, and he had been helping her and Caleb pack up their belongings, but this sun he ascended to the fourth tier to see someone different.

Elder Grooms was his teacher and friend. He had taught Telep about the ideology of Eveloce and had counseled him through many trying times. Telep had greater respect for Elder Grooms than any other elder, even greater than the high elders of tier five who meditated at the Temple of the Mind. Telep wished Grooms had been present at the hearing. He needed his counsel now more than ever. He needed someone to straighten the swarms of conflicting ideas in his head.

As he walked, he imagined how the meeting would go. He would tell Elder Grooms about the unjust hearing and the obvious bias of the presiding elders. He would talk about the hordes of progressive achievements that both Caleb and Ell had made and could continue to make for Eveloce. He would lay out all the facts and articulate the injustice. When he was finished, Elder Grooms would be moved to intervene by appealing to the High Elder Council for a retrial.

Elder Grooms's home was a light gray stone. The house was burrowed into a hillside as if a lush green landslide had consumed the back half, making it appear smaller. The dark wood door opened before Telep could knock. Grooms's handshake was firm, but his skin was soft with age. The inside of the house was quaint, but the dark grain furniture gave it an expensive appeal. The early morning light poured through two windows on the same wall, which cast stark shadows in the main room.

Grooms offered Telep dark tea. He initially declined but then reconsidered to stay in his good graces. "I'm glad you came to see me," said Grooms as he settled into a heavy wood chair, leaning so far back that his eyes seemed to peer down at Telep. Light from the window shone brightly on one side of his face.

"I've wanted to come for a while now," replied Telep as he sat on the edge of a creaky stool, resting his elbows on his knees. The steam from his tea warmed his face. "Well, since the incident with Caleb on the South Rim."

"Yes, yes. Tragic, tragic. Such a skilled laborer and admirable man he was." Grooms blinked his shallow blue eyes as he drew a deep breath. "And very fortunate to have you to pull him off that ridge."

"Elder, he's worked his whole life for us, for me, for you, for every son or daughter of Eveloce. For nearly two hundred seasons he has given all of himself. His birth debt was declared paid when he was eleven solars aged, and he's paid it off nine times over. Doesn't that mean something?"

Since newborn children cannot immediately contribute to society, the care given to them is referred to as their birth debt. When they are able, each son and daughter of Eveloce begins working the debt off through labor. Once they contribute enough, their birth debt is declared paid, and a formal ceremony celebrates them as a positive asset in Eveloce. It is a rite of passage that most people reach in their late teens. Elder Grooms had presided over Telep's birth debt ceremony on the eve of his thirteenth solar, though he was frequently told he could have done it by his twelfth.

Grooms set down his tea.

"Listen to me, son. I know you are close to Caleb, but remember he is a son of Eveloce, the same as you, the same as me. And *She* must come first." Silence settled in the space between them. Grooms leaned forward in his chair. "Tell me, what does Eveloce mean?"

Telep looked down at the dark liquid steaming in his cup.

"Progress."

"Sacrifice, for the *sake* of progress . . . Were Caleb to stay in these mountains, he would be lessening everything he has done, cheapening all the greatness. He may not realize this right now, but as a son of Eveloce I believe time will bring perspective."

Telep looked around the room. He had been here so many times, but now it felt different.

"Couldn't he still teach? He's the most knowledgeable climber—"

Grooms shook his head.

"Thinkers teach with voice; laborers teach with body."

Telep stared vulnerably at the tea swirling in his cup, not wanting to meet Grooms's eyes. He took a deep breath, biting his lip.

Grooms kept a calm demeanor while waiting. The room remained silent.

An unquenchable dryness filled Telep's mouth. His lip throbbed from the constant pressure between his teeth. His toes dug into the coarse wood floor as a fearful breath quivered through his nose.

"What about Ell, Elder? Should she not be able to stay in Eveloce?"

Telep pressed his hands against the steaming cup as Grooms took a deep breath.

"As far as Eveloce is concerned, she has done nothing to individuate herself from her father."

Telep looked up, meeting Grooms's gaze.

"How can you say that, Elder?"

"My son, these are hard truths, but Eveloce is built on hard truths. It aspires to them, to make difficult decisions and accept painful realities."

Everything in Telep's body wanted to bolt out the front door and not look back, but he couldn't.

"Telep, you are a relational man, you always have been. But sometimes relationships can get in the way of what is truly paramount. And what you put first in life defines who you are."

Grooms rose to his feet and walked forward, the floor creaking under his gentle steps. His face darkened as he left the light of the window. He became a silhouette until the next window's harsh rays illuminated half his face. He cupped his hands under Telep's chin. Something in Telep wouldn't let him look away, his eyes remaining fixed in his teacher's fervent gaze.

"You have more promise than any climber in Eveloce. You can be a real part of human progress. A *real* part."

Telep stared helplessly into Grooms's eyes, which seemed to be locked on something inside him that he couldn't ignore.

"And in time, my son, you will have both your loves."

———

Telep spent the next six suns with Ell, talking with her, holding her, lying with her. They mused about their future, promising each other so many things. When the time for her and Caleb to leave drew nearer, their interactions became strained. The last two suns found little to say between them. He touched her more, wishing she would feel how much she meant to him, but something had changed. Telep felt this change most when looking at the mountain's rock faces as he walked between the tiers. Looking at them felt strangely like looking at a part of himself, a part that if lost, would render him like Caleb.

Though he didn't agree with what Elder Grooms told him, his words provoked true insight. He was a climber, and Eveloce was his home. And though he loved Ell, he forced himself to contemplate the possibility of letting her go, just for a while.

On the sun before Ell and Caleb were to leave, Telep went to see Elder Roh for permission to escort them out of Eveloce, as there was no way Caleb could traverse four tiers in his condition. All sons and daughters of Eveloce needed permission from a high elder to leave the mountains.

"Start early and you should reach the bottom of tier two by nightfall," Roh instructed, removing three pieces of silver from a ring inside his robe to pay for lodging. "Spend the night but be sure to wake with the sun. Leave them at the North Gate at mid-sun and return up the mountain. They will be met with a carriage in the evening. Do you understand? You leave them at the North Gate by mid-sun and return up the mountain," repeated Roh with cautious precision.

"I understand."

"Now, you will be leaving the North Gate at mid-sun. Let me buy you a bed for the night." Roh reached into his robe for another piece of silver.

"That's okay, Elder. I can make it back to my bed by nightfall. Keep it for the next shipment of dark wood."

Roh chuckled. "Grooms was right. We are fortunate to have you."

The dawn had not yet broken, but Telep could tell from the song of flutterbirds that it wouldn't be long. He could see his path in the light of the full moon. He was reminded of the last time it had been so bright and full, how he had been with Ell at the Temple of the Moon. He was hit with a wave of regret, realizing they hadn't been back there since that night. The beauty of the moon always brought Ell to his mind. This morning it was particularly bright. Telep looked to one of the lacus spots near the top of the moon that resembled a bird's wing. Sometimes a colorful light would hover above the spot, making it appear to be on fire, though this morning it didn't burn.

He reached Caleb and Ell's home just before dawn and was surprised to see them waiting by the gate, bags in hand. Ell's face was blackened in silhouette as the moon sank in the sky behind her. Telep yearned to be alone with her for there was so much he needed to express but didn't know how, especially in front of Caleb.

The going was slow but not as slow as Telep anticipated. Caleb had carved himself a new crutch, and it was obvious he had been practicing with it. On flat ground, he took long strides and kept a normal pace, but it wasn't long before the path turned downhill, which slowed his speed significantly.

The sun broke the horizon as they reached the base of the fourth tier. It was there that the terrain started to slope more sharply. For the steeper sections, Telep stood behind Caleb, holding onto his upper body, then they stepped down together, their three legs making a tripod. Telep soon felt foolish for thinking he'd get to spend time alone with Ell during their journey. Assisting Caleb was a constant task. It felt strange having the once greatest climber in Eveloce cling to him for stability.

It was mid-sun when they reached the base of tier three. Caleb sat on a large flat rock to rest.

"I'll go refill the waterskins," Telep volunteered.

"Actually Ell, why don't you do that? I'd like to have a moment with Telep."

Ell put down her satchel and gathered the skins, disappearing toward the stream. Telep took a seat next to Caleb, carefully stepping past him to be on his leg side.

"Beautiful sun."

"Yeah," Telep replied, though neither one of them made an effort to look up at the sky.

"What have you and Ell decided to do?"

Telep thought aloud for a moment. "You know, what's happening—it doesn't change anything."

"Sure, it doesn't change the way you feel, but it does change things. Eveloce is a way of life. You can't bend it to fit your own desires . . . Even if she comes back, she'd need to reach tier three before any notion of marriage could be considered. I'm assuming you'll be top tier by then."

The stark words hung a weight in Telep's chest. His gaze roamed the dirt between his feet.

Then Caleb said, "You know that drive inside of you to climb to new heights, to go where no one has been, to forge new trails? That doesn't go away. Remember that when making life decisions."

Telep's eyes widened. Caleb's words formed a bridge to a piece of himself he had never discussed with anyone or even fully understood. It was something he always felt inside of him—an innate force that weighed on every decision he ever made, that guided him and pushed him . . . pushed him toward something . . .

Telep thought of his own penchant for innovative climbing routes and urge to explore new places.

Caleb sees it in me; he must feel it too. And he gave it a name—the drive.

He looked at Caleb and felt a new closeness to him, like he understood him in a way no one had before. Then he thought about Caleb's drive and how it seemed entwined with Eveloce.

He doesn't want me to sacrifice Eveloce for Ell because I'd be cheating that part of myself.

Telep wondered if his drive was dependent on Eveloce the way Caleb's was.

After a silence, he asked, "What will happen to your drive away from Eveloce?"

Caleb turned to him with a piercing stare, restraining an intense torment.

The inn at the base of tier two was a small establishment, receiving most of its business from hired farmhands during the harvest season. Though arriving well after sundown, they still agreed to leave at first light. There had been some close calls in the later portion of the sun where fatigue visibly plagued Caleb. Now he wouldn't even receive a full night's rest. This concerned Telep, but when he lay his head on the soft pillow and his eyes rose to the ceiling, all he could think of was Ell.

Suddenly the leather partition separating his room from the next drew back, and Ell stepped before him wearing a white nightgown with thin shoulder straps and a hem well above her knees. The white of the garment glowed like the white of the moon and shimmered in its light drifting through the open window. A slight breeze blew through the room, pushing the shear fabric against her body, illustrating every curve. Telep blinked and blinked again, his mind losing the ability to evoke a thought. She only stood there for a moment before crawling into bed, but he knew he would remember that image of her forever.

He didn't know how she had slipped away from Caleb and didn't much care. She was here. He was here. And he needed her.

Ell slid under the wool blanket, facing him, though never meeting his gaze. She brought her hands up to his neck, then touched his chest, softly sliding her fingertips across the fabric of his shirt. She pulled herself close. Telep drew down the blanket to their hips, and Ell made a gentle sound. He brushed the hair from her face, gliding his hand down her arm, over her hip, and lightly landing on the small of her back to pull her closer. He moved his other hand into her soft hair and cradled her head under his chin. Feeling her warm breath on his neck, he pushed the strap of her gown off her shoulder.

Sadness overwhelmed him.

So many times he had lain with her, felt her body, held her close. But now the beauty in his grasp felt perishable, like it could turn to ash and crumble between his fingers.

She was leaving with no spoken plan to reunite, and he would go back to serving Eveloce, the governing body that deemed her *unfit*. The truth of the thought flooded Telep's consciousness in a way he couldn't ignore. To do so would be a delusion. There was a reason Ell couldn't look at him; this truth weighed on her too. He could feel it thickening and suffocating the air.

Telep's hand closed around her hair, squeezing so tight because he never wanted to let go. He kissed her, and he rolled on top of her, and he felt a powerful force swell inside him; he knew that nothing could wring out the hope he held.

———

When Telep awoke, the sun was already situated well over the horizon. The pervading light sent a sting of nerves through him that chased the fatigue from his eyes. *There's no way we'll make it to North Gate by mid-sun*, he thought, gazing out the window to check the sun's angle in the sky.

He took a breath and turned his attention to Ell, still asleep with her back pressed against him. Pulling her close, he kissed the side of her neck. She stirred with a groggy groan.

"S'it morning?" she murmured, squinting hard. It always took her a while to wake up, a trait Telep loved and hated. "It's so bright." She burrowed her face into the pillow. After a moment of stillness, her hand felt around for his, and interlocked fingers. Watching her calmed him. The last thing he wanted to do was rush, but the bright grassy landscape outside reminded him they still had a journey to complete. He forced himself out of bed with a grimace.

It was just before mid-sun when they departed the inn. Telep kept a brisk pace while his mind remained on Ell.

When they reached North Gate, the sun was gone. No carriage was waiting. The road was empty. *Has the carriage come and gone?* Telep wondered in dread, but he was relieved to see there were no fresh carriage tracks in the mud.

When he looked to Ell and Caleb, a heaviness came over him. Telep stepped close and gripped Caleb's broad shoulders.

"You taught me so much. I'll never forget, and in time I'll pass it on to future sons and daughters, and they will be better for it. Because of you, we all are better."

Caleb nodded. Then he grabbed the front of Telep's shirt. "You know I've come to think of you as a son, and this isn't going to change that."

Telep nodded. Caleb turned and crutched to the arch of the gate, his chin up and his eyes focused on the road. Telep took Ell by the hand and led her aside. Looking into her deep blue eyes, he couldn't bring himself to say what he had originally planned.

In that moment, those words disappeared, and new words came flowing out.

"We will see each other again . . . and it will be sooner than you think. . . . I hope you can find a way to believe me."

She bit her lip and looked down, then stepped into him, pressing her cheek to his chest. They held each other for a long time, but it felt like only an instant.

Telep's empty stare followed his footsteps as he made his way back up the mountain. But his mind remained below. The words he had spoken echoed in his mind.

Trees covered the lower part of the mountain, but when he came to a small clearing, he could see North Gate, where Ell and Caleb were still waiting. As the light on the horizon dimmed, a shroud fell over them, and they were soon left in darkness. Then off in the distance, the flicker of torchlight appeared, jittering as if attached to a carriage rattling up the bumpy road. As it neared, a strange feeling gripped Telep.

Three figures jumped from the vehicle and ushered Caleb and Ell into the back. Not until hearing the clang of the iron hatch slamming shut did Telep realize: *That's not a carriage . . . that's a prison cart.*

Chapter 6

The precision of Elder Roh's instructions rang in Telep's mind as he raced down the mountain. *Leave them at the North Gate at mid-sun and return up the mountain.* He knew that was a prison cart. When he was a boy, his father had taken him out of Eveloce for a moon, and they stayed with Mainland farmers. He remembered seeing the subdued, beaten faces riding in the back of prison carts traveling north, past Eveloce, to North Hold, the felonious dumping ground of the whole Mainland.

Telep's foot struck the side of a rock, and he hobbled to a slower pace, dreading the pain that was sure to come. He had hurt his feet numerous times while climbing and knew this would be painful from the sound. It began throbbing, but he kept hobbling down the path. The thought of Ell and Caleb in the back of a prison cart spurred him faster. He began to feel dizzy. A constricting blackness narrowed his vision, but he pressed on.

By the time Telep reached North Gate, the torch fire of the cart was out of sight, escaping down the southbound road. Telep thought for a moment, trying to make sense of things. *Did the elders arrange for that cart or have Ell and Caleb been abducted?* He deduced that they had to be going to Nexus. On the Mainland anyone who didn't live in Nexus or Eveloce was a farmer, hillsman, prisoner, or from the West Isles.

Telep stepped on the main road, trying to remember exactly what he had seen. He closed his eyes. It had been so dark, but he thought he remembered the crisscrossing iron on the back of the cart as the torch passed in front of it. He cursed his uncertainty.

The chirps of grass bugs accentuated the silence as he walked alone in the darkness. Fear prodded what he did not know—which way to go? Should he return to Eveloce and appeal to the elders, or follow the cart into the Mainland and ensure Caleb and Ell's safety for himself? There was no guarantee he could track down the cart, and yet, there was no guarantee the elders would know what happened. It could be an unrelated band that had abducted them. And even if the elders did offer a plausible explanation, he was aware that he couldn't be certain of its truth. Realizing this brought him to a decision.

He looked up to the torches burning high on Eveloce. Then he turned and hobbled down the road that led to the Mainland.

Keeping his weight on his heel, he pressed on into the night until his movements became sloppy with fatigue. He laid down under a merce tree, making a pillow out of his nearly empty waterskin.

He tried to scavenge for food the following sun but found very little fruit growing near the main road. He grew faint from hunger. It wasn't long before the road merged alongside a river, though its water was not as pure as up in the mountains. He refilled his waterskin several times trying to keep his stomach full, ignoring the bits of sediment passing over his lips.

Suns passed, and moons went. Time became erratic. On some suns, he limped down the road through the light and into the night, while others he moved sparingly for the sake of his toe. Eventually he started passing farms.

Every sun he saw new things; every night he slept in a new spot. Routine was gone. It exhilarated him.

When climbing in Eveloce, he worked to create novelty, and

novelty excited him in a way far more enduring than the fleeting high of taking a risk. The unfamiliarity he experienced on this road every sun flooded his chest with a feeling that only strengthened his resolve to continue on.

Still, with every step he moved away from Eveloce, he felt its growing pull on him to return. Desperately, he wanted things to be the way they were. He longed for his consciousness to jump to an alternate existence where the strap of Caleb's satchel hadn't snapped, but with each setting sun, he saw a different life for himself rising on the horizon.

There was no certainty as to how the elders would view his transgression or how their inevitable punishment would affect his ambitions of advancing to the fourth and fifth tiers.

In truth, he worried more about his parents. Sometimes at night, he would look up at the points of light in the sky and picture his parents doing the same. He would pick one light and stare at it, imagining the stream of his gaze would make that point swell so it might attract the eyes of his mother and father. He hoped that somehow, in the nebulous aether of conjoined consciousness, they would know he was all right. Thoughts of his mother concerned him more. His father always trusted him to keep himself safe, but his mother had no such trust. It sickened him at night, thinking of his parents' worry. Yet each morning, he continued south toward Nexus.

Suns passed, and moons went. The mountains fell away, transforming into tall grass and flat ground. Never in his life had he seen terrain so subdued. The calluses on his hands softened from lack of use. While he missed climbing and the feeling it gave him, the new sights and experiences filling every sun sparked a fire in his chest that he couldn't ignore. It was alive with unknown possibilities. The fire seemed to illuminate the image of Ell's face in his mind, and together, the images pushed him further away from Eveloce. He pictured her face, her lips parting in a full smile . . . then her haunting eyes behind the iron weave of the prison cart.

Slowly the landscape became hilly again with lush greenery.

Each sun, he would see a plant or tree or bug that he'd never seen before, and it comforted him, quelling the worrisome thoughts of Ell and Caleb, his parents, and his status in Eveloce.

One morning, Telep awoke to a loud buzzing. The incessant hum shot around his head chasing away any lingering reverie. At first, he thought it was an enormous drekk fly, and he shielded his face with his arms. But through a squint, he beheld the delicate frame of a bird, the tiniest bird he'd ever seen, smaller than any on Eveloce. As it hovered in the air, completely still, he could see its unusual pattern of white feathering, so fine it resembled fur. A blur of its wings surrounded its body, flapping as fast as an insect. It darted this way and that, dragging up the pitch of its hum as it moved. It looked at him with its little head cocked while the sun glinted off its black cherry stem bill.

Telep's eyes widened. He felt a buzzing in his chest as if the bird was flapping between his lungs. It was still, and then it was gone, zipping over to a bright pink flower. He studied the flower. Its shape almost resembled the bird, as if its reflection settled in a rippling pink pond. The bird fluttered its long-curved bill into the flower's corolla. Telep eased up to his hands and knees, mesmerized by the creature getting its nourishment. When the bird got its fill, it zipped out of sight.

Telep looked down at the grass and smiled. When he glanced back at the flower, he noticed it changing. Opening. Then as a breeze blew across the stem, the flower coughed out hundreds of crystalline spores. They floated past him like a plume of feathers. Never had he witnessed such a coalescing of animal and plant. Never had the natural order felt so elegant.

The bird drank from the flower, enabling it to release its spores and reproduce. Telep thought about this for the first part of the sun as he continued down the road. He decided to name the bird Still Bird because it could stay so still in mid-air.

The road persisted and food became scarce. He was lucky to find a few handfuls of berries each sun by foraging along the side of the road and the riverbank. As he walked farther, more farms appeared and with them, better foraging.

One sun he discovered a shortcut through the hills where he ran into a tribe of hillspeople. He spotted them standing in a semicircle around a swine carcass, still convulsing after having its throat cut. A shirtless man with dark skin stood over its quivering body with bloody hands shaking the swine's belly fat and laughing hysterically. Telep slowed his stride when they noticed him. After a moment of stillness, the shirtless man stepped forward and held out his hand, still dripping red. Telep reached for it, trying to signify that he meant no harm, but the man pulled it away. Laughing, he held up his palms and shouted, "Hey! I got blood on my hands!" The group erupted in laughter. "You hands keep clean, ya." Telep's face cracked into a nervous smile.

The group passed around an old knife taking turns cutting fur off the animal. Each acted as if they had the best technique, jabbering and pointing; some having a fast stroke and some having a long stroke. It seemed a slow process no matter who held the blade. Another man rose over the hill with a pot of steaming water. He snatched up the knife, splashed the water over the carcass, and scraped its body with the blade. The fur detached much easier. They shared the swine with Telep for supper.

Telep found himself bemused by the hillspeople. Everyone in Eveloce pushed hard in one direction for the sake of the whole. These people laughed and drank and joked. They didn't seem to have a higher pursuit. Their complacency made him uncomfortable, but he was grateful for the hot meal.

———

Many suns passed. The moon shrank and grew. Thoughts of Ell pulled him forward in his journey. Many nights she consumed his dreams; past memories playing over and over like a calming mantra.

He dreamt of the time he fell into the river on tier four and became tangled in the water root. Struggling and thrashing, he felt Ell's hands grip his body and pull him to the bank. He awoke in a tangle of tall weeds. He pictured the curve of her smile, a lure affixed in his chest. She had saved him. She hadn't even known him then, but she saved him. He pictured them standing on the shore of the river, the sand gathering between their toes, holding each other like the bond of humanity lived in their embrace.

The clang of the prison cart's iron hatch shutting rang in Telep's ears. He rose to his feet and walked on.

Chapter 7

When Telep approached the outskirts of Nexus he came across a hot spring. He knew about their existence, but none could be found on Eveloce. The sight of it struck him—bubbles churned the grayish, green water and sent steam into the air. Removing his sandals, he slowly dipped a foot into the water, and the heat sent a shiver through his body. It seemed so unnatural. Hot water without fire? He hadn't planned on putting more than his feet in, but before he knew it, his clothes were off, and he was up to his chin in the frothing water. His eyes closed, and his head slipped under the surface. He hugged his knees to his chest.

When putting his clothes back on after indulging in the relaxation of the hot spring, he noticed an odor of foul eggs. The scent became more pungent as he walked further down the road. He didn't realize it then, but it was the first time in a long time he had walked without limping.

He saw men exiting a small cave. They were carrying pails of a yellow substance into a nearby hut. He wanted to stop and find out what it was but forced himself to continue on.

Over the next suns, he made it past the outskirts, and the city itself swelled before him—Nexus.

The enormity of the metropolis dwarfed Eveloce. Buildings and streets and people extended as far as he could see. He wondered how so many people could live in such close proximity. Everything was condensed, and it seemed to go on forever.

Hordes of muddy feet stomped through swampy puddles peppering the town square. Telep squeezed his way through the crowd. He couldn't remember seeing such a striking gathering of people before. Assorted wood buildings of differing colors surrounded the square, and in the center was a rectangular stone basin filled with brown water. It looked primitive in relation to Eveloce, but Telep didn't let himself think about that now. He needed to look for someone who could help him. Thinking about the best way to locate Ell, he decided it would be more effective to ask about the one-legged man.

"What's my brother done now?" snapped one woman in response to his inquiry. He stared at her worn leathery face, and when she scratched the back of her head, he saw burns on her forearm, like scalding oil had splashed her. It dawned on him how many people outside of Eveloce had scars, physical ailments, or deformities. Far removed were the unblemished hills of Eveloce. Apparently in the Mainland, missing limbs were common. He decided searching for the prison cart would be best.

He looked around the town square. All the carts and carriages he saw were either transporting or selling goods, and those that did carry people had no iron confinements on the back.

After several lacking conversations, Telep took a deep breath. Normally he would stand back, observe how things worked in the city, and slowly wade into his new surroundings; but now, the pressure of time forced him through the people and workings of Nexus like meat through a grinder. And he enjoyed it about as much.

Making things more difficult was the fact that he didn't want to tell anyone where he was from or what he was doing there. As

Telep had been taught, many people of the Mainland aspired to live in Eveloce, but most were denied. He didn't think it would be beneficial to speak of his house on tier three.

Further down the main road, he came upon a carpenter sanding the large wooden wheels of a carriage. The man's large calloused hands reminded him of Caleb's, though not quite as massive.

"Excuse me?"

"Yea?"

"Could you tell me where carriages are made?"

"All over, yea."

"So, there are a lot of carriage makers throughout the city?"

"Of course, O."

"Who makes the carriages with the iron confinement on the back?"

The man stopped sanding and faced Telep.

"Te prison cart fa confine, eh? Ah, more o'dem been croppin' up hè, but I don do tat."

Telep stirred with excitement.

"More are passing through? Where are they taking people?"

"Na, no people. De jus buildin' em. Den dey go South End."

"To South End, but they're not carrying people?"

The man shook his head and turned back to his wheel as if he had spent his last word.

Telep stepped away and took a breath. It would take several suns to reach South End, the southernmost point of the Mainland. By nightfall he was exhausted. He lay down under the curving bark of a swaying tree but hardly slept. The moon shone through the branches above, and he thought about Ell. Tired and cold, he began walking before dawn. He reached the center of the city by first light, and it was soon dense with people. Shoulders nudged and people pushed. Someone knocked the satchel from his shoulder, and he quickly snatched it up, gripping it close. The churn of the crowd overwhelmed Telep.

He tried to move faster but speeding through the mass of

people only heightened the feeling. He walked awkwardly with short strides, trying to protect his sensitive toe from the hundreds of feet stomping all around. He moved to where it was less crowded but had to be extra vigilant of passing carriages and carts—their large wooden wheels rumbling over the street's uneven brownstone. It beguiled Telep how people could be at ease in this bustling fray, and yet everyone seemed comfortable enough.

Telep watched a fruit cart with uneven wheels wobbling down the road. He wondered why the cart makers in Nexus didn't use the same methods as in Eveloce to make their carts roll smoothly. He was grateful when a large bump in the road jarred a few fruits to the ground, and he was able to snatch them up before they were trampled. Though his stomach ached, he waited until he was away from the crowded street to eat, where he could sit under a tree and enjoy the podfruit, which tasted terrible.

As the city thinned over the next few suns, Telep noticed a lot of smiths, masons, and carpenters. Gradually things felt different, the marketplace becoming lost in a slew of industrial factories.

One sun, as the light neared the tree line, a cart rumbled past filled with battle-axes. They were new, with clean wood and fresh sharpening lines. Before he could think what to make of them, a pungent odor struck him. Its strength intensified as he made his way toward a stone building in front of a large mass of rock. It had a hay roof with sections that had been swung open leaving two large holes for ventilation. Next to the building stood a small stable. Not wanting to risk sleeping on the side of the road, Telep looked inside and was happy to see a small hayloft. Though he did not enjoy the smell migrating in from next door, he scraped some hay into a pile and slept.

Hot slits of white light woke him in a dizzy haze. He stretched, rolled to his knees and then to his feet. To his surprise, the sun was already over the tree line. He stepped out of the stable, the bright light shriveling his face, and walked to the shadow between the stable and the stone building. He noticed a cave extending into the cliffside. It sloped downward before disappearing into blackness. Approaching the opening, wet cool air pushed against his face, and pulled past him as if the cave was breathing. The unknown of it drew him in. He stepped forward.

He walked hesitantly, moving slower and slower. Light retreated from him, the entrance gradually becoming a small white dot. Telep felt the darkness envelop him. His outstretched hands connected with cool moist stone. Slowly, he walked his hands along its curve. The slap of his sandal on the cave floor carried a rippling echo. The wall curved so much he thought he must have reached the rounding of the back wall. He turned around. There was no white dot. No nothing. Fear swarmed through him as he realized there was nothing he could do to make his eyes see anything, like a sense had been erased. He stood frozen, his own breath shouting in his ears. Biting his lips together, he heard nothing but the ring of silence, disrupted only by the echo of a distant drip.

Then there was something else. Murmuring. A crack. He recognized the sound through the echoed distortion. Metal hitting rock. More murmuring. Voices. People were in the cave. Men. Out of the darkness a faint redness appeared, dancing on a distant wall, at least he hoped it was on a wall. He worried that it could just be the kind of color seen through closed eyes, but when he swiveled his head, the light remained fixed. Then it slowly brightened, and the voices became clearer, though still incomprehensible.

A pattern appeared in the brightening haze. Two glass torches swung into view. Their light made a bright circle around two figures that shifted with the changing shape of the cave as they walked closer. Telep backed into the moist rock. On impulse, he called out to them. At the sound of his voice, they shuddered and dropped their torches. Darkness flooded the cave.

"Who's there? What do you want?!" one of them yelled.

Someone was frantically rummaging through supplies. Telep thought of what to say next. He heard sounds of leather sandals scraping the cave floor, broken glass being kicked, a stick dropping.

"Shit!" cursed a low voice.

"I said who's there?!"

Telep stammered. "It's . . . okay."

"Who are you?" shot the low voice.

"I'm a visitor. I don't—"

"What are you doing here?"

"I just wanted to see the cave."

Silence.

"Alright, you bring a light with ya then?"

Then came sounds of a bag being packed up. *CRACK.* Iron striking rock.

"No, I don't have a light, but we're close to the entrance."

CRACK. A spark. *CRACK.* Light sprang around the men from the head of a pickaxe. Telep's eyes adjusted. One of the men screwed on the lid of what looked like a tin of oil and placed it in his pack before walking forward, careful not to step on any glass. The other man followed close behind carrying two pails. Telep remained still, squinting and leaning away from the flaming axe.

"Yeah, I know we're close to the entrance," declared the low voice disparagingly, making sure to catch Telep's eye before whisking the flame away. The man had a scar stretching from his eye to his chin.

Exiting the cave, the man shoved the flaming axe into the dirt and sat on a rock. He was stocky and strong, his black hair short enough to stand up straight but thick enough to hide his scalp. His scar was thin like a tear trail but protruded off his face like a seam. The other man was thinner and taller with a pointy face that remained taut and anxious. They both looked about his age.

Telep thought it best to wait for his nerves to calm before launching any inquiries into their business, but as he stepped out of the cave it was the low voice that posed a question.

"So, you're just a visitor, huh?"

"Yeah, I'm just—"

"Shit man, why you have to make us lose our shit?" chimed the pointy man looking over the supplies.

"Yeah, I'm sorry. I'm sorry about your lamps."

"Damn man, so you not from Southy?" The taller man began pacing.

"Pardon?"

"South-E, you're not from South End."

"No no, I'm headed there, but no, I've never been."

"So, you're from Eveloce," stated the scarred man.

Telep froze.

"Shit wait, you're from the mountains?"

A short silence passed.

"I'm not from South End, so I must be from Eveloce?" As he spoke, he watched the scarred man's mouth curl into a grin, and he knew how he had known his origin. The dialect and speech pattern of this man was the closest to his own that he'd heard since leaving Eveloce. The hillspeople were terribly difficult to understand, and he relied heavily on reading body language with the farmers on the outskirts. The tall pointy man sounded rather uneducated, but the short man with the low voice spoke with fluent precision. He wondered how this scarred man on the other side of the Mainland could maintain Eveloce proper. "So are you—"

"My father lived on tier one for seven solars. He taught me how to speak correctly."

Telep's eyes shifted to the pointy man, checking to see if he'd taken offense to the comment. He hadn't.

"Well, what is *correct* is really subjecti—"

"No," the low voice interrupted. "What is *proper* is subjective. What is *correct* is not."

They looked at each other a moment. Telep sensed the man's esteem of Eveloce, but he also resented his blatant piety; it made him want to expose the man's admiration for Eveloce as an unfounded naïveté. After all, what could this man know of Eveloce and its ideals? He had never lived there. But Telep decided to hold off.

"I'm Hal." The man leaned forward on the rock and extended his hand.

Telep shook it. "Telep."

"This is Peda," Hal said, gesturing toward his pointy colleague.

Telep shook Peda's hand, and Peda spoke.

"Telep is it? Well Telep, the cave dweller from the mountains, it's a pleasure. You know the mountains ain't the only place that speaks proper. My folks, born 'n bred in Southy, two of the originals, and they taught me."

Telep glanced at Hal's condescending expression over Peda's assertion and clenched his jaw.

"People speak proper in South End?" Telep asked with just enough emphasis on 'proper.'

Hal shot Telep a smirk as if to bond with him over Peda's laughable belief that he was speaking properly. But Telep immediately shot him a look of scorn, judging him for taking pleasure in his partner's ignorance.

Telep rarely disparaged people, hardly ever without feeling at least a tinge of guilt afterward, but in this case he didn't. There was something about Hal that stirred him. Eveloce is a beautiful thing because of the purity of what it strives for; that is commendable. Respectable. But the concessions that must be made to filter its ideology so purely are horrific. Those concessions are what tore Ell and Caleb from him. Taking pride in what Eveloce strives for is fine, but only if you understand the human connection that is being sacrificed. And smiling derisively at a fellow man's ignorance is not honoring that sacrifice; it's spitting in the face of it.

Hal's face stiffened into a piercing stare.

"Yeah, they speak proper," Peda assured. "They speak unproper too. All kinds in Southy."

"So, what are you mining here?"

"We mining bile. What, you don't smell that?" Peda gestured to the stone building behind him.

"Bile?"

"Well, that's what it smell like, don't it? I'm the one dredging it up. I'm the one kneeling by a pail of it all sun. And I'm the one sitting next to it on the carriage. So as far as I am concerned, it is bile."

"Is there a carriage coming for you soon?" Telep asked.

"Na, three more suns of bile harvest. Then we have a load."

Telep felt Hal eyeing him. He wanted to leave but needed more information.

"Do any passenger carriages come by here?"

"Yeah lots, every now and then," Peda replied.

Suddenly Telep wished he was getting this information from Hal, but the man remained silent on the rock, holding his stare. "Why all the questions, eh?"

"Did either of you see a one-legged man come by here in the last cycle?" Telep looked to Hal who didn't move.

"A one-legger?" Peda questioned. "No. I woulda made fun of that."

Telep glared at him.

"Why would you make fun of that?"

"To get it out of the way, ya know. You gotta bring it up I think. Or else it's just the thing that no one's talkin about. If you don't make fun of it, it just stays what it is, a missing leg, ya know . . . Man, Southy's gonna be overrun with one-leggers. The singing man, the bile burner, uncle Sal, the new climbing guy, and now whatever prisoner you're rootin' caves to find."

A wave of excitement rushed through Telep.

"What, wait. What new climbing guy?"

"He just started a few suns back. I wouldn't a noticed 'cept he's a one-legger."

"A one-legged man just started climbing in South End?" His eyes darted between the two, searching for confirmation.

"Ha! He's not climbing. Ep Brody hired him to teach."

Telep stepped forward with eager interest.

"And he started a few suns past?"

"Yeah yeah, pretty funny, right?"

Telep took another step, grabbing Peda's hand from his side and gripping it in both hands.

"Thank you. Peda, that helps me out a lot. Did he have anybody with him? A girl about our age?" He held on to Peda's hand waiting to hear the answer.

"I don't know ye, I just hear he a one-legger," Peda replied, a little confused by the excitement his words were provoking.

Telep looked away in thought until Peda's hand went limp, awkwardly seeking release. It occurred to him that now that he had decent reason to think Caleb and Ell were at least safe, he should lessen the mental footprint of his interaction. He had been so worried he didn't realize he'd been brutishly and shamelessly asking questions that he'd provided no basis for. Dropping Peda's hand, he looked down the road like he meant to get going.

He felt Peda and Hal exchange a glance.

"Your family run off on you, man?" Peda asked with a smirk.

"No, just want to pass along a message. Not sure if he took this road or the east road." He took a breath, about to offer departing pleasantries when Hal spoke.

"You a climber?"

"Pardon?" Telep stalled, trying to think how to answer.

"You express a lot of interest in a crippled climbing instructor."

There was something unnerving in Hal's voice. Telep looked

at his face, his chin raised and his eyes frozen in a taunting expectancy.

"He from Eveloce too?" Hal brushed his thumb against the scarred side of his face.

Not knowing how his answer would affect Caleb and Ell or the amount of influence Hal had in South End, Telep thought it best to appeal to what he knew of Hal's family.

"No," he answered sullenly, "not for a long time now." In his periphery Telep saw Hal's body soften, but just for a moment.

"He must be an important man for you to be granted leave to track him all the way out here."

"Indeed, he is. And afforded expedient notification of his daughter's birth debt celebration." Telep knew he tended toward larger words when he was nervous, but he hoped Hal wouldn't notice. Hal's jaw clenched. He was wrong. What he mistook as admiration for Eveloce was only respect. He resented Eveloce.

"Though I doubt he'll attend," Telep added. "He made it very clear that South End was his home now." He watched Hal's eyes light up for just an instant, and he knew he had found Hal's weakness—pride for South End. This surprised him as he had never heard any distinction articulated between South End and Nexus, other than it being the southernmost point of the city and of the Mainland. He felt confident he had lessened the animosity Hal felt toward him; he could head to South End with little ill will between them. With the exception of the scare in the cave, this whole encounter would be a faint memory by the next moon's cycle. But one thing remained curious: "What climbing is there in Southy?"

"None," started Peda, unwrapping parchment from a chunk of bread, "the climbing is south of Southy. For Brody."

"*Ep* Brody. His name is Ep Brody," Hal corrected.

Telep blinked in confusion. "What is *south* of Southy?"

"Da brig," Peda tried to answer through a mouthful of bread.

Telep looked to Hal who was staring back at him with a smug grin.

"Who is Ep Brody? How can I find him?" Hal rose and stepped within a pace of Telep, his eyes almost sympathetic . . . almost.

"Go to South End. If you're anybody, he'll find you."

Chapter 8

Deep blue light radiated overhead as Telep started back down the road toward South End. The shadows lengthened but then faded as a blanket of gray clouds rolled over the sky. A fine falling mist collected in his hair and dripped down his face. He moved faster, confident he would reach South End before dark. Before, he thought of South End as the southernmost point of Nexus and the end of the Mainland. Now, it seemed, there was more to it. What would inspire such pride in Hal?

The road curved along with a large river that Telep waded into to fill his waterskin. The water was warmer and darker than it was in the mountains where it flowed fast and loud through channels of brown rock. Now, close to sea level, the river browned and thickened and slowed to a walking pace.

Telep was relieved and excited when he saw a falling hill on the far side of the river merge into the dark gray and red stone of the seawall.

I am at the edge of the walkable world.

An emptiness formed inside him—a feeling of undeserving, like he was reaching the summit without climbing the mountain.

His pace slowed. He started to feel sick, the emptiness emanating out from his chest. He felt like the possible landscape he had so longed to see was fading in front of his eyes, and the sadness formed a lump in his throat. While back on Eveloce, the outside world felt limitless. He had then seen a very small percentage of it. Now that he walked across the foreign lands, it felt like it wasn't enough; an ocean reduced to a washbasin, a world reduced to an island. If he didn't see it, his wildest dreams could imagine that it could be anything. But once he saw the coast, the end of land, possibilities vanished.

Sickness clutched his heart, and his only comforting thought was of Ell. He imagined holding her hand as he walked, but after a while he felt like she was leading him somewhere he didn't want to go, and he resented her for it. His mind became light and dizzy. The lump in his throat extended down into his chest and stomach. He tried to keep from vomiting but couldn't.

He cursed himself for coming here, though he knew he would do it again given the circumstances. He wanted to see new lands more than anything. The trip here from Eveloce gave him some of the most exhilarating feelings he'd felt in his life. He didn't want the end of the Mainland to become a reality. The comfort of knowing the bulk of it was still to be discovered was about to be lost.

He came to a bridge extending over the river connecting another road that ran along the seawall. He noted the bridge's ingenuity and design. Its style looked so different from what he was accustomed to seeing in Eveloce. It was made of wood and had four curved arch beams, two on each side. They were stacked vertically with beams running between them connecting the two trusses. Never before had he seen such large wooden arches.

When he stepped in front of the seawall, the mass of it struck him. Each stone cube was as wide as his extended arm. The low reverberations of crashing water coming from over the wall resonated in his chest and seemed to take over his feeling of sickness. He continued on. From the other side of a rolling hill in front of him, he saw wafts of smoke rising over the horizon, just starting to turn orange with the setting sun.

When he mounted the top of the hill, he looked out and beheld South End. The sickness he felt dissipated as he took in the view, not just of the city but of the largest structure he had ever seen lying beyond it—a colossal tapestry of iron and wood. It started in the city square in front of him. Its massive iron girders rose high above the seawall and formed the base for a long platform that extended out over the water and jagged rock, far into the blue. It rested on a mountain rising out of the sea far higher than the jagged rocks littering the water. It was a seacliff. Even the highest tide wouldn't come close to covering it.

More land! This is a bridge leading to more land beyond the wall! Telep's chest fluttered.

As the sun neared the sea, its light reflected off the water in a shimmering stripe that diverged from the bridge, creating a 'V' that extended out to the horizon. Telep saw this as the most breathtaking intersection of man and nature, and in that moment, he felt the two converge on him. Tears filled his eyes.

Looking out to the south and the west, he walked along the stone path overlooking the city square, where the start of the massive structure was the centerpiece. There was wooden scaffolding scattered around the base of the structure, still under construction, though it appeared to be fully functional. Men and women walked on the girders, carrying thick planks of wood. Similar planks spanned the iron beams, extending out over the water to create the bridge's platform.

As he began his descent into the square, he noticed the smoothness of the stone path. Even on the decline, it retained a consistent and gradual slope far superior to the stonework in the city square of Nexus, though not quite matching that of Eveloce.

As he continued, he noticed a grassy hill to his right. In the middle of it stood a stone building with a hay roof overlooking the square, much like the building he had passed earlier after soaking in the hot spring. A familiar noxious odor leaked from it, reeking of foul egg. It smelled like the air itself had been burnt. *Is this where Hal and Peda's 'bile' is refined?* He snorted it from his nose and looked ahead.

There was much going on in the square—the clanging hammer on a blacksmith's anvil, the rhythmic buzz of carpenters sawing wood, the intermingling footsteps of workers and pedestrians, the call of merchants announcing end-of-the-sun sales, even children laughing and playing. Despite all of it, he found it difficult to keep his eyes off the gargantuan structure.

As he descended lower, he noticed more intricacies. Underneath the wood planks of the bridge was a zigzag pattern of iron girders providing support, but they were much thinner than the enormous beams making up the base. These beams extended down into large stone shoes scattered around the square. He watched a group of kids run after a young boy who used one of these stones as a barrier to hide behind. When the group came around one way, he ran the other. It didn't take the group long to split into two and go around both ways at once.

As the sun fell into the sea, the workers walking high up on the beams began moving toward the seawall where a large wooden ladder extended down to the courtyard. One man remained on one of the crossbeams next to a platform. He was looking down at a pallet of planks being hoisted up by five men on the other end of a pulley.

How could I have not known what was going on here? Telep thought, realizing he had little idea what was actually happening. *Perhaps they are mining that mountain out in the sea. Is this what Peda meant when he said the climbing was being done south of South End? How could something this large be kept from anyone on the Mainland? Surely the elders knew about it.*

Wanting to make good use of the remaining light, he entered

the square and immediately sought someone to ask about the new climbing instructor. Looking around, he noticed a man staring at him. The man stood in front of a blacksmith who filed sparks off a tubular piece of metal. Next to him, someone held up a piece of parchment for him to see, but the man's eyes looked past the parchment; they were on him. Telep turned around to see if there was anything of note behind him. When he turned back the man hadn't moved.

CRACK.

Gasps came from all around the square. Telep spun around. Five men retreated backward, yelling in rapid succession. Past them, a large pallet of planks exploded against the stone, bouncing in all directions. Telep looked up where a man dangled helplessly from a crossbeam, his safety line wrapped around his neck, and one of his arms caught in the noose now strangling him. The man's other hand grabbed for the safety line but couldn't grip it, as if it was broken. Everyone in the square fearfully watched him struggle to free himself, but every time he grabbed for the line, it slid through his fingers.

Telep spotted the vertical beam nearest to the man and followed it down to the stone shoe securing it in the square. He ran closer along with several other onlookers, but no one seemed to know how they could help. Workers sprinted toward the ladder by the seawall, but all were a ways off. The people running next to Telep slowed their pace, while he ran faster, straight toward the beam. With a burst of athleticism, he sprang up the stone shoe and leapt as high as he could, grabbing the beam with both hands. The metal was still hot from the sun, and it made his grip firm and sticky. He lifted his feet and pressed his sandals into the iron. He pulled his body up and grabbed higher on the beam, one foot and one hand at a time. In this way, he found a rhythm of extending and contracting his body to ascend the pillar. Gasps and yells emanated from the people in the square.

The higher he rose, the more their sounds faded, and the

more clearly he heard the gurgled choking and gasping from above. Shooting glances upward he saw a large crossbeam merging with his girder. It looked so much smaller from below. He adjusted his holds so that his last one was just under the crossbeam. Pulling his feet up as high as he could, he leapt up with all his strength. His hands barely made it above the obstructing beam, but he seized it, though he had to extend his body too much to brace his feet against the girder. He hung awkwardly, his hands slowly sliding down the hot metal until they met the crossbeam. He tried to bring his feet back up against the bar, but his sandals slipped, and he hung once more. A wave of exhaustion shot through him. His core muscles throbbed. His hands were weakening. He hung for a moment with his face pressed against the metal.

After a breath, he kicked his legs away from the girder and swiftly pulled his knees up toward his chest, pressing his toes against the beam. They stuck, and he reached up, resuming his climb. He adjusted his rhythm to utilize different, less exhausted muscles. The pace was slower, but he could sustain it longer. The gurgled coughs sounded much nearer now. He was as high as the hanging man. He adjusted for the final crossbeam, marking the top of the structure. He gripped just under it and leapt. His hands seized the top of the beam, and he dragged himself up. Jumping to his feet in a breathless daze, he ran across the beam looking down at the dangling man's blue face. Sprawling out on his stomach, he grabbed the safety line and began pulling the man up. His lungs burned with exhaustion, but he ignored it. Some line slid through his fingers.

Not now, hands.

He kept pulling. When the man was close enough, Telep grabbed under his chin and yanked his head back behind the safety line, freeing his throat and arm. His hands gave out, and he dropped the rope, letting the man fall until yanked to a halt, now hanging from his waist.

Telep listened to the man gasping for breath. He watched him swing limply over hundreds of people looking up from the square. They were jumping and screaming, but all Telep could hear was the sound of his own labored breath as he rolled on his back and stared up at the darkening sky.

Chapter 9

A purple lizard crawled across the ceiling in sporadic bursts over Telep's bed. It had a white stripe down the center of its back, and its hands looked almost circular with webbing. He watched it as the morning light permeated the room, not wanting to move, not wanting to stir the new pain sure to be in his muscles. Even lying still, he felt sore. He gripped his wool blanket, angry he had gone so long without climbing.

He thought of what he should eat for breakfast, but then realized he was still full from the feast the night before. Everyone had been so kind to him, offering him rare meats and drinks long aged, but his thoughts let him enjoy none of it. Someone told him the new climbing instructor was away, off training somewhere, and no one knew anything about a daughter.

The lizard hadn't moved in a while. Then it started crawling differently. Slowly. Like a cat stalking a bird. With a sudden spring forward, it devoured a moth Telep hadn't even seen. A small piece of wing hung out of its mouth, just for an instant before being swallowed completely.

Did that lizard really move like that? Like a cat? He wasn't sure. *Lizards don't move like that.* Maybe he'd just imagined it. After a while, he became frustrated with his uncertainty.

The lizard scurried away as a loud knock jostled the door. Before Telep could ask who it was, the door flung open, and a very large man stepped up to his bed. Telep sat up with wide eyes. Ell flashed in his mind. She would describe this person as a "large, large man" like she always did when describing someone both tall and fat.

"Your presence is requested at the seawall," the man stammered as if struggling to remember the words. He wore a long brown robe with mud stains just above the light rope belt. Telep shook away the thoughts of invaded privacy and looked into the man's eyes. He was middle-aged with thick facial hair, but somehow, he resembled a child.

"By whom?" Telep regretted asking as the man's head cocked to the side, and his eyes shifted around as if searching for an answer. "It's okay, just give me a moment," he assured, rising out of bed and pulling on his shirt.

"It's a beautiful sun," the man smiled.

"Yeah?"

"Oh yeah, beautiful." The man continued to smile at him.

Telep hobbled after the man. It was still early. The sun had not yet broken the horizon. The city looked different than it had the sun before. Calm and peaceful. When they neared the seawall, Telep saw a man sitting atop it facing the water. He was just to the side of where the massive bridge reached over the wall and out to the cliff rising out of the sea. Telep couldn't help admiring the structure as he walked next to it. As they neared the wall, the man stopped, and Telep stopped with him.

"Thank you, Sereph," said the man on the wall without turning around.

"Welcome." Sereph walked off.

Telep looked up at the man sitting well over five times his height. "How'd you get up there?" Silence. The only sounds were the rumblings of the sea coming over the wall.

"Do you need help?" His voice was so calm.

Telep almost asked his pardon, but then realized he had

heard him. He almost laughed as he put his fingers into the grooves of the seawall. In no time, he was lifting his legs over the top. The seawall was wider than anticipated, and Telep scuffled across it like a crab until he could hang his feet over the side. When he looked up, his lips parted, and his eyes widened.

The seacliff he had seen the previous sun was suddenly not alone. Two more cliffs rose behind it. From this new perspective, the first seacliff no longer blocked the view of the others. Not only that, but the bridge appeared to stretch from the first to the second to the third. Telep's mind churned outward in possibility.

His cheeks rose in a fervent smile that only dissipated when his peripheral vision reminded him of the mysterious man sitting a few arm's lengths away. Glancing over, he saw the man was not hanging his feet over the edge but sitting cross-legged. He had short dark hair and a well-kept beard. He wore thick but tattered wool trousers and a tight-fitting wool shirt with sleeves extending just past the elbow. Though he didn't look it, he was obviously a man with some influence, and Telep didn't want to make more of a splash in South End's social pond than he already had. And he certainly wanted to stay in the good graces of those in power.

The man never looked over; he just kept his gaze forward. His eyes were open, but he seemed to be meditating, being bothered by nothing. His mind was somewhere else, experiencing something.

A wave crashed into the wall sending a gust past Telep. His eyes followed the receding water out over the endless jagged and twisting rocks reaching to the horizon. They then moved to the cliffs that rose up like carnivorous teeth. He pressed his eyes shut, and when he opened them his vision receded into his mind and the landscape in front of him became a giant beast—its face appearing in the thickening clouds, the sky an all-knowing eye that could form clouds to interlock with the seacliff teeth, the wind a salty breath emanating from within, the waves a tongue lapping at the edge of man's platform, tasting it, wanting it. He felt a peace and an excitement harmonize in his chest.

When his gaze returned to the man beside him; he knew he felt it too, and he understood. This was a special place, the edge of our land. The man hadn't moved, but he felt close to him now, like they viewed nature the same way. Maybe not the same, but they both respected it. *Or maybe he sees something completely different.*

"You're not from here."

The man's voice startled Telep, though he spoke calmly like a mother waking a child. Telep's rationality interpreted the remark as an accusation, but something inside told him all would be fine for telling the truth.

"No, I'm not."

The man pulled up a long husk from next to his leg and began tearing away its tough exterior.

"This is your first time in South Nexus?"

"Yeah," Telep replied, "don't most people here call it Southy?"

"Most people don't think about the importance of this bridge being considered a city project of Nexus, which has three times the taxable population as 'Southy.'"

The man never removed his attention from the stubborn husk.

"Are you a politician?"

"Only when I have to be. Politics moves slow. I want to see consistent progress. Guess I'm impatient like that." He took a breath, and they sat in silence a moment.

Then the man turned and looked at him. His face was kind and inviting, but his eyes pierced Telep with a weight that sank into him like a brick in the sea. The morning light glinted off his forest green eyes, surrounded by a host of converging lines that made him appear older than the rest of his physique would suggest.

"Husk fruit?" he offered, holding out a second husk.

Telep had never seen a husk like it before. It was as large as his forearm. Most of it was dark brown, but it faded into a milky orange on the rounded bottom. Telep held up a hand to decline the offer but then wished he had taken it.

"Named it 'husk fruit' myself. They grow on the seaweed out yonder." His eyes pointed out to the seacliffs.

Suddenly Telep remembered Hal's words from the cave: *"He will find you,"* and he realized who this man was.

"I enjoy working with people," the man continued, "not those pretending to represent their interests. It gets frustrating sometimes, but to do something, the correct channels need to be open."

The man seemed so relaxed, talking like they were friends sharing a smoke pipe. But this didn't bother him. In a strange way it felt right and comfortable.

Telep recalled his knowledge of Nexian politics. In Eveloce, the elders were the politicians. They were the greatest thinkers, philosophers, and governors, and to be such was a formidable honor. It wasn't a stepping stone for furthering other ambitions. In Nexus, however, those who held power were the established families, all of them being landowners. Some owned land with deposits of precious commodities; others owned influential amounts of farmable land. But even devoid of commodities or nutrient rich soil, land meant power.

Centuries ago there were countless wars fought over it, eventually leading to a small colony taking control of the largest cluster of mountains and declaring it separate from the Mainland. They devoted the mountains to peace and human progress, naming it Eveloce. Several armies tried to overtake it, but the higher ground always held. Eventually, the different armies dwindled, and the Mainland became more or less united, the major landowners coming together and deciding the best way to use the land. Some peoples wanted to remain separate, most notably the West Isles, but such rebellions were put down, and the overall collective remained intact, the heart of which was called Nexus. They even sanctioned government projects like building the seawall. Before, South End was a marsh caught in the influx of tides.

Telep looked at the man and the bridge extending out to sea behind him.

"So, this is your project?"

The man laughed.

"This is humanity's project." He was finally making progress on his husk.

Telep smiled. Somehow, he did want to be a part of this project. It was extending the platform of where people could go.

"This must be quite different from what you're used to being around."

Telep felt his chest tighten. As he thought of how to remain ambiguous yet polite, the man looked at him with gentle unassuming eyes. The eyes of a friend. Telep took a breath.

"Yes, Eveloce is very different."

The man smiled. "Thank you for trusting me. My name is Ep Brody. What's yours?" He extended his hand, and Telep leaned over to shake it with both hands.

"Telep." He smiled at how Ep Brody introduced himself as though they were children about to become fast friends.

Ep Brody finally split the husk open revealing three pink pods of soft fruit. He popped one into his mouth and immediately spit it out. "Terrible," he declared, throwing the husk into the sea.

"I want to show you something." He rose to his feet, grabbed the other husk fruit and stepped past Telep, continuing along the seawall.

As Telep rose, he looked out once again at the jagged rocks and sea before him. He pictured the massive bridge extending out to the nearest seacliff as a string wrapped around nature's tooth, ready to pull it out. He grinned to himself and followed behind.

There was a soothing familiarity about Ep Brody. Somehow

the weight of being so far from home subsided in his presence. Many governing elders back on Eveloce were the same way—personable and charming, talking to everyone as if they were dear friends. They utilized their social prowess to advance their position of power.

Ep Brody pointed out elements of interest as they walked along the seawall, gesturing with his husk . . . "over there is where the town square used to be, and over there is where the sea rocks claimed their last vessel, and right there is the best cheese mill in the world!" A genuine love of the city emanated through his words.

Soon, they entered the residential part of town. The stone houses stood close together, their orange clay roofs contrasting the light gray stone of the street. Ep Brody continued talking.

"That is where the architect for section one lives. This is the home of my chief welder, and right behind it is the home of my chief welder in training. We used part of this guy's design for section three, but the bulk of it came from her over there."

It struck Telep how geometric the community was. Everything was laid out in a grid, and the homes were surprisingly similar, making it all the more impressive that Ep Brody could pick out specific residences. The only thing breaking the pattern was the sporadic curves of the seawall.

"Section three?"

"Yeah, the bridge starting in the square and leading to the first seacliff is section one." Telep felt his mind churn at the implied possibility that the number could be higher than three—more than he could see.

"How many sections are there?"

Ep Brody stopped, turned, and smiled. "I'll show you."

Telep felt a happiness in his chest that he wished would last forever. When he arrived in South End, he thought it was the end of the world. Now the world had been pushed back, and he didn't know how far—a fact that stoked a fire inside him.

"But first," Ep Brody continued, "you see that house there, with the smoke and the bent chimney?"

"Yeah."

"That is the house of the man you saved last night . . . I don't know how you did that—scale that beam . . . you rose faster than the people on the ladder. I don't know anyone else who could do that. Roda is alive because of you."

Silence. It didn't feel like flattery, just . . . recognition.

"He lives there with his wife; she's probably cooking up some breakfast now. And his brother is staying there while his new home is being readied. I'm sure they would love to thank you."

Telep's gaze dipped to his feet and he shifted his weight.

"Oh, that's okay. The city showed me enough thanks last night."

Ep Brody became serious. "Look through their eyes. What is 'enough?' Wouldn't you want to say thank you?"

Telep took a breath and nodded.

———

A middle-aged woman answered the door, the scent of cooked meat greeting them with her. She smiled at Ep Brody, and they embraced. Ep Brody introduced Telep, leaving out his being from Eveloce. As soon as she realized who he was, she gripped the sides of his shirt and pulled him close, trying to express a feeling beyond herself. Telep felt the emotion in her sustained embrace and looked to Ep Brody, who nodded.

With a sniff and a smile, she whisked them in and offered to wake Roda.

"Oh no, let him sleep," said Ep Brody. "Is brother Benya around?"

"Oh, he'd love to see you. You just missed him."

The inside of the house was quaint and organized. In just a few steps, they were in the kitchen. The scent of the meat intensified, and the smoke of the fire could be seen wafting across an open doorway from the backyard.

"No bother, we'll get him next time," Ep Brody smiled.

"Went to the bridge, I think," she offered.

"Hey, we were just heading that way. But you enjoy your breakfast, it smells divine."

She pleaded that they take some food for the road, and Ep Brody accepted immediately, telling Telep to try wrapping the lamb in the merce bread. Telep left the house admiring the rapport Ep Brody had with her. When Telep bit into the lamb, he thought of the woman's face when she learned who he was; and he was glad he had made the visit.

Walking to the bridge, they took the main road instead of the seawall. Along the way they came across many workers just starting their work sun. Telep thought he noticed several of them exaggerate their efforts upon seeing Ep Brody. He looked to see if Ep Brody would get angry, but only saw flashes of disappointment in his eyes.

While they were walking, Telep saw a gray cat saunter out of an orange berry bush and onto the road. A baby vole hung from its mouth by the scruff of its neck, its eyes calm and demure. The cat crossed the road and disappeared under a house. Telep wondered if the cat was caring for the vole like a mother but then felt naïve for considering it.

Ep Brody spoke. "You know, while you're here it would be wise to get to know people before mentioning you're from Eveloce. There is a lot of pride here in South Nexus and a lot of pride in this bridge. You understand?"

"Okay."

"But this bridge is humanity's creation, a devotion from all the people of the Mainland. Humanity's bridge into the unknown. Any pride taken in it should be shared with all. We use the best people because they are the best. A lot of greatness comes from Eveloce, and we're not going to dismiss them for lesser natives of South Nexus. The work will not be compromised. It is my job to make sure this is the best we can do as a species."

"You bring in workers from Eveloce . . . how do you get them here?"

"Prison colony is at the north end of the Mainland. After dropping off the prisoners, the carts are empty for the trip back. I hire them."

A grin crept onto Telep's face. All the worry, confusion, uncertainty—the catalyst that had brought him here—now rescinded with a few simple words.

Ep Brody seemed like a man who would do whatever he needed to get what he wanted, but he also seemed like a man whose direct spoken word could be trusted. And more than that, Telep felt a connection with him. He believed him.

Telep thought back to the night he saw Ell and Caleb being loaded into a prison cart. Having all the dreaded possibilities extinguished in just a couple sentences . . . he felt as if some part of him always knew they were all right, that they weren't prisoners.

Prisoners—such a bizarre idea it now seemed. The thought fled his mind when they neared the town square, and his eyes once again beheld the enormous structure.

Telep's stomach churned with excitement, but he was able to force down the last of the lamb and merce bread. He took a deep breath.

"Are we going to see Caleb out there on the bridge?" He realized after he said it that he hadn't yet revealed he knew the one-legged climber.

Ep Brody turned to him. "Caleb?"

Telep tried to remain nonchalant, but something in his face must have betrayed the intent.

"You two pals from Eveloce?"

"Yeah."

"And you're here to see him, make sure he's all right."

Telep took another breath. "And his daughter, too."

Ep Brody studied him. "Well of course his daughter."

Telep's pace slowed. "So, they're both all right?"

"Better than ever. They're doing great work."

A weight lifted from Telep's chest.

"And I can see them both?"

Ep Brody smiled. "I'll tell you what. Come with me out on the bridge, and we'll see what we can arrange."

There was something in his voice that Telep didn't like. He was determined to see both of them whether it was "arranged" or not.

"Where are they working?"

"Caleb's out on the bridge training young climbers. That's where we're going."

"What about his daughter? Is she out there too?"

"No. Ell's working in South End."

Telep's heart beat faster. "I need to see her."

"She's probably busy right now. If you're going to come with me out on the bridge, we have a lot of ground to cover before dark. Come with me now, you'll go see Caleb, and Ell will be here when you get back."

Telep stopped walking. After a few paces, Ep Brody stopped and looked back at him.

"I need to see her now."

Ep Brody sighed. "Okay. Then we better keep walking."

Telep's chest churned, and they continued on.

———

They passed the last of the residential homes, and the large city square lay before them bustling with people. The scattered planks from the incident the night before were all picked up, and the pulley now lifted new ones up to the top platform. Business as usual. No evidence of a life-threatening event.

Ep Brody veered onto a narrow dirt path leading up the grassy hill that overlooked the square. They passed a sign that read: "No Smoke Pipes Beyond." The path led to a single building, sitting alone on the hill, set apart from the rest of the city. Telep remembered walking down the same grassy hill when he'd entered South End. He remembered the same building with the ventilated hay roof that smelled of rotten eggs and burnt air. The same odor filled his nostrils.

Ep Brody turned to him. "This is where Ell works."

Telep's hands shook with raw excitement.

Ep Brody knocked on the door and a heavyset woman opened it. A black rag covered her mouth. Her eyes were dark and gloomy, though they widened at the sight of Ep Brody.

"Good morning, Eve. We need to borrow Ell. It won't take long."

The woman stared at Ep Brody, then glanced at Telep. She coughed a raspy cough.

"She's not here. Left this morning for the Tocs."

Telep's excitement evaporated in the pungent air. Ep Brody turned to him.

"She's far away. The Tocs, that's several suns west. I'm impressed. That means she is in the final part of her training."

"How far west?"

"It's far. Far too far. We can't go there. It's only for refiners, and she shouldn't be interrupted during her training."

"What if—"

"Let's go out on the bridge. You will see Caleb. I'll show you around. And when you come back, Ell will be returning, and I'll make sure she gets a couple suns off work."

Telep looked out at the bridge and the cliffs in the distance.

"Okay."

They headed back down the hill, Telep's chest aching with disappointment. He forced himself to think of other things. One of Ep Brody's comments stuck out in his mind.

"What did you mean earlier when you said: 'bridge into the unknown?'" Telep asked.

"I meant exactly that."

"You're not mining the seacliffs?"

"We are using them as supports for the bridge."

"And you don't know what it's leading to?"

"Sure we do. Every sun we get a little farther. Every sun, we push the veiled horizon a little further back." He paused. "How much of the Mainland have you seen?"

Telep didn't need to think about it, but he left a pause anyway.

"I've been to the north. I've seen all of Eveloce. And I walked to South Nexus on the east road."

"Well I've seen all of it. I spent my youth traveling around, seeing new places, meeting new people. It was a great time in my life. Everything was new, and then nothing was new. There was a sense of . . . possibility lost. And as depressing as that was, I felt so fortunate being able to explore the land I was born to. Hundreds of solars ago we weren't afforded such luxury. We spent every waking moment working just to survive. Later, we lived and died in the blood of battle, deciding who owned what. And now, we are unified enough to build a wall that holds back the sea. We can alter the platform of our existence. We have filled the land we were given. It's not enough. There is more inside us . . . why shouldn't there be more out there?" Ep Brody's words hung in the air.

Telep felt his mind swell. This man just expressed an idea he had always felt but couldn't articulate. He thought a moment.

"How do you get a government to fund something like that?"

"The possibility of land . . . The land of the Mainland has been distributed among the same families for generations. Land is power. And power always seeks more power. I should know. I'm from the crimson house of Ep."

"But how do you sell that to a government? What evidence is

there that a sizable chunk of land even exists away from the Mainland?"

Ep Brody smirked. "You know, Eveloce produces some great but sheltered minds." Telep shot him a look, but it went unnoticed. "Many solars ago, we found a body over the seawall, on a raft snagged in the jagged rocks. A body . . . not from here. It came from out there." Ep Brody pointed his husk down the stretch of bridge over the jagged rocky sea.

Telep's mind went in free fall. He looked out where Ep Brody pointed, his eyes wide with interest, but his rationality begging the falsity of such a claim.

"What do you mean 'not from here'?"

"I mean the body did not originate on the Mainland. The sea brought it here from somewhere else." Ep Brody spoke with a calm, assured lilt.

"Where?"

"Excellent question."

Telep's eyes darted around with his thoughts. He thought back to his education from the elders, which suddenly seemed incomplete. His tongue scraped the side of his dry mouth. He tried to swallow the bareness in his throat. "How do you know it wasn't from the Mainland?"

"Its native skin was dark, much darker than anyone here."

"Native skin?"

"It was damaged, but there were traces of the original pigment. Fortunately, this took place in the cold season when the sea's current flows inward. There were also strange markings, patterns dyed into the skin that we couldn't duplicate. It was pierced in several areas that aren't customary anywhere on the Mainland. And it was ornamented with shells that aren't found here."

"Did you see it?"

"I was one of the last to see it. The body was found as I was returning from my travels. It was big news by the time I got back. It was under the protection of my brother, Ep Salo, and he let only a select few handle the body or its dressings, noblemen from some of the influential families. Shortly after I returned, people got sick. A terrible, terrible sickness spread. Very painful. Within a moon cycle, everyone who had significant contact with the body was dead. That included my nephew. Those infected were quarantined. Their families had to watch from a distance . . . the body and its ornaments were burned."

Telep struggled to wrap his mind around this new information. He took a breath, letting it sink in.

Then Telep looked at the side of Ep Brody's face. He could tell the man was just saying words, recounting events without feeling them. To somebody else, Ep Brody might have come off as callous or uncaring, but to Telep it added to the story's potency. Ep Brody couldn't bring himself to feel those things again, so he recited the facts like a chronicler at the Temple of History.

Telep could tell this was a very heavy story for Ep Brody. The way he said "nephew," "family," and "brother." It seemed the more casually he said something, the more hurtful it had been, and the more emotional distance he kept from it. In Telep's mind they were details not vital to the story, but vital to Ep Brody's recollection of it, and he couldn't leave them out. It was also apparent that a lot of the pain Ep Brody felt was through his brother, Ep Salo.

"So anyway," Ep Brody continued, "we received funding for the bridge project shortly after, and I've been overseeing it ever since."

They stepped off the dirt path and onto the smooth stone of the city square. The bridge took up more and more of Telep's view. An excitement grew inside him. Sparks floated across his vision. His mind drifted to Ell. Cupping his hand at his side as if to hold her hand, he realized how much he wanted her there with him. He wanted to be looking at this with her. He wanted her to come on this adventure. He summoned the memory of the last night they spent together . . . the image of her in the white gown . . .

"You alright, Telep?"

Looking up, Telep realized he was five paces behind.

"Yeah, yeah," he assured, taking long strides to catch up. It took him a moment to remember the last thing that had been said. "Yeah, running such a project must be really stressful." It felt strange saying this.

In Eveloce, stress was considered a necessary and positive element in the pursuit of progress. Complacency was in the established; stress was in the unknown. That was where sons and daughters of Eveloce were expected to push their trades. As the elders would say, "the pursuit of perfection requires the path untread."

Telep thought it was wise to practice acting like a Nexian, but it felt strange doing so with Ep Brody since the man seemed so driven toward progress himself, almost like a son of Eveloce.

"Fe, stress will end, and it's necessary to create something that will last," Ep Brody said.

This man belongs in Eveloce.

Then looking to the massive bridge disappearing into a rapidly descending cloud of white fog, he figured Ep Brody couldn't belong anywhere but here.

This bridge . . . this is a beautiful thing.

Telep thought of some of the ideas that Eveloce perpetuated about Mainlanders and felt shame as he remembered them, most of them from his childhood.

"Hey, Sereph," called Ep Brody.

Telep looked up to see the large large man carrying a wood brace on his shoulders with a big bucket of water hanging from either side. Sereph spun around, and a young woman walking behind him had to duck under the swinging bucket, some of its water spilling on her. Ep Brody hopped forward. A smile lit up Sereph's face. He opened his mouth to say something, but nothing came out.

"How ya doin'? Ya workin' hard?"

Sereph nodded as if already exhausted.

"Well good, it's good to work hard. Hey, what kinda sun is it?"

Sereph brightened. "It—it's a beautiful sun."

"Alright, we got a beautiful one, just what we wanted." He poked Sereph in the belly with his husk fruit. "You keep working hard now." Sereph nodded and turned away, making Telep lurch his head back to avoid getting smacked by the bucket.

They continued across the square toward the tall wooden ladder by the seawall. Telep could feel the pulse of social recognition for Ep Brody as they moved among the people. Silence, averted gazes, smiles, nods. Many bridge workers once again became extra productive. And once again Telep noticed the tinge of disappointment in Ep Brody's eyes. But this time, Telep thought he saw something else—a trace of anger in his clenched jaw.

Telep's stomach churned with anticipation as they passed under the bridge. When they reached the ladder, Ep Brody motioned for Telep to ascend first. Then he held up a hand. "Or would you rather take the girder?"

Telep grinned. The wood rungs were worn smooth. He stepped up. Looking skyward, he watched the top of the ladder approach. He thought of a story the elders used to tell about a boy climbing a magical ladder. The noise of the city square faded away, and all he heard was his hands on the wood and the wind blowing past him, fiercer now that he was above the seawall. Wisps of fog floated by overhead. He looked up in the sky to the east where the thickening fog reduced the sun to a perfect white disk. Pulling himself above the last rung, a calm lucidity overtook him. Standing atop the platform of the bridge, his fingers interlocked and rested on his head. He looked to his right where long metal girders extended over the square; to his left, wooden planks disappeared into white fog. His chest fluttered. He knew he would never forget this moment. This image would stay with him always.

He felt a tap on his ankle.

"And it never gets old," smiled Ep Brody, standing up next to him.

Telep looked back at the green hill on the far side of the square. They both took a breath, turned, and walked into the fog.

Chapter 10

Telep watched the seawall pass beneath him. Ep Brody explained some of the bridge's specifications with passionate precision and childlike enthusiasm. As he talked, Telep stared ahead into the white fog, his thoughts drifting back to Eveloce. *Why would the elders keep this a secret?* The fog continued to thicken, and soon they were in a white abyss. No top, no bottom, no sides. Even the sea was lost from sight. All they could see was the bridge disappearing ahead and behind. A large gust roared past, and the bridge swayed. Telep's stomach twisted.

"Feel that? She's breathing." Excitement animated Ep Brody's words.

The rocking nauseated Telep. The thickness of the fog seemed to weigh on his mind, and he started to feel lost, his only point of reference quaking under his feet.

Why didn't the elders tell us? Why wouldn't they want to be involved in this? Isn't this bridge a grand realization of what we believe and strive for? This is exploration. This is progress.

Ep Brody's voice arrested his thoughts.

"You know, I have a lot of respect for Eveloce. This bridge

would not have been possible without the minds of the mountains. They are hard-working, progressive people."

Telep blinked rapidly. There was something he didn't like about the statement. It felt like an attempt to distance him from his people.

"I agree," Telep said matter-of-factly.

"I just wish the elders would allow Eveloce to interact more with their Mainland brethren. They are like a beacon of greatness, of progressive aptitude. But greatness is everywhere. The West Isles has the best bridge and ship makers; South Nexus has the best miners and refiners. I want to bring these people together, but the elders keep things very closed off." Ep Brody's tone was not accusatory but hopeful. "The people they banished have advanced this project considerably. There's a collective now on the Mainland, and Eveloce is part of it. Few things give me more pleasure than taking people like Caleb who have so much left to give and providing an outlet for them that not only stretches their abilities but is part of the collective growth."

Don't bring Caleb into this, Telep thought, though part of him resonated with what the man was saying. He knew how important an active purpose was to Caleb. He wanted to see Ell and Caleb more than ever. They would make things clearer.

Ep Brody seemed so sincere when he spoke. Something in Telep couldn't help thinking that even if only part of him is genuine, he still might be right . . . Maybe Eveloce's stringency and isolation was doing more harm than good. He feared he was being manipulated but even more afraid that he hadn't yet heard the truth.

Look where I am. Even if this bridge is being built on exploitation, lies, and deceit, it has a noble purpose—an inherent truth.

This bridge . . . There's something innate in it. It is a platform of exploration. Any person to walk over these planks and deny that truth is denying part of their humanity.

The fog lifted slightly, and they could see more of the bridge and the rocky sea below. Telep kept looking back to view the Mainland, but it was never there. He noticed that Ep Brody never looked back. The man didn't even turn to glance at Telep as he talked. His eyes remained fixed ahead.

A figure appeared through the fog—his dark cloak pulled tight around him; his chin tucked to his chest. The man wobbled toward them. Ep Brody seemed not to notice, but then he stopped. They waited as the man hobbled past, the harsh wind whipping the tail of his cloak. Telep looked to Ep Brody who held his fingers over his mouth, his gaze down and to the side. The dark cloak disappeared into the white abyss behind them. The wind blew harder, and Telep could taste the salt in the air on his dry lips.

"Rise," Ep Brody said.

Telep looked at him unsure. "Wha—"

"RISE!" he yelled as if commanding the fog to obey his will.

A plank creaked. Looking down, Telep saw two hands gripping the side of the bridge. The fingers shifted and strained. A foot swung up, then a knee. The dark clothing stood out from the fog. A man stood before them, his downward gaze locked between his feet.

CRUNCH—like a thick carrot snapping in two. The man's head snapped back, blood running from his mouth, his two front teeth bent in, pointing down his throat. Telep's eyes fluttered in confusion. His impulse was to reach out and pull the man away from the edge, but he stopped himself when Ep Brody stepped to the man, seized his hair and yanked it back. The same *CRUNCH* sound rang out as he smashed his husk down on the man's face. Telep froze. Another *CRUNCH*. Then another, and another, each one sounding wetter. The man tried to squirm away but was held in place. One hand gripped Ep Brody's shirt, the other feebly tried to shield his face. He arched his back not wanting to step back any further, his heels already kissing the edge of the planks. He buried his nose behind his elbow. Ep Brody pulled the man's head close to his mouth.

"When you hide . . . you risk being found." Then he pulled the man even closer, almost in an embrace, and whispered in his ear. The man's grip on Ep Brody's shirt softened. His destroyed face sucked in one final gasp before being flung over the edge and fading into the white abyss. Ep Brody swung the husk hard through the air and a spatter of blood painted a red stripe across the bridge. Then he flung it down where it made a weighted knock on the wood before bouncing off the edge.

Telep's eyes were wide with fear, his heart pounding in his chest. He looked over the side and could barely see the limp body snagged between two jagged rocks, swaying with the waves —the tongue of the beast rolling him around in its mouth.

Telep looked back to Ep Brody, who was sprawled out on his belly in the place the man had been hanging, and looked under the bridge.

Telep stared at him, frozen.

Ep Brody gripped the side of the bridge and shimmied his body over the edge until he was hanging. Then one hand disappeared. When it returned, it was holding a cylindrical metal contraption the size of his forearm. He set it on the bridge, swung his leg up, and reached out his hand. Telep stared at it, the calloused palm smeared with red. He grabbed it and pulled him up.

Ep Brody held up the metal contraption for Telep to see.

"You see this? Remember it." Then Ep Brody looked over the edge and hurled the cylinder down, presumably at the corpse snared below.

Telep's thoughts raced so fast, they blurred into nothing. Never in his life had he witnessed such an act. He looked at the anger on Ep Brody's face, at the red stripe spotted across the bridge, at his own hand stained with blood. He felt afraid but not of Ep Brody. When he looked at him, somehow, he still felt safe. Shining through his shock and fear, he felt an ineffable trust in the man—like somehow this *had* to happen, and no one was to blame.

Ep Brody stepped on the red stripe; Telep stepped over it, following in stunned silence, listening to the wind, and watching the red footprints in front of him become fainter and fainter until finally they disappeared.

Telep could hardly think, his mind suddenly empty from shock. He struggled for some form of understanding. He didn't know what to do. Part of him wanted to turn around and run the other way. He felt surprised at himself for continuing to follow Ep Brody, but it wasn't a conscious choice. It felt like his body was acting on its own, continuing to follow this man who remained quiet, leading him deeper into the white abyss.

The simplest questions filled Telep's mind, but somehow, they couldn't make it to his tongue. The back of Ep Brody's head gave off an aura that seemed to outlaw even the most reasonable queries.

This man just brutally killed another human being.

Telep visualized the man's face after the first blow from Ep Brody's husk, the husk he'd offered Telep on the seawall.

What would have happened if I had accepted the husk and eaten it? Then perhaps the man would still be alive. I would have cracked open its hard exterior before it could crack the skull of that man. The pods of fruit inside would have nourished me instead of being forever encased in a weapon of—Telep shuddered when the word came to him—*murder.*

Telep's gaze bore enmity into the back of Ep Brody's neck. *You are a murderer! You murdered that man!* Telep screamed through his gaze, but his tongue remained silent, paralyzed.

He started telling himself that it must have been justified. It must have been inevitable.

What was inevitable about it? The occurrence was instigated by a conscious choice and deliberate action, but still Telep couldn't shake the feeling.

The shock of the moment continued weighing on him as they walked. They didn't speak. The longer the silence endured, the more it insisted upon itself. After a while his thoughts drifted to what lay ahead, and he immediately felt guilty for thinking about anything else.

The planks continued passing under their feet. The fog began to thin.

The bridge was empty save for the occasional construction crew either replacing a damaged plank or widening a section of the structure. Ep Brody stopped to interact with the managers of these crews; his demeanor was sullen but still personable.

The enormity and spectacle of the first seacliff almost distracted Telep from the crushing weight consuming his mind and chest.

The cliff was massive, both in girth and height. The top of it where the bridge lay was unnaturally flat. All around, iron supports driven into the rock secured it and then rose into the sky, converging like a coned tent as if to complete the mountain that had once been. From the top of the united beams, thick iron cables extended out to the bridge in both directions. Telep marveled at the architecture before him.

The plateau that the bridge rested on perplexed him. It had clearly been shaped that evenly by design, but he knew of nothing that could sculpt such an immense area of rock. Without thinking, he asked Ep Brody how it had been done, then realized he had broken a silence that had lasted a good portion of the sun.

"There is a powder we use to shape the cliffs as needed."

It was clear the man did not want to speak.

They passed the first seacliff and continued on to the second stretch of bridge. It was similar to the first by way of design, but the planks covering it looked newer.

Salt built up on Telep's lips until his mouth was too dry to lick it off. They became pale and cracked. He stayed a few steps behind as they walked, staring at a tiny rip in Ep Brody's collar.

What happened with the man on the bridge started to feel like a dream, though he knew it wouldn't fade as such. But there was something about it; the way he felt about it was dreamlike, both in the moment and now. It then dawned on him that while it was happening, he hadn't even considered stopping it. The thought gripped him with guilt.

Who was that man? Why was he hiding? Why did he need to die?

As time passed, his recollection was reduced to a handful of images. His mind could no longer replay what happened. The more he thought about it, the more distinct the images became. He could see the movement of only certain portions—Ep Brody moving toward the man, bringing the husk down on his face, the man's hand releasing Ep Brody's shirt, his chest rising as he took that last breath, and his lifeless body shrouded in fog snared between the rocks. All of these motions were short; almost instantaneous in his mind. The rest of his recollection was in precise images—Ep Brody's face, his eyes, the man's bent teeth, his arched back, burying his face in his arm, and the red stripe across the bridge.

Telep felt comatose as he cycled through the motions and images, each becoming more selective. One part of each appeared clearer and more detailed—the hand, the face, the teeth, the blood—while the rest became dark and hazy, disappearing into the surrounding fog. He went over them again and again until they started to change; his imagination began creating new elements.

He saw the man look into Ep Brody's eyes as he was being bludgeoned as if to ask for pity. Telep shook his head in a grimace. *That never happened; he never looked at him.* Then he saw the man try to push Ep Brody off the bridge and Ep Brody grab the man's hair to stay on. *That never happened either . . . I am trying to alter my memory. In reimagining it, I am wetting the ink of my recollection and creating new details—details driven by my guilt. I am changing the incident in my mind so I can justify what happened, or at least the way I feel about it . . .*

Telep shook his head violently. His face like stone, his breathing sharp. He feared he wouldn't be able to remember the event the way it happened. Though he tried to think of other things, the images and motions kept invading his mind. He tried to push his thoughts elsewhere so the images could solidify. Justification through delusion was for the weak; Telep wanted his memory to reflect the truth.

Planks continued passing beneath his feet. He stared into the fog like a drone, his mind paralyzed.

When they reached the second seacliff, the fog lifted enough for Telep to see the water below. This cliff was as high as the first but narrower. Workers built platforms where the rock started to slant down toward the water. Ep Brody stopped behind them and listened as they argued over the angle at which a support beam should be drilled into the rock. In efforts to impress Ep Brody, many of them who had been silent before now fought for their ideas. Among them was a woman with pale skin and short black hair. She pushed around drawings with calculations of her design. She had an accent Telep had never heard. The only one remaining silent was the manager of the crew, designated with a green armband. Ep Brody didn't appear to be listening to their arguing. He looked over their shoulders at the platform and at the slope of the rock. Then he caught the manager's eye.

"I need to talk to you about tomorrow's shipment of lumber," Ep Brody said as he stepped away. The man followed.

"Alright," started the man, hurrying to keep up. "I was told it would be here shortly after—"

"Use Leta's design," Ep Brody interrupted.

The manager blinked and tilted his head. "Wha—"

"Leta. Her idea is best. Use it. Just make sure there aren't any cracks on the underside of the rock. Send whoever has the biggest problem with her design to check."

The manager nodded. "Yes sir, no problem."

"Wait until I'm gone to select her design."

The man gave a nod and returned to the group.

When Telep looked back, Ep Brody was already at the end

of the cliff glaring back with impatient eyes. He shook his head and followed.

———

The third section of the bridge was shorter, but by the time they crossed it, the light had started to fade. Ep Brody said they would spend the night on the third seacliff, which was larger than the first two. Only the side of it had been flattened for the bridge to rest on. The rest rose high into the air, and large cables passed through the high rock and out in both directions. A fleeting wave of excitement pulsed through Telep's chest when he saw a fourth section of bridge extending out to another seacliff in the distance. *How far does this bridge go?*

There were more workers and more supplies on this cliff. It was a diverse group, men and women, old and young, light and bronze. Their clothes looked strangely varied, from flowing robes to tight-fitting woolens.

Ep Brody spent the twilight looking over assorted projects and making suggestions. Later in the evening, he conversed with the workers, asking about their families, embracing them and kissing some on the cheek.

Telep watched Ep Brody with unblinking eyes, his mind still in a haze. He watched his face and his gestures. He watched because he needed to understand; he needed to know who this man was. He needed to know who was running this project. He needed to know who stained his hand with blood. He watched until he saw what he was looking for. He watched until he saw a gravitas behind his eyes. He watched until he saw the masked solemnity of a pained man. He watched until he could fathom some rationale for this sun's horror.

———

In the last vestige of light, Ep Brody ordered everyone to the top of the cliff. Ladders connected platforms all the way up. The top of the cliff had been flattened just like the first and second seacliffs. Pulling himself atop the sizable platform, Telep gazed out in the distance at the dark shape that lay ahead. The view was better from up here but limited by the growing darkness. He took a breath and rested his hands on his head. The thought of being here, in this place, on this bridge, which a few suns ago he hadn't even known existed, excited and calmed him.

For supper they had goat cheese, assorted vegetables, and a goat cooked whole over a large fire. At Ep Brody's request, three hens were added over the fire. Telep couldn't tell if this was an act of generosity or a way of silencing the clucking from below.

The people were receptive to Telep. They introduced themselves and made him feel welcome.

"Is this your first time out here?" one man asked.

"Yes, it is."

"That's good. You enjoying the food?"

"Yes, very much."

"Well if you need more salt, just keep lickin' your lips."

Telep smiled along.

To drink, they passed flagons of spiced rum and coconut milk. The drinks long outlived the food and bolstered their stories with laughter. After a while, Telep joined in commenting on stories and sharing his own, trying to take his mind off the grisly images. After the meal, he looked next to him to see Ep Brody sitting still, staring into the flames.

New logs were added, thinner than the others and wrapped with braided green and brown vines that smoked and crackled in the flames. The rich smoke rose into the air. More and more ripples of laughter. Someone plucked the strings of a lute, while people danced and moved freely. The sky grew darker, the points of light brighter. Telep lay back, resting his head on a hard stone. He heard Ep Brody's breath not far away.

"I want you to work on this bridge, Telep." Ep Brody's voice was soft, but his tone was sharp. "That is why I brought you out here. We're at an impasse and we need the best. I don't want you to do it for the money. I don't want you to do it to be near Ell. I want you to do it because you understand what it is that compelled you to come out here." He drew a deep breath. "Don't answer now. I'm asking this of you because I think you understand something, because I think there is something in you that you can't deny. Don't answer now. When you see tomorrow's sun shining on the edge of the known world, answer then."

Telep's eyes searched the sky. He knew what Ep Brody was saying. He recognized the inner drive that compelled him to come out here. It was something he wanted to fully understand.

Telep watched the billows of smoke rise off the fire. It was so thick, but it rose so slowly. He'd suspected that Ep Brody had a purpose for him. His immediate reaction was no, he couldn't leave his life in Eveloce. Then guilt hit him.

He knew the longer he was away, the harder it would be to explain his absence to the elders. But even with that knowledge, he found himself longing for Ep Brody to keep talking, as if part of him wanted to be convinced. But silence persisted. He knew he couldn't entertain Ep Brody's proposal without first asking the question heaviest in his mind.

"Who was the man on the bridge?"

Ep Brody took a deep breath. "Remember that metal contraption I showed you? That was filled with the powder we use to shape these cliffs. It's an explosive powder. That man was a weed. It was his intention to detonate the powder on our bridge, which would set us back solars."

Telep felt a weight leave his body and float away with the smoke pouring off the fire. A wave of anger swelled in him at the mere prospect of impeding this bridge. This project embodied the ideals he'd revered and worked toward his entire life. The idea of sabotaging such an endeavor struck him as a crime of the worst consequence. A crime against humanity. He imagined how he would feel if the collapse of the North Rim on

Eveloce had been the result of mindful sabotage. His breath became rigid with anger. But in the silence that followed, the anger seemed to float into the air with the colorful smoke.

Ep Brody continued: "If you focus on the small, there may be incidents on this project that you find reprehensible or wrong, but that is just a blip on a stunning tapestry. The man on the bridge couldn't see the beauty of what we are doing. The greater picture. It's a beautiful thing. I don't want to cause hurt. I don't want to cause pain or suffering. It hurts me, body and mind . . . but I can't let snakes into our garden. That man had passion. He was acting on his convictions, but what are good intensions when the action is pure evil? His fear of growth and change is a disease that cannot coexist with our progress."

Ep Brody's words shook with the tremor of a tortured soul. Telep realized he was hearing something few people had heard, maybe no one. He thought back to the incident on the bridge. Ep Brody's action had been extreme and brutal. He had taken a life, and that fact filled Telep with a guilt that he couldn't let go. Despite that knowledge, Telep still felt the connection between him and Ep Brody. Ep Brody's words aligned with the ideology of Eveloce, and it made him feel at home.

His chest rose and fell. He raised his hand and tried to touch the thick smoke in the air.

"I can't let one skeptic ruin our sanctuary, our temple. It needs to stay sacred." Ep Brody's breath trembled.

Waves of laughter echoed around them.

"All these people, you, everyone on the Mainland—they all count on me to keep it sacred, to push us as far as we can go. Sometimes that means doing very hard things . . . These people, they want to be pushed. Even if they don't realize or admit it, they want me to be hard on them. Deep down everyone wants to give their best. It's just so often that their best is the hardest place to reach."

Telep felt a bubble around himself and Ep Brody. They were isolated, alone, away from all else.

"Do you know why my people work harder when I'm passing by?"

"No."

"Because I'm not a good enough leader to inspire the part of them that wants to give their best. To get results, I've instilled fear. But you know, we need results."

Telep rubbed his eyes for a long time.

"Tell me, what makes us different from animals?"

"We can reason. We know right from wrong. We're more than instinct and learned behavior," Telep said.

"Exactly. We are. Our consciousness is a living thing. It gathers, it collects, it stores. It passes on knowledge to its children. What kind of stewards would we be if we said, 'Thanks, human ancestry. Thanks for slaving to make our lives better' and then do nothing to add to the lives that follow us? 'Thanks for developing methods of farming so we can eat better than you in a fraction of the time. Thanks for fire. Thanks for the wheel; now we can transport our abundant harvests to our weatherproof shelters where we spend most of our time. Thank you for sharpening mathematics into a useful tool. Thanks for dying in battle to protect our land. Thanks for giving us leisurely lives so we can do just enough to get by.' All these things are just stepping stones, tools to be used. We can expand the teachings of our fathers. So, when I say, 'bridge into the unknown,' I mean the Mainland is a stepping stone, and the bridge is our stride to the next one."

Telep's mind floated through the haze of colorful smoke in the air. He couldn't remember how Ep Brody's speech began, but his words resonated with something deep in his core.

"You have done a lot," Telep assured, sounding as coherent as possible. "No one can take away the strides you've made."

Ep Brody let out a long pensive breath that seemed to push away the smoke and reveal the deep black of the sky. Points of light shining brightly illuminated the sea of black. Their brilliancy swelled. But Telep did not marvel at them. Instead he marveled at the blackness between them where he felt his consciousness being siphoned into the dark unknown abyss.

The smoke cleared; the vines burned away, and the fire dwindled to an orange glow that brightened when a breeze swept past.

Ep Brody swallowed and took a breath. Then he said, "The strides . . . the strides are necessary for all of us." He hesitated. "But for me . . . I just want the next stone."

Chapter 11

That night, Telep dreamt of an old story the elders used to tell him. It had several different endings but always started the same way—with a young boy climbing a ladder that grew higher and higher as he climbed. The endings were always something that changed the boy's life forever. Sometimes it was good, sometimes bad, sometimes neither. One ending had the boy climb until his ladder caught the sun's fire. In another, he climbed until all the matter in the world had gone into the ladder itself and he had nowhere to return. His favorite had the boy climb until his ladder merged with the ladder of a young girl climbing the other direction—they passed each other and continued to the other's world where they both had to walk on their hands. Though the stories were memorable, it was the virulent gaze of the elders while telling them that now gripped Telep's dreams, the high flames of the burning pyre reflected in their eyes.

He woke up thinking about the body that had washed ashore, and the disease it had spread, and its unforgivable omission from his education on Eveloce.

When Ep Brody awoke, he strode around the seacliff with renewed energy. He paced in front of Telep as he ate his breakfast—fried egg and dark tomatoes, goat cheese and bread. He spoke with vigor about a new nut discovered on the next seacliff.

"The organic growth, it changes rapidly out here. Once you leave the Mainland, things start happening. From North Point to South Nexus, the aquatic vegetation changes modestly. But out here it gets bizarre, like we passed a threshold. It changes from seacliff to seacliff. Even the marine life varies."

Telep's brow furrowed at the enthusiasm so contrary to his demeanor the previous night. He wished Ep Brody would give him one solemn look acknowledging the raw sentiment they'd shared under the smoke and black sky. That look would affirm so much, but it did not come. Telep was about to speak, but Ep Brody walked off to make his rounds amongst the workers. Telep watched him, waiting for the veneer to slip. It didn't.

Clouds rolled in to soften the morning light. Telep could see farther than the previous sun, but the distance only showed shapes of gray. His tongue stuck against his lips, and he realized how thirsty he was. Looking down by the bridge, he spotted the water barrel where people filled their skins before the work sun. As he climbed down, the sun broke through the clouds, warming his back.

When he reached the bottom and turned around, the fog was gone, and he could see far into the distance. The sky radiated shades of yellow and red around the rising orange disk. He could see the fourth seacliff ahead and the second seacliff behind, all connected by the bridge. The sight swelled his chest with excitement. He wished to be back on top of the cliff so he could see farther. It was one of the things he loved about climbing. The higher the climb, the wider the view, and the broader his perspective. When he climbed, he felt like he was seeing a larger picture, a truer picture, above the hordes of bias below.

A breeze blew over his dry lips, and he hastened to the water, still cool from the brisk night air. He filled his skin and raised it to his mouth, gulping down half of it before taking a breath and filling it back to the brim. He looked up the cliff and was disappointed to see Ep Brody and the last of the workers descending the ladders. He suspected Ep Brody would want to get moving straight away and he wouldn't have time to go back up to see the view.

As they stepped off the third seacliff en route to the fourth, Telep looked ahead with bright eyes. As they walked, he noticed a change in the sea.

The jagged rocks that had always riddled the water as far as the eye could see began to thin. Telep shook his head in amazement. Even when looking from the highest mountains, rocks plagued the sea from the coast to the horizon. It was a geographical constant making seafaring impossible; A pervasive maelstrom enclosing the island.

Naval endeavors had been attempted several times throughout history, but all became cautionary lore. In some areas, it was possible to navigate between the rocks with a smaller vessel but only at the height of the tide, which never lasted long enough to make sea travel practical.

Now, as Telep walked toward the fourth seacliff, the composition of the sea began changing. Distance grew between the rocks. The farther they went, the scarcer the rocks became. Telep gazed out at the deep blue expanse ahead to watch the waves swaying freely.

He noticed that the direction of the rolling waves on one side of the bridge was different than on the other. They angled slightly toward each other. The water looked so calm and peaceful . . . inviting even.

The end of the bridge connected high on the rock of the fourth seacliff, which looked sizeable but narrow. It had an unusual shape, much different than the other seacliffs. A large, rocky spine stretched the length of it, effectively curtaining it into two halves. Carved paths connected wooden platforms where laborers worked on various projects.

When Telep looked beyond the cliff, his mouth fell open. He was shocked he hadn't seen it until now. Past the fourth seacliff was a giant mass of bulbous rock rising out of the sea. It was different from the other seacliffs; larger and darker, almost black. It stretched into the sky like a plume of black smoke.

"Come with me." Ep Brody's voice startled him. He led Telep across the fourth seacliff, passing many platforms and workers. He led him out onto a narrow ledge leading to the end of the cliff.

"That is the farthest point anyone has ever touched," he said. Telep met his gaze and then shimmied past, edging his way along the narrow ledge. When he reached the end, he knelt down and cupped his hand around the last nub of rock, feeling its coolness on his palm. A void formed in his chest. When he looked out to the dark cliff ahead, he felt Ep Brody's eyes on him and knew this is how he'd meant for him to feel. A chill went through him. It seemed so close, yet somehow unreachable. Large waves converged and crashed violently into the cliff's base from both sides, cutting into the rock like two woodsmen thinning a massive trunk.

The way the waves cut into the rock made it appear softer than the other seacliffs. Its shape was not sleek or elegant but bulbous and oblong.

No leg of the bridge extended to the dark cliff and no construction was underway.

"Come on," Ep Brody said. Telep turned from the massive rock and followed him back along the narrow path to an odd-looking hold in the rock leading up the cliff's spine. It looked unnatural, having been discolored by the scraping of metal tools. Ep Brody seized it and started ascending the side of the cliff. Looking up, Telep saw a string of manmade holds extending up the rock. Ep Brody scaled the wall cleanly and swiftly. Even though the holds were manufactured, Telep was impressed with his form and speed. It was clear he had climbing experience.

Telep followed behind, the holds feeling good in his hands.

The cliff did not take long to ascend and when Telep reached the top, he rested his hands on his head. Then he heard a familiar voice and swung around to examine the other side of the cliff, his eyes settling on a man standing before a group of young men on the stony shore below. It was Caleb.

"Caleb!" he shouted without a thought, immediately scanning his route down the steep ravine between them.

Ep Brody looked to the carved-out path to the left, then to Telep flying down the treacherous gorge, and he smiled.

Telep jumped the last body length to the platform below and threw his arms around Caleb, ignoring the shock and bafflement on his friend's face. Caleb's crutch slipped from under his arm and fell to the ground.

"What are you doing here?" Caleb asked.

"What, too soon for a visit?"

Caleb hopped to his crutch, finagled his toes under it, and kicked it up to his hand. Telep grinned. Caleb looked back to his students who were standing around, unsure what to do.

"Let's have a practice," Caleb yelled. Some of them remained frozen, dumbstruck at how Telep effortlessly sailed down the ravine. A young man with a helmet of thick black hair exchanged glances with a tall red-haired lad as the young men started jogging over to a section of the cliff's spine with numerous large holds chiseled into it. Telep's eyes narrowed. The red-haired lad looked familiar. Telep noticed he was missing the small finger on his right hand. There was a boy on tier two who looked similar, though he was missing no appendages. In fact, he was a climber, as Telep recalled, and a few solars younger. Telep used to see him on the practice wall of Eveloce.

"Why did you leave Eveloce?" asked Caleb. Telep looked at him, then glanced at a wave crashing into the rocks behind him. He knew speaking his thoughts would upset Caleb, whose loyalty to Eveloce was unshakable.

"I needed to make sure you and Ell were alright."

Caleb's stare dropped. "Because of the prison cart?"

Telep nodded.

"Believe me, son, Ell and I are being treated well."

"Have you seen Ell in her new workplace?"

Caleb nodded. "Taking to it very nicely. You haven't seen her?"

Telep bit his lip. "She was away . . . training."

"And you came out here?"

". . . Yeah."

"Well, she's doing well. Making the dark powder that shapes these rocks."

Hearing this from Caleb lifted a weight from Telep. He took a deep breath, the first he'd been able to relish in a long time. He wanted to hug Caleb but settled for putting a hand on his shoulder. He bowed back like a thin branch, and Telep had to stabilize him. Caleb suggested they have a seat on a nearby rock.

In front of them, the rocky shore sloped down into a bay channeled by piled rocks on either side. There were no jagged rocks in the bay, only the rich blue water that deepened the farther it extended. In the middle, a black cliff rose toward the sky. It was smaller than the others.

He hadn't seen it initially because the spine of the cliff had obstructed his view. It stood out from the surrounding rock. Much darker. It looked to be the same composition as the enormous seacliff beyond.

Telep looked back to Caleb. "So, you are okay?"

"Yeah." There was a pause where Telep prepared the question both of them were waiting for him to ask. It was the same thing he'd been wondering since entering South End.

"Why did they keep this from us?"

When Caleb finally spoke, his words were calm and calculated. "Eveloce thrives on progress."

"I know, so why wouldn't they—"

Caleb raised a silencing hand.

"Eveloce thrives on progress, and so far, this bridge has not yielded sufficient returns. The elders are not needlessly keeping people in the dark. They told us about the seawall that expanded the Mainland. But this . . ."

"How could this not be seen as progress? They—" Telep recalled Ep Brody's words: *"This is humanity's bridge."* "We found new vegetation and marine life."

Caleb remained silent a moment.

"Many people lost their lives making this bridge."

Telep's eyes fell to the ground, and a lump formed in his throat. He shook his head, pushing the images of the man on the bridge from his mind. Telep surprised himself with how little he wanted to hear a defense of Eveloce and the elders.

"This project is venturing out, and that itself is progress . . . That itself is progress," Telep repeated.

Caleb swallowed, his eyes narrow, looking far out to sea.

"The collective is always wiser than the individual, Telep. When people come together, they can build something better than any of them could do on their own. Using the best of each person, they become more. Something greater than the sum of the parts. That is Eveloce . . . I'm surprised how quickly you've forgotten. You feel betrayed because the elders didn't tell you about this, but it's not for you to question. Don't forget what Eveloce is."

"Progress."

"No." Caleb swallowed. "It is sacrifice for the sake of progress. The best components of a machine do their job and nothing more. When was the last time you climbed for Eveloce? When was the last time you served the collective? You won't find a better one . . . And you have been blessed. You have what it takes to be the best among the best."

Telep bit the inside of his lip, his eyes fixed on the rocks by his feet.

"What if I can't sacrifice what I need to?"

Caleb remained still.

"Then you are not a son of Eveloce."

The words stung. Never had Telep's devotion been questioned. He looked over at Caleb's stub leg, a sight he'd avoided until now. It was no longer wrapped in bandages. The scar tissue had closed over the wound, though the middle remained dark red and purple. When Telep looked back up to Caleb's face, he saw him in a new way. Not as Ell's father, not as his climbing instructor, friend, or mentor, not as a cripple, but as a man who devoted his entire life to Eveloce. It was a vital part of him. A lifetime on its mountains, yet he couldn't rise high enough to see its faults. Even after being banished, he defended it as he would defend himself.

A sadness descended on Telep as he suddenly felt distant from the man who had given him so much.

"I'm thinking about staying here to work on the bridge."

Caleb drew a long breath.

"You have so much potential. Use it as best you can, still being true to yourself. And if that means joining the bridge . . . then I suppose there are worse ways to spend a life."

Telep suppressed a smile and peered to the students where one young man had skinned his knee and hobbled around in a circle.

"But promise me something, Telep." he looked back to meet Caleb's gaze. "You are tier three. People would sell their families to have what you were born with. I know you don't take that lightly. And you know you could reach top tier—the precipice of knowledge, wisdom, and ability; the forefront of human evolution. Promise me you won't give that up without taking a good while to make sure it is what you want."

A silence passed between them. Caleb's eyes were on the horizon. "Eveloce reaches toward an ideal. What does this bridge strive for?" Telep was about to answer but was soon glad he didn't. "Another chunk of land for greedy houses to fight over."

Another long silence.

Then Telep said, "Maybe that chunk of land will impart infinite wisdom and untold knowledge, and we'll all be better for it."

Caleb chuckled.

Telep looked down to the rocks between his feet. One stone

stood out to him. It was pale blue, turning a faded orange on one end. Telep stared at it, then nudged it with his foot, feeling its weight. It looked like it would fit perfectly in his hand. He wanted to pick it up and hold it, maybe carry it in his satchel, though he couldn't have said why. He left it alone, not wanting Caleb to think his attention was divided, though it wasn't until the thought passed that he realized Caleb was speaking.

". . . The nice thing about climbing is you can see the top of the mountain. You can see the steps and the holds you need to navigate. You can watch the progress, watch the summit come down to you . . ."

Telep followed Caleb's gaze to his students. Some of the young men were halfway up the wall unsure how to proceed; others were at the base in the same predicament. Four of them already sat atop the wall, the tall red-haired lad among them. It struck Telep how each of them had a different hair color—red, brown, gold, and black.

". . . I'm watching what is happening here, and I don't see a summit. I see greed and death."

Caleb seemed farther from him, and it squeezed his chest with an ache. He looked to the horizon where flat, gray clouds speckled the distant sky. Then he looked back to the stone between his feet. He stared at it, his eyes pulled into its shape, contour, coloring, the tiny bumps roughening its surface. There was nothing noticeably special about it, but he continued to gaze, smothering it with his eyes.

He imagined that his stare gave the stone some sort of power; that his consciousness formed a stream that built up like water behind a dam, waiting to be unleashed. He picked it up and gripped it, his hand becoming a claw around it.

Telep blinked, suddenly feeling the silence between him and Caleb. He smiled, but just for an instant. He didn't know if Caleb had heard the story of the otherworldly body washing ashore, but he didn't want to bring it up. Maybe he already knew and thought it was a hoax—very understandable. It was a far-out tale. Thinking over why he himself believed it made him realize it was because he believed Ep Brody.

Then Telep said, "You know, I just feel like this is something . . . there is just something about being out here."

Caleb's chest rose and fell with a long, silent breath. Telep knew this wasn't what he wanted to hear.

"You're attracted to the unknown, always have been. That's part of what makes you a skilled climber. You make things work that shouldn't work. You find steps and holds that others wouldn't think to use. You don't see the obvious holds as being obvious and that frees you in a way. Each time you climb a mountain, you rediscover it. But everything cannot be new all the time. If you climb a face enough, eventually you will have to climb it the same way twice."

Caleb cocked his head and wet his lips. "When you build a life, certain things get put *in place*. These things rarely change. Maybe it's your work, maybe it's a relationship. But the older you get the more things get established, and they become fixtures. They get familiar, comfortable. These things ground you, remind you who you are. You learn to rely on them and to trust them . . . *Trust them*," Caleb emphasized the words. "Everything can't be new all the time."

Telep remained silent.

"Things may seem dull at times, but trust me, things happen in life that'll make you glad you have those fixtures in place."

Telep thought over what he had "in place" in his life. Eveloce, his parents, Ell, Caleb, Elder Grooms. He thought of what Caleb had "in place." Eveloce, then Ell, then climbing.

Looking back to Caleb, he saw his lips pressed tightly together. Telep had asked Ell about her mother only once, and she had been vague. It was obviously a source of great pain for her and Caleb. He wondered if Caleb was thinking about her now.

Caleb continued: "Right now your relationship with Ell is new. I know you've been together some time, but trust me, it's still new. You're learning about each other. It's easy to surprise each other. And that's great. That's what it should be. But that doesn't last." Caleb paused and took a slow breath. "Sometimes when people are pulled apart by circumstance, the loss of control blinds them. It narrows their perspective."

Telep stabbed his thumbnail into the crook of his finger, but when he looked at Caleb's eyes, his hand softened. Telep couldn't deny the weathered sincerity—almost vulnerability—in Caleb's voice.

Climbing commands being shouted from the practice wall broke the silence that followed.

Then Telep said, "Doesn't it inspire you to work every sun on a project where . . . where anything is possible?"

"I know what's possible. The first sun I arrived, they were carrying two bodies away—fallen climbers." His voice was strong, his tone accusatory toward the unseen powers behind the bridge project.

Telep saw the pain in his eyes and remained silent a moment. "Where did they fall?"

Caleb nodded toward the dark seacliff rising out of the bay.

"The rock is soft and unpredictable. It would be dangerous for anyone; it just wasn't meant for climbing."

Telep thought a moment about why climbing that cliff in the bay would be worth the lives of two climbers.

"Were they practicing for the larger cliff?" Telep asked.

"They weren't ready, they just—" Caleb stopped, shaking his head.

Shadows stretched on the stony shore. Telep watched the waves strike the small seacliff in the bay; he studied the dark foam accumulating at its base. They stayed silent, and the longer they didn't speak, the more it seemed like a silence of respect for the fallen climbers.

Finally, Telep spoke.

"So how is this bunch doing?" he asked, tilting his head toward the students.

"Some show real promise. A couple are already quite skilled. Most are just starting out. They're mostly drillers now learning to climb."

"Drillers?"

Caleb nodded. "That's the main thing they need climbers for, to drill into the rock and set the dark powder."

Telep leaned forward with interest. "Yes, I heard about that, but I haven't seen it. Did you know about it before coming here?"

Caleb slid a finger across his brow. "No."

"That boy that you're teaching, the one with the red hair, is he from Eveloce?"

Caleb nodded.

"What happened, why did he leave?"

"He was on the West Wall, and his small finger got wedged in a crack. His step broke, and when he fell, his finger stayed in the wall . . . Still the best climber of the lot. He'll probably be the one attempting the cliff out there." Caleb gestured toward the bay.

"How soon?"

"Sooner than he should," Caleb sighed, adjusting his position on the rock. "They're putting a lot of pressure on me. When I got here, they asked what I could do in three suns. I told them I could find other work. I'm trying to give these kids more time, but there's a lot of urgency to do things now. And I think before the next full moon, they'll take that boy and put him on that cliff."

"And he'll go?"

"He wants to go. They all want to go, even the ones who can't make it up the damn practice face."

Telep looked back to the stone between his feet.

"They want to hurry him on that cliff just so he can practice?" Telep suddenly had another question.

"No, well, they want him to practice, but they are more interested in the dark powder and how it will affect that kind of rock. It's very rare. It's much softer than what they're used to blasting."

"Who is 'they'? Who is pushing for all this so soon?"

"A man of a man of a man. I don't know how long the chain is, but I deal with a guy named Vercillian. He oversees a lot of the projects here on the fourth cliff. Apparently, his superior is holding the silver."

"And they want to use dark powder on that cliff?"

"That's the reason for climbing it. They want to test the dark powder on it, learn what they can."

"Why?" Telep asked.

Caleb paused, scrunching up his face as he looked high in the sky.

"See that slope leading into the bay? If you follow that up, there are boats. Boats they are gonna take to the final seacliff."

Telep cocked his head. He had other questions but knew Caleb wouldn't want to answer them. They remained there for a while, both staring out to the horizon.

———

Ep Brody sat on a smooth rock atop the ridge overlooking the stony shore. One hand steadied a seanut on the rock in front of him, while the other adjusted its grip on an axe. Another man stood behind him staring intently at what lay below. Gold chains circled his wrists and neck and fastened his deep vermillion tunic blowing in the wind. His hair was short and receding. His face was gaunt but strong; the look in his eyes, intense.

Ep Brody hacked at the seanut, but its hard shell—the size of a man's head—resisted each blow. The man behind him became annoyed with the hacking. He turned, letting out a sharp breath.

"How could you let him talk to Caleb? Have you met that man? He's obsessed with Eveloce," the man snapped.

"Relax, Golden Boy. I know what I'm doing."

"*You* know what you're doing. How can I do my job if I don't know what's going on? You want to give me a hint? Because I don't see this doing anything but setting us back a full cycle, if not longer. And don't call me that."

Ep Brody placed the nut between his feet and gripped the axe with both hands. He took a breath as he adjusted his grip.

"This is my decision," Ep Brody intoned. "When it comes to my brother, you are protected, all right?"

The man's eyes shot back just in time to behold a fury of loud, violent chops, each one making the skin around his eye twitch. The barrage ended with a loud crack as the nut's shell finally succumbed to the metal blade.

Then the man said, "Believe it or not, I share your brother's vigor for this project. It fills my eyes by sun and my dreams by night." He walked toward Ep Brody, circling around to his front. The intensity of his voice swelled as he continued. "I'm always thinking of ways to increase production, to condense the timeline. And I am paid because of it. Not the other way around. So when I see you risking a resource that could save this project cycles, not to mention lives, and I ask you about it, it is because it is my job to know, not because I want to protect myself from the possible, and in this case likely, repercussions from Ep Salo." His taut gaze loomed down on Ep Brody who glanced up from his nut.

"You know, I always found it interesting. Your name is Vercillian . . . and you constantly wear vermillion."

Vercillian looked to the sky in aggravation. Ep Brody returned his attention to his seanut. "Oh look, there's a whole other layer I have to peel." He dug his fingers inside, peeling back a squishy membrane.

"This is serious, Brody. This is a resource we can't afford to squander."

Ep Brody pulled back the membrane, and it dripped a milky yellow liquid. Inside, three round pods jiggled with a green jelly. He scooped a dollop onto his finger and whisked it into his mouth. Immediately he spit it out, throwing the whole nut off the cliff and trying to wipe the taste from his tongue.

"I know," he said, now sounding serious. He stood and walked to the edge of the cliff. Vercillian followed. They looked down at Telep and Caleb sitting on a rock on the stony shore.

"If the kid is going to work on this project, he needs to know he is not letting that man down."

"But that man eats, drinks, and bleeds Eveloce. He'll never support the kid leaving."

"Telep doesn't need his support, just to know he's still loved. He bleeds something else."

Chapter 12

Telep wanted to attend Caleb's evening practice session to meet some of the climbers and assist in the training, but he knew if Caleb had been okay with it, he would have extended an invitation. With no such offer and Ep Brody nowhere to be found, he decided to meet some of the other people and see the projects on the seacliff.

This cliff's height fluctuated more than the others which made traversing, even a short distance, take longer.

Telep went back to where the bridge met the cliff. He looked at the large but thin sheet of rock jutting out to the left of where the bridge anchored in the rock. From there, it formed a long ridge that snaked back and forth down the length of the cliff as if a giant serpent had died and fossilized to form the curtaining spine.

Telep stepped up on the ridge and started following it back down toward the end of the cliff, this time giving more thought to the people and projects along the way. Narrow trails and small platforms scattered the cliff, but he hardly used them. He wanted to practice climbing since he hadn't challenged himself in some time. Telep made his way down the center of the cliff, climbing up and over the ridge each time it snaked in front of him. Most of the projects had to do with boat construction and supplies.

He still hadn't seen the boatyard leading into the bay that Caleb mentioned, but he hoped to discover it soon. Telep had learned most of what he knew of sea vessels at the Temple of the Sea where likenesses and models filled the chambers. Covering its walls were accounts of the famous shipwrecks that had claimed the lives of so many Mainlanders.

As Telep climbed along the cliff, he thought about that word, "Mainlander." Growing up, it had always referred to anyone who was not a son or daughter of Eveloce. Occasionally he'd heard it used as an insult or jibe, but he never liked such usage, especially when it came from his friends. He had to admit, though, that his distaste for the term was the direct result of his father. When he heard Ep Brody talking about the whole of the Mainland with such pride, including Eveloce among the Mainland brethren, he felt deprived. How much had he missed being isolated up in the mountains? *I am a Mainlander.* As he thought about it, he gained more appreciation for his father's worldview.

He snickered to himself recalling the time a few classmates came to his home for an Accomplishment Celebration. They were playing a game outside when his mother called from the window that supper was ready.

"Last one in the house is a Mainlander!" shouted one of his classmates. That classmate, however, never made it into the house because Telep's father caught him at the door. The image was still clear—he and his other friends racing into the house, past his father holding that very confused classmate by both shoulders. He remembered that night; he remembered his father returning from taking the lad home. He walked in, wiped his feet on the mat, gave a nod, and headed to bed.

Picturing his father's expression, Telep buried his face in his hands. He wanted to see his parents so badly, and it made it worse that he didn't know when he would. Sometimes at night, he could feel his mother's worry from tier three, and he would look at the points of light in the sky and think: *Comfort her, Pa. You know I'm okay.*

As Telep climbed past one of the platforms, a voice called out. Not understanding what had been said, he kept moving. The voice persisted. He didn't realize a man was yelling at him until the voice became quite aggravated. When he turned, he saw a small bald man with dark skin staring at him.

"Com, com," the man ordered, waving him over. Telep followed the man to his work platform where long wooden rods rested on waist-high brackets. The man introduced himself as Chandradaul, a common hillspeople name. After that, the conversation became difficult. The man was unintelligible. Sporadically, Telep caught a word or short phrase and raised his eyebrows and nodded as if he'd understood, but the man's dialect made it nearly impossible. Telep found himself unable to look away from the man's three crooked, yellow teeth bouncing up and down in front of him. Telep realized the long wooden rods were oars meant for the boats. Chandradaul moved a sanding plane steadily through the air above one of the long wooden poles. He pushed Telep's head very close to the wood.

"Fine, fine, very fine," he repeated several times with pride. Telep winced at having the man's sweaty hands press against his hair and face, though he had to agree that the grain of the wood was as smooth as glass. Then Chandradaul angrily flipped the plane over, revealing its broken blade. Whipping out a large knife, he pushed Telep's head over to the other end of the pole. The wood looked the same. Chandradaul moved the knife steadily above the wood as if to carve it, an intense concentration in his eyes.

"Fine," he said with a tilted head and a shaking hand as if he had some reservation. Then he told Telep to look again. This time he noticed the grain was slightly coarser than on the other side but still very smooth. It was hard to believe it had been done with a knife. Telep was equally impressed that the bridge project had recruited a carpenter from the hillspeople tribe.

After removing himself from Chandradaul's company, Telep came to a platform where food was being prepared which made his stomach churn. A table was set up with many bowls of food. A large, large man in a butcher's smock hacked a slab of meat and tossed the chunks into a pot of steaming stew that made Telep salivate from halfway up the ridge. Behind him on the platform, people talked in groups. It was a diverse bunch. Many of them appeared young, around his age or slightly older.

Telep went straight for the table with lamb, nomo, beef, and swine, each served in their own seasoned sauce on a bed of onion and pepper. Next to the land meats were some colorful sea meats, including luna, which caught Telep's eye. Next came an array of land vegetation including turnips, corn sheeths, purple lingins, potato pods, and radishes, which appeared untouched. As Telep grabbed an empty wood bowl from the corner of the table, he felt eyes on him. Not passing eyes, but watchful eyes, the kind that itch the skin.

Though famished, he scooped modest portions into his bowl. The piercing eyes intensified, and in his periphery, he saw a figure step up to the table beside him. He grabbed the wooden spatula from the platter of luna, eyeing the one remaining piece. Suddenly the spatula meant for the whisker fish was in the luna platter scooping the last fillet.

"Beat ya. Wow, you slow."

Telep turned to see a petite girl pitching the luna steak into her empty bowl. Her short black hair contrasted her ghostly white skin and pale blue eyes. She was skinny, the bone of her elbow thicker than any part of her arm. Her chest was as flat as a washboard. Her neck was wrapped in an olive scarf that hung past her lean shoulders and over her thin wool shirt with string straps. The shirt didn't quite reach the waistband of her trousers, and his eyes widened at her hipbones sticking out farther than her stomach. Several silver ornaments adorned each ear, as well as one in her nose and lip. She appeared a few solars older than Telep and, despite her thin frame, she looked healthy. After shaking every morsel of luna off the spatula, she began filling her bowl with other selections.

"Oh, he can't believe it gone. No luna. No luna tonight," she taunted, never turning to look at him.

Her voice was low but not unfeminine. Telep took a breath and stretched the back of his neck.

"That's alright, plenty of other food here."

"Oh yeah, no luna though. Got me the last one right hee."

Telep watched her scoop gob after gob of food into her bowl, all with the same spatula. He took another breath.

"You enjoy it."

"Aw, he givin' up so easy. No fight for he precious luna." Telep really wished she would stop saying "luna." A vague memory of her dialect flashed in his mind, but he couldn't remember where he'd heard it.

"Hardly worth fighting for at this point," Telep said, watching the growing heap in her bowl.

"Fe fe naw, no shrug off small victory. Small victory make up life." She glanced at his food. "You con take more naw ya know," her voice sounding sincere for the first time.

Telep stared at her bowl, at least four times heavier than his. Her bony hand looked like a claw holding it up. He turned to face her. After slopping a heap of potatoes on top of her mountain of food, she stepped around him to the other side of the table. His eyes followed her scrawny arms carrying the heaping feast, and he couldn't help but smile.

Then she swiveled around and locked eyes with him.

"You eat wit me."

"Pardon?"

"You com. When you done replacin' luna, you com eat. You eat supper wit me, okay?"

"Okay." He scooped up the largest remaining lamb shank along with a chunk of merce bread and followed her.

They sat on a carved trail, bowls resting in their laps, feet hanging over the water below.

"So how long have you worked out here?" Telep asked, immediately wishing he had asked her name first.

"So fe, ya eva drill rock?" she asked, ignoring his question.

"Pardon?"

"Rock—ya eva drill rock?" she asked again screwing her spoon deep into her mountain of food.

Telep stared at her a moment thinking of something Caleb had said.

"Yeah, I'm a climber so I work with rock."

"Good good, that'll make easy." Her voice was intelligible despite her mouthful of food.

"Make what easy?"

"I to teach ya to drill rock."

"I know how to drill rock. Do you know who I am?"

"Um-hmm. You are climber." She lifted another spoonful to her mouth.

Telep glanced down at the dwindling heap in her bowl, her food all mashed together in a jumbled casserole.

He drew a deep breath of salty air and held it in his lungs as he looked out to sea. The water shimmered in the colorful light of the setting sun. A gust blew the hair from his forehead, and he exhaled into the wind, which calmed when he had no more breath. Tearing off a piece of his lamb shank, he wrapped it in merce bread and took a large bite.

"My name's Telep. Nice to meet you."

"Vetra," she answered, nudging his arm with her elbow. "So ya eva work wit dark powder?"

"No, I haven't."

"It simple enough . . . ya part anyway."

"What's my part?"

"Drill, pour, light, run."

Telep nodded. Then he tore back into the lamb, trying to keep pace with Vetra.

As the sun neared the horizon, Telep's excitement about learning how to use dark powder grew. He thought it strange that Ep Brody disappeared, leaving him in the hands of Vetra. It seemed clear that Ep Brody expected him to stay and work on this cliff, though Telep never said he would do as much. They never discussed the duration of his time out here, but after hearing from Caleb that Ell was safe in South End, he knew he did want to stay a little while longer at least. The more he thought about it the more he wanted to contribute, to be forever part of this project, to do one thing, give one thing that could not be given by anyone else. Then he would always be a part of this venture and anything and everything that spawned from it. And no one could ever take that away from him.

By the time he finished his lamb and merce bread, Vetra was drumming her fingers on her knee.

"Com," she said, "I show ya tools."

"Tonight?"

She had already sprung to her feet and was starting down the path. One last spoonful of lingins and he was up and following her.

The platform with the drilling tools was on the other side of the ridge. When they got there, the sun was just starting to meld into the horizon. Vetra was meticulous in the way she unwrapped them from their burlap cases and showed them off. Telep had used many of the tools before, carving out holds or setting anchors for safety lines. He had seen his father use some of the others.

"Good, ya know tools. Tomorrow ya learn boom."

They agreed to rise with the sun and meet back at the platform.

"Wait, I don't know where to sleep," he told her when she turned to leave.

"We all sleep together, com."

The sun was gone when they came to a large square hole in the rock, near where the bridge met the seacliff. He missed this while exploring earlier. As he leaned down and peered inside the dark shape, he saw two straight rows of hay beds, most filled with sleeping workers. It resembled a cave but was too perfect, too geometric. The depth wasn't clear with just the moonlight. Vetra and Telep were two of the last to arrive so they took beds near the entrance.

Telep chose the last bed on the end where he'd be able to see the water in the morning. Vetra climbed into the bed next to his. They covered with wool blankets. Their pillows were thin sacks of lumpy cotton. Moonlight reflecting off the water danced on the roof of the cave. Watching the faint glimmers of light swaying back and forth seemed to quiet the noxious snoring echoing from within.

"That luna taste so bad. Okay goodnight." Vetra rolled on her side to sleep.

Telep's brow furrowed for a moment but then softened. Soon his mind turned to Ell. He gripped his blanket tight, pulling it to his chest.

Chapter 13

Cawing birds woke Telep as the light of dawn burned his eyes. Sitting up, he looked at the water—small waves cresting on the stony shore. His mouth was dry, his lips caked with salt. He reached into his satchel and felt his waterskin. Empty. Vetra was gone, though most of the other beds were still filled. He rushed to the platform to meet Vetra who was already there filling a leather bag with tools.

"You late. Late, late luna."

He cocked his head and took a breath hoping that would be the last time she called him that.

His first word of the sun cracked in his dry throat. He forced a cough.

"Sorry, I came as soon as I woke." It dawned on him how foolishly accurate this statement was as a stinging reminder radiated from his bladder.

"Drink before sleep, then ya rise on time."

"Speaking of drinking—"

"Here, ya take this," Vetra interrupted, tossing him the leather bag.

Telep swallowed, and a burning dryness crawled down his throat to his chest. Telep liked working in the morning but never before breakfast. He followed her to the edge of the cliff where large jagged rocks lined the shore. Along the way, Vetra talked about what they would be doing and what might be new to him. He answered her questions with as few words as possible, each one paining his throat.

Vetra knew rock—the different types, the strength and malleability of each, and how they meshed with the drilling and blasting processes. Any uncertainty Telep had concerning her professional ability was quelled by the time they reached the cliff's edge. He knew he could learn a lot from her.

Vetra's approach to teaching was fast and direct, clear and without repetition. It impressed him how she could naturally infer what he already knew. Few things she said lacked new information.

A lot of what she told him had to do with drilling depth and dispersing rock dust. She showed him many drill bits, some the size of a nail, and others taller than him. One of the tools she showed him was a fine spike with a cupped lip spiraling around it.

"This for shallow hole rock dust."

Choosing a large rock, she handed him a hammer and a spike as long as his forearm and told him to pound it in. The rock was soft, and the spike went in quickly. When the spike was halfway in, she stopped him, pulled it out, and told him to blow into the hole. A fine mist of rock dust plumed from the puncture. He licked the dust from his lips and tried to spit but had no saliva. She handed him the tool with the fine spike, and he fed it into the hole, turning the crank on the handle. After a few turns, rock debris started dispersing.

She showed him a few different tools for getting rid of rock dust in holes of differing depths.

"It weakens boom. Must not dilute powder."

He slipped a small pebble in his mouth to try to take his mind off his thirst and kept shifting his position to distract his bladder, which hadn't been emptied since before supper the night prior. As he listened to her speak, it struck him as strange that he'd only met her the preceding sun. Somehow it seemed he had known her longer.

It wasn't long before Vetra stopped, packed up the tools, and conceded that it was time for breakfast. Telep sighed in relief.

"You go ahead. I left my waterskin in the cave and I want to fill it up at breakfast," he told her. She didn't care enough to shrug. As soon as he was out of sight, he relieved himself on the nearest rock.

When he arrived at the breakfast platform, only a few people were eating. Most were still in the cave sleeping or just waking up. He stormed to the water barrel and gulped the cool liquid. Once satiated, he walked to the long table of food. The selection was not as diverse as last night but was still impressive. There were eggs—boiled, scrambled, hard, and wet—all served on cooked bread. There were swine strips and tomatoes, brown onions and raw corn. On the back of the serving table stood large colorful casks of juice—orange, purple, brown, and green.

After taking some wet eggs, brown onions, a thick strip of swine, and half a wrinkled tomato, he started over to a smaller table with a variety of breads and spreads. One spread in particular caught his eye. It was black and purple with swirls of gold like a mixture of heavy cream, crushed blackberries, and honey. Telep took two slices of dark bread and spread a generous helping on each. When he sat down next to Vetra, she had nearly finished her meal. He rushed to catch up, hardly savoring anything.

Soon, others climbed over the ridge and filled their plates, Caleb among them. As Caleb waited in line, a tall man in a red tunic and chains of gold pulled him aside. The man appeared to scold Caleb, his face taut and agitated. Telep wondered if that was Vercillian, the man Caleb spoke of. He imagined Vercillian was setting a deadline for the climbers to attempt the seacliff in the bay again. Caleb remained still, his face calm and detached.

Two competing thoughts swelled in Telep's mind. It bothered him seeing his friend spoken to harshly, but he couldn't help feeling excited at the notion of the project moving forward. It sent a flourish through his stomach and into his chest. That feeling fled from him when Vercillian shook a finger in Caleb's face, sneered a final word, and stormed off, his long red tunic hurrying to keep up.

Telep looked at Caleb's expression. He wanted to honor Caleb and Eveloce. In that moment, he thought about returning home.

Then Telep shifted his gaze to the horizon where the light from the rising sun pierced his eyes and set something aglow behind them. His teeth clamped down on his lip. He knew that if he returned to Eveloce, he would not come back. He looked around at the different people on the cliff and felt a responsibility not only to them, but to the ideals of Eveloce as he understood them.

Telep looked up to the ridge behind him where it dipped down just enough to see the top of the smaller seacliff rising out of the bay.

That cliff is the tip of this project's spear, the Mainland's spear. I am that cliff. I was meant for it. Telep turned back around, seeing nothing, his eyes lost in the fire raging behind them. *I am the tip of the spear.*

The food tasted of nothing. Telep's jaw fell and rose like a drone. He imagined himself climbing the dark cliff in the bay. He imagined reaching for an overhang, but the rock crumbled between his fingers and he fell. When he watched his body slam into the cliffside, he jerked and nearly elbowed Vetra.

Suddenly he felt a pain in his lower lip and tasted blood. He looked back at Caleb crutching his way from the serving table to a wooden chair set out for him. He thought of Ell. Telep pictured himself with one leg and imagined Ell following him around, watching him struggle to learn how to function. She couldn't help him, and her face never changed. It was locked in the sorrow of perpetual discontent. He pictured his parents the same way, but they were reacting to his death, constantly embracing and always alone.

Telep blinked rapidly and shook his head, the world reappearing before his eyes. Taking a breath, his gaze locked on the red and purple splotch at the end of Caleb's nub. He forced his eyes back to his food, perturbed that so much remained. He stacked the slices of bread and wet egg and was about to chomp into both when he heard a strong voice.

"Vetra," it commanded.

Telep looked up to see Vercillian standing before them, his gaze fixed on Vetra who swallowed her last mouthful and stood to follow him. She glanced back at Telep, seeing him awkwardly clasping a dripping stack of food. Her brow furrowed.

"Relax, enjoy ya food." She followed Vercillian over the ridge and out of sight.

Telep sat still for a while, much longer than he planned. His eyes looked back over the ridge to the small seacliff. Then he began devouring his food, his mouth struggling to keep up with his hands constantly offering something new. The different flavors combined in his mouth, first the bread and wet egg, then a big spoonful of soft brown onions, then a large bite of swine, each one adding a burst of new flavor before fading into obscurity.

For a moment, all he thought about was the taste of the food, its flavor, temperature, texture, and smell. Soon only the dark bread with black, purple, and gold spread remained. He left that out of his eating frenzy because it was something new, and he wanted its taste to be pure. When he bit into it, a mesmeric potency of flavor filled his mouth. He savored every morsel. When he finished, he went back to the serving table for more, but it was gone.

The next sun, Vetra brought a separate pack to the large rocks at the water's edge. After the mid-sun snack, she opened the new pack and pulled out an iron cylinder as long as her forearm. The bottom of it was welded shut, the top covered with a fitted burlap cap. Telep recognized the cylinder as what the saboteur on the bridge had tried to detonate.

"Now ya learn boom," she said, carefully closing the bag and setting it down in the shade of a large rock. Telep smiled. "Choose a rock."

He looked back and forth for one to pick out.

"Okay, ya choose this one." She pointed her foot to the rock right in front of them.

She gestured for the tools, and he brought over the bag. Squatting over it, he awaited further instructions. Vetra stared at the rock, her head moving, her eyes fixed. She analyzed it, circled around it, ran her hand over it. She held out an open palm to Telep, who guessed correctly that she wanted the most used tools—the hammer and chisel. She chiseled a small mark into the rock and handed back the tools. Pulling a charcoal pencil from the cuff on her wrist, she drew several lines around the mark, encircling it, all equal distance away. She made sure of this by measuring each line with a marked string. The diameter of the circle was about as wide as Telep's forearm. She pulled out a new string and marked it precisely with the charcoal pencil. Then she handed him the string.

"Pick another one," she said.

"That one," he said immediately, his pointing finger catching up to his words. She nodded with a slight smile and started carrying out the same procedure on the new rock, which was similar in size, shape, and composition to the first. When she finished, she handed Telep another marked string and told him to drill a hole in each rock, both toward the center, and each to the depth marked by the string. Telep carried out the task quickly and efficiently. Just as he finished drilling the second rock, Vetra spoke.

"Ya see second marking on string?" she asked.

Telep looked at the string and saw another marking about two finger-widths from the end.

"Yes."

"Drill into rock that much."

"That much more?"

"Yes."

When he finished, he turned and saw that she had packed dark powder into two small burlap bags, both the same size, comparable to his closed fist.

"Ready to pour powder?" she asked.

"No."

"Why no?"

"Rock dust?"

She nodded and took a breath, which Telep took as a cue to begin removing it. When he finished, Vetra looked bored.

"Pour slow 'n careful," she instructed, handing him one of the bags and pointing with her nose to the first rock. Watching the dark powder pour into the hole made Telep think of Ell in the refinery and wondered if she had looked at this powder, perhaps even worked on it as part of her training. The thought made him happy, but his face remained in deep focus. When he handed the empty bag back to Vetra, she gave him another tool, which he used to pack the powder to the end of each hole. Then she gave him a long string speckled with a foul-smelling, yellow powder.

"Feed hole, all way to bottom."

The string was long enough to extend a couple body lengths outside the rock. Vetra stuck a thin rod into the hole until the string descended a bit further. Then she pulled the other end of the string away from the rock as far as it would reach and removed a stick the size of her charcoal pencil from her bag. A yellow substance coated the tip of it, the same shade as the string. Telep recognized what the stick was, though it looked different than the fire sticks on Eveloce.

"Hold fire to this, then we run, yeah?"

"Run where?"

"Just ya stay close."

Telep nodded, and she handed him the stick along with the

cylindrical metal contraption. Telep fed the non-coated end of the stick through until it came out the other side. An unusually large wave crashed into the rocks, and Telep felt a ball of energy swallow his stomach. He gripped the stick and yanked the coated end through the device lighting it aflame with a pop and a hiss. The fire jumped to the string as if with a mind of its own. Telep started laying the string down but dropped it when Vetra pulled him away by the neck of his shirt. He stumbled along with her when she didn't let go. Looking back as he ran, Telep watched the fire and smoke creep closer to the rock. She pulled him into a small crevasse in the ridge, its narrowness pressing them together. Telep leaned his head out trying to see, but Vetra yanked him back in. He looked at her. Silence.

BANG.

The blast rang out followed by the sound of debris raining down. A small pebble rolled near their feet.

"That why ya no look," she said, gripping his shirt.

He nodded.

When they walked back, Telep was amazed to see that the blast had carved out a hole in the rock right in line with the circle Vetra had drawn around it. Almost exact.

"How did you do that?" he asked her.

"That what I do."

When they stepped out of the crevasse to examine the blast of the second rock, Telep was confused to see it had blown in half. He looked up at Vetra who held up two fingers, measuring their width with her other hand.

"That why we must be precise."

They spent the next two suns practicing blasting. A lot of what they practiced had to do with the direction of the hole being drilled. She taught him how to use tools that directed the bearing of his chisel bar. It impressed him how, through calculation and measurement, she could harness the power of this new invention, and turn this complex function into a precise science.

Telep became nervous and excited when Vetra told him that

Vercillian meant to have the small seacliff blasted in three suns' time. He talked to Caleb a couple times during meals, but Caleb remained stressed about the approaching climb and the readiness of his students.

When the third sun sank into the horizon, Telep watched it from the edge of a trail, Vetra sitting on one side of him, and an empty bowl crusted with dried stew on the other. The scene calmed him. Over the last three suns, his liking and respect for Vetra had only grown. They had become a team.

It felt strange thinking about what he had not known five suns past. Vetra had immersed him so much in drilling and blasting that now it seemed innate. He cringed at the very real possibility that he wouldn't get the chance to use what he'd learned.

Telep closed his eyes and his mind raced. He imagined himself with Ell. He imagined what he would say to her.

"What should I do?" he would ask.

"Do what makes you whole," Ell would respond.

"I feel like I can't be whole. If I climb tomorrow, we can be together, but it will break your father's heart. And I'll be giving up a way of life I've always held dear, a way of life my father and his father served loyally all of their suns. And if I don't climb, I will go back to Eveloce, and something inside of me will have been cheated, wasted . . ." Then he'd have to turn away to say, *"If I go back to Eveloce, I don't know if I'll ever return. If I go back . . ."*

"What do you want?" she would ask.

"To satisfy everything driving me."

"What fears you?"

"Having regrets and leaving others broken."

Then she would tilt her head and smile.

"I'm here if you need me."

Telep sighed knowing he'd reached the end of the advice that his own mind could draw from Ell. He pictured her face, visualized her expressions, but they weren't as clear as they'd once been. He covered his face with his hands.

That night he dreamt he was climbing a ladder made of all the people he had ever loved. He climbed and climbed, trying to step lightly on his loved ones. Then he realized it was not a ladder but a giant wheel that rotated as he climbed. So, he stopped climbing, refusing to go nowhere. And slowly he melded into the wheel itself, becoming part of it, unable to move but at the behest of another climber.

———

The next morning, he watched the dawn break.

This is it. This is the sun.

Walking to the cove with Vetra, Telep suddenly wished he had talked to Caleb about climbing the cliff. He felt nervous, but Vetra's look of unwavering boredom calmed him.

They arrived early, before the sun broke the horizon, but several people were already standing on the gradual slope leading into the bay. Among them were many of Caleb's students. The pale-skinned boy with a helmet of black hair was there but the red-haired lad was still absent. Ep Brody and Vercillian stood at the water's edge. Vercillian clad in his usual red and gold, and Ep Brody in thick green trousers and a wrinkled cotton shirt.

Vetra stopped next to a large rock close to the water, and Telep placed the bag of tools at her feet. Giving her a nod, he started over toward Ep Brody but slowed when he saw him entangled in conversation with Vercillian. The thought of walking past crossed his mind, but there was nowhere else he could be going, unless he was walking into the sea. So, he stopped next to him and waited. Ep Brody paid him no mind. Inferiority pressed into Telep's chest as neither one of them acknowledged him. He didn't care about Vercillian, but Ep Brody . . .

When Telep was about to turn and walk away, Ep Brody's eyes wandered over to him, though from the look on his face, he may as well have been looking at a rock. He asked Vercillian if he would pardon a momentary absence. Vercillian stared at him a moment with prodding eyes before stepping away. Ep Brody's face was flat with expectancy.

Telep swallowed. He opened his mouth, but nothing came out. A wave of anger rippled up his spine. Images of the man on the bridge sprang to his mind—his face, his teeth, his hand, his blood. *His blood!* What happened on the bridge was a bond between him and Ep Brody, a bond of the worst kind. When Ep Brody explained why he had done it, somehow Telep didn't hate him, and that meant something. Now with this empty expectant stare, that bond was being betrayed.

Telep forced words from his mouth.

"I am curious what capacity I'm to be in this sun," *and if you don't stop looking at me like that, I'm gonna bloody your face.*

"Capacity?" Ep Brody asked dryly.

Telep swallowed hard, biting the inside of his lip.

"Am I going to climb this sun?"

Ep Brody smiled, resting a hand on his shoulder.

"Telep, Telep, I didn't hire the best climbing instructor on the Mainland so I could make these decisions myself." Then he turned and walked up the slope.

Telep's eyes narrowed. Something was off. He stretched his shirt away from his chest, and his eyes rose to the horizon.

He thought of Ell working in the refinery back in South End, using her talents to push this project forward. She would be returning from her training soon, if she hadn't already. He wished he were there to greet her. But even more appealing to him was the idea that he could tell her he was employed out here; that he had purpose out here. If he climbed this cliff, he would be ingrained in the project, and the silver he earned could help provide for both of them. If he worked on this bridge project just a little longer, he could offer her more than a visit. He could offer her a life they would share, here, on this side of the Mainland.

A wisp of red caught the edge of his vision, and he followed the tip of Vercillian's windblown tunic back to his gold-laden sandals, now firmly planted in front of Vetra. She nodded as Vercillian spoke, but Telep could tell she was waiting for the conversation to end.

He took a breath and turned toward the bay. His gaze drifted up the dark cliff as he mapped out routes to the top, all of which avoided the tempting overhang near the summit. He rested his hands atop his head but quickly pulled them off. Taking a slow breath, he scanned the setting all around—the small rolling waves folding around the base of the cliff, the line of the horizon perfectly bisecting sea and sky, the practice section of the ridge where several of Caleb's students now waited in stillness save their hair in the sporadic wind, Vercillian's taut face and large gestures, Vetra's quick glance of growing impatience. Then a calmness descended on him. *Caleb loves and respects me.* He hoped this sun Caleb's respect would outweigh his love.

When Vercillian finally left Vetra, Telep asked her what he'd said.

"What, you try to torture me? Wit that man, one time more than enough."

Telep chuckled, feeling more relaxed. Then he saw Caleb crutching down the incline. He turned to Vetra and asked to go over their starting procedure even though he knew it backward and forward. Vercillian met Caleb at the bottom of the slope. His lips moved, and Caleb's face became rigid. Once again, large gestures seemed to add weight to Vercillian's words. When he turned to leave, the wind blew his tunic in front of Caleb's face and when it whisked away, Caleb's gaze shone directly on Telep. A jolt of nerves shook him, but he remained still. Caleb took a deep breath and nodded him over.

"How are you feeling, Telep? You alright?" Caleb's voice was solemn but firm, matching the look on his face.

"Yeah, I feel good."

"How are you doing with the drilling and blasting?"

A strange feeling came over Telep. This was becoming real. Images of Eveloce and his parents and the elders and the temples flashed in his mind. Sadness, excitement, joy, fear.

"Well, I've learned a lot, and I feel very comfortable."

Caleb nodded slowly. The air became quiet.

"You don't have to do this."

Excitement rushed into Telep's chest but subsided when he looked in Caleb's troubled eyes. The wind filled the silence that followed. An understanding settled between them and they shared a breath, accepting the decision Caleb had made. Each knew the feelings of the other.

"You're a good enough climber to know your limitations."

Telep nodded and looked to the dark cliff before him. It rose higher than before.

Chapter 14

Telep felt the eyes of many as he waded out to the cliff. The pale-skinned boy with a helmet of black hair waded next to him carrying the bag of tools and a long coil of rope slung across his torso. His name was Salai. He was quiet, competent, and most importantly, Caleb's choice to assist him. Telep wanted to know where the red-haired boy from Eveloce was, but something kept him from asking.

A ladder leaned against a large boulder on the short side of the bay wall. Vetra stood atop it, and Caleb sat next to her. The boulder was close enough to the cliff that Vetra could talk to Telep by yelling through a wooden cone. Telep wasn't worried about hearing her; her voice carried.

The water rose above his naval. The cliff loomed over him. He looked around. Something didn't feel quite real—the people on the shore were motionless save their clothing and hair blowing in the wind, his old and new teacher on the boulder, everyone's consciousness converging on the back of his neck. It was like everything around him was the background of a dream waiting for the influence of his actions. He stopped. He had the power to carry his body amid this scene any way he liked. This was his time, frozen with the collective consciousness weighing on his chest. The moment stood still, waiting on him, time moving only with the rolling waves, wafting clouds, and salty breeze.

Telep's thoughts swelled—the Mainland two suns away, his parents over a full moon away, the horizon a vicious illusion of infinity away. But the next seacliff was only a short boat ride away. He gazed over the rim of the cove at the towering dark mass of rock flourishing the end of known land. Then he looked back to the smaller dark cliff looming over him, obstructing the mouth of the bay.

At that moment, he felt a sting at his back—a sting carrying a noble weight—*the point of humanity's spear.* He looked at Salai, then back at all the eyes on the shore trying to push him forward. *Who's wielding the spear?* For an instant, his feeling of power disappeared—a pawn in a larger game controlled by an unseen force that, if needed, would control him like a puppet. He took a breath. *This is for progress. For who I am. My entire life has shaped me for this moment.*

He looked at the calm water around his waist. Everything was quiet.

Then Vetra's voice echoed through the cone.

"What, is it ya monthly blood?"

A smile crept over Telep's face, and when he glanced down at his hand, he felt the power of the world. *This is what I want.* And this time the "I" meant more than him, more than all the people standing behind him, maybe more than he would ever know.

A swell of excitement flooded his core, and he turned to Vetra and held up his left hand with all his fingers turned in toward his palm, a large smile on his face. Vetra chuckled and sat down on the rock. Telep turned back to the dark cliff, Salai still staring at him.

"Just had to piss," Telep said, stepping past.

Waves crashed against the cliff. Low gurgles and a frothy simmering emanated from the dark foam around its base. Telep spotted his first hold and lifted the rope from Salai, slinging it over his shoulder. He took a breath.

"Keep me in sight, yeah," Telep said.

"I will."

Something in the way Salai said it made Telep wonder if he had been given a separate set of instructions. *Stop being paranoid. Focus.*

Telep gripped his first hold. The rock was cold in his palm, its texture coarse and mealy. He pulled himself up and reached for his second hold, his foot finding a step under the water. His other foot swung up near his waist and planted firmly on another step. Hold after hold, step after step—he pulled himself up. The sound of the crashing waves turned into a daunting groan as he rose higher. As his body brushed against the face, the cliff shed small fragments of rock. From mealy crumbs to coarse pebbles, they broke from the cliff with alarming frequency, creating a steady rain under him.

Caleb had said it was soft, unpredictable rock, but Telep had never experienced anything like this. Suddenly he felt in a foreign place, something he had never felt while climbing. This wasn't a rock. Rocks were hard and sturdy. Trustworthy edifices. They wanted to be climbed. Telep had always felt a kinship with mountains, but no such connection existed here.

This is a rock like a corpse is a man. The realization sank into him like betrayal.

He was now considerably higher than Vetra and Caleb. As he reached for the next hold, he saw a crack surrounding it. Grabbing it with just the weight of his arm, the entire hold cracked off the face of the cliff. A wave of fear gripped him, but he forced it away, throwing the hold out to sea behind Salai. Looking down, the jagged rock face stung him like quills.

I can't trust this rock for anything. His mind began to race but he seized it with a breath. He had been here before, in situations much more dangerous than this. *I don't need to risk my life.* But he felt the collective gaze from the shore boring into his back. The stinging nudge of the spear. *Just get up. The best way down is up.* Scanning the rock face within his reach, he could not find another hold that would allow him to keep the same route. Looking to his left, he noticed the rock became uncharacteristically smooth with no holds or steps. To his right was a hold that looked firm, but he would have to go slightly lower to get it. Seeing no other option, he took a step down and swung to it. Again, as he had anticipated, there were no holds above him, but there was another one further to his right. This happened again and again and again.

After a while, he lost sight of Vetra and Caleb, and after moving over a few more holds, he was lost from the sight of everyone on the shore. With no holds to give him options, he found himself trapped in a rut spiraling around to the backside of the cliff where the waves crashed in full force. On a comfortable hold, he stopped, a smooth bulbous overhang above him. He looked down. The wind had calmed, but the waves were still large enough to smash him to a pulp against the cliff if he made a mistake.

The horizon darkened with gray clouds, though the sky above him remained such a bright deep blue that looking up to the top of the cliff required a hard squint. Salai had set the bag of tools on a small rock at the front of the cliff and followed him around to the back. But the water had grown deeper. He stayed to the side of the cliff so as not to get carried in by a wave and thrown against the rock, a fate that flashed in Telep's mind before reaching for the next hold.

Get your mind straight Telep. Never picture a fall. Picture what you want. Picture making your hold.

He swung next to a large crevasse running up the cliff wall, seemingly all the way to the top. The sides of it were rough, but it had no obvious holds, though it did cut through the bulging overhang above. Telep scanned the rock for anything he could grip but found nothing. Hesitancy seized him, and he looked back the way he'd come. He looked down at his current step and saw a crack surrounding it. Ice-cold nerves shuddered through him as he tightened his grip on his only other point of support. He knew he had to move, and fast. His eyes darted to the hold he had come from. To reach it he would have to switch hands on his current hold, and he didn't want to risk putting all his weight on the cracked step. His gaze darted back to the crevasse. *CRACK.* Falling. His body tightened as his fingertips jolted his full weight to a halt.

A gust howled past him, blowing fragments of rock into his eyes, but he forced his eyes to stay open, fighting the jagged rock bits burrowing into his soft tissue. His burning gaze shot to the crevasse desperately seeking anything he could grip, hold, or brace, but his vision blurred with tears. The rock under one of his fingers broke, and his body swung and twisted as he clung to the hold with his three remaining fingers. An ominous gurgling sound echoed from below like a giant throat waiting to swallow him.

His free hand clawed at his eyes, trying to rid them of the debris and tears. Still, he couldn't see. He grabbed a handful of rope from his chest and rubbed his eyes into it like a frightened animal nuzzling into the ground. The shards of rock tore against his eyes, but he didn't stop.

Survival consumed his mind. The weight of his entire body pulled down on his three fingers. His heart pounded in his throat. Every instinct screamed at him to find something else to grab, anything at all to keep from falling to the base of this decrepit cliff. Flashes of Ell, Caleb, his parents, the featureless faces of those who had fallen from this cliff before him.

The flashes scattered when he pulled his searing eyes back from the rope, his sight partially restored. *I am not those climbers and that is not my story.* Another finger broke through the hold. The strength of the world fought through his two remaining fingers.

His eyes flew to the crevasse. Kicking at the wall, he began to swing. With just a little momentum, he released the hold and flung himself toward it. Rock whipped past him in a blur. He fell three body lengths before the gorge wrapped around him. His shoulder slammed into the wall. Immediately, he pressed his feet against the opposing side trying to brace himself. Twisting, he forced his back, protected by the coil of rope, against the wall. His hands gripped the rope at his chest, and he pressed harder with his feet, feeling his momentum slow down. The soft rock shed a landslide of debris as he slid down the gorge. Pressing with all his strength, he came to a grinding halt. He breathed, his body both numb and in pain at the same time.

He focused on his position. One small move at a time, he worked himself into a position he could hold.

I'm okay. I can work with this. I'm not dependent on small dead steps and holds. If this rotting bastard wants me off, it's going to have to shed a lot more than that.

Looking down, the water was still far below. Salai was swimming away from him back to the front of the cliff. *He is going for help.* Telep tried to shout but his voice failed. Coughing and swallowing, he tried again.

"Salai!" No response. "Salai!" Still nothing, and he was almost out of sight. Telep swallowed once more. "Stay there!" he screamed with all the voice he had in his cramped lungs. Salai disappeared out of sight but then reappeared looking right back. Telep shouted the same thing again. Salai swam back a little ways and then stopped. He understood.

Bracing his body between the walls of the crevasse, Telep pressed his hands into the wall near his lower back and pushed his body up. Then he adjusted his feet and pushed up again. Slowly, he rose up the trench. After a while, he felt drips of sticky liquid rolling off his palm. He ignored it. He rose past the broken step, through the bulbous overhang, all the way until the crevasse curved inward, and he could step down to the back of the gorge and climb up the steep, rocky hill. Soon it leveled off, and he stood on top of a large burgeoning plane. Though he had already reached the point needed to carry out the plan, he wanted to stand atop the highest spot where the feeling of conquering the cliff would be most potent.

He rested his hands on top of his head as he sucked the salty air through his dry lips. His lungs were depleted, his body scathed, but his nerves were lost in the pulsating delirium of accomplishment. An almost overwhelming sense of achievement emanated deep in his core. He had climbed bigger rocks, much bigger rocks that required a lot more skill, but this rock gave him that feeling more than any of them.

His wet, sticky palm stained his matted hair red as he took in the sea far below. Peering down at Salai, he yelled for him to return to the front of the cliff where it would be easier to pull up the bag of tools. A smile gripped his face as he maneuvered to the front of the cliff. The shore of the bay erupted with waving limbs and distant cheers. He waved, using his less bloody hand.

Caleb nodded in relief, and Vetra raised the cone to her mouth, though Telep could hear nothing.

An exceeding elation took hold in his chest, and his eyes glistened with collective pride.

He lowered the rope to Salai who attached the tools and later, the dark powder.

Chapter 15

When the first blast went off, the cliff shook, and a large section, including the summit, fell into the bay. The chunk of rock was so massive, it seemed to fall slowly, and Telep knew he would not forget it. Actualizing Vetra's plan required little adjustment. She walked him through where and how to drill for each blast. They performed three blasts the first sun. The second two were not nearly as large as the first, but they were not meant to be. Each time, what Vetra said was going to happen, happened. At the end of the sun, after he had secured the new climbing rope with three deep anchors and waded back to shore, he asked her how they did. She bunched her lips on one side and handed him a drawing on a thin piece of parchment, part of several pages fastened together.

"What you think?" she asked.

It was a detailed charcoal drawing of the cliff. Telep held it up to the live cliff and was amazed to see it nearly a replica.

Swallowing his amazement, he said, "You're not a bad artist. You may want to pursue that," and she smiled.

When Telep flipped the page, there was another drawing of the cliff, but it was smaller. The next page showed it smaller still, and smaller still, until it was a large flat nub in the water. And then the last page was blank.

Over the next several suns, the cliff disappeared precisely as Vetra had planned. Other teams of climbers and blasters blasted large chunks off the cliff and laborers removed them from the bay.

The mood on the cliff was happy, but Telep grew tired. Sleep eluded him. Dark circles spread from his eyes. The images of the murder on the bridge weighed on him. Being away from Eveloce weighed on him. Vetra recognized the burden.

She told him about growing up in the West Isles, what she thought about when she watched the sun set, what the ornaments on her face meant, and why she wore them.

Telep told her about Eveloce and his journey. He confided his doubts, fears, hopes, and insecurities. Talking about such things felt strange. Only Ell had shared such conversations with him, the kind that are hard to happen upon, the kind where vulnerability becomes a strength between two people.

Telep wondered if Vetra had delayed opening up to him until after his initial climb because the two climbers before him had died, but he didn't ask her. Each sun, he learned something new about her and shared something about himself; sometimes they were small things, and sometimes they were things they'd never shared with anyone.

Every sun, the work rolled easier but slower. The more they decimated the cliff, the broader it became, and the more blasting was required to shorten it yet again. When they had reduced the cliff to nearly its thickest point, the process slowed, and it became apparent to Telep that they were not simply destroying it but were shaping it. The blasts became very small and precise. They were creating a flat surface; a platform. When he asked Vetra about it, she told him it was a test to see if they could do the same thing with the larger seacliff at the end of land. Suddenly, he knew the reason why.

The final seacliff was to be a hub, a giant platform on which to build a large ship, maybe more than one, that could venture far into the open sea. The bridge had pushed them past the jagged rocks where seafaring was possible. Telep's mind swelled with an elation of realized potential for all of humanity.

After the platform had been completed, more teams came and performed tests on the rock. They lifted large weights, pieces of lumber, a heavy iron apparatus—things with functions and purposes that were not obvious to Telep. He asked about them. Sometimes he was given answers, and sometimes he wasn't.

As his work slowed, the elation he felt waned, and he began to feel empty. The exclusivity of his job was over. The tip of humanity's spear no longer prodded his back. He had completed the part that no one else could do. Other climbing teams could ably perform the tasks that now filled his suns. In fact, they were better at it.

Harsh shadows stretched amid the fourth cliff's swerving spine as the sun neared the horizon. Telep looked down to his feet, one on either side of the ridge's crest—one in light, one in dark. He felt the temperature change in the cold, black shadow. The salty air burned in his nose. He looked out over the water at the setting sun, its golden rays extending out like luminous lashes of a divine eye staring into him. Hearing sandals scuffling against rock, Telep could feel the eyes on his back, a man he had not spoken to in many suns.

"How are you?" Ep Brody's voice was calm and sincere.

After the man's unexplained avoidance over the past work period, the calm inquiry stirred a little anger in him. He figured Ep Brody's avoidance was intentional. That was the only reasonable explanation for not occasionally running into him. On an island this small, paths crossed often. The only other person Telep did not see regularly was Chandradaul, and that was no accident.

"I'm okay."

When he turned around Ep Brody was sitting peacefully on the ridge, feet apart, head leaned back. He wore loose, white pantaloons ending halfway down his calf and a light gray shirt with the same half-arm sleeves that all his shirts seemed to have. How could a man who presented himself this casually maintain such control among the workers? Perhaps Ep Brody didn't have as much power as he asserted. Perhaps he was a figurehead, a sociable distraction who took his orders from a higher power.

Telep sat down next to him, suddenly feeling tired. A silence passed between them. The images of the man on the bridge flashed in his mind, and it occurred to him why Ep Brody's presence exhausted him. The guilt had subdued during the time he was at the forefront of the project, the tip of the spear, which had produced a feeling that seemed to trump all others. But that feeling had waned now, replaced by self-reproach. Often, he would wake with an aching jaw and overwrought muscles, still seeing the images and motions he'd so deliberately secured in his memory.

Telep recognized Ep Brody's influence on him. He watched him bludgeon a man to death with no thought of stopping it. That was what plagued him most. Why hadn't it at least occurred to him to try to stop it? The guilt prodded his lack of consideration. To Telep, intention meant nothing to the world, but in his chest, it mattered.

"You sure?" Ep Brody asked.

"I'm just tired."

"Fe, fe. Lot of people tired here. This is the last cliff where we can work. It's a good place to be tired."

Telep nodded, his eyes on the ground, his hands kneading the strap of his satchel.

"So, you should head back to the city."

Telep's hands froze.

"W—What, why?"

"You're tired. Fe, you left your home, family, friends. You're depleted. You should go back, get some rest. Spend some time with your lady friend. We have people who can handle the remaining blasting. And it won't be long before your specific skill set can be utilized. You should be rested."

Telep smiled. The words resonated in his ears like musical notes.

Ell! A wave of pride rolled through him. He would tell her about his journey, and what he had accomplished for the bridge project. And that he intended to stay. He looked over to Ep Brody who was sewing a small tear in the bottom of his pantaloons. Telep wanted to look him in the eye when he thanked him, but Ep Brody didn't look up.

"Thank you."

"I am leaving in the morning for South End. So, you will come with, yes?"

"As long as you're sure you don't need me here. I don't want to . . ."

"No. No one will begrudge you for taking a leave now."

"Okay."

"Don't think you're special. I would suggest a leave to anyone who looked as shitty as you. You look like you've aged ten solars." Ep Brody glanced over and briefly met Telep's eye to emphasize this point. Telep nodded.

"Is anyone else coming? Is Vetra coming?"

Ep Brody shook his head.

"Just you, me, and Chandradaul."

Telep bit his lip, trying to suppress a large sigh.

"I'm just kidding. Chandradaul isn't coming."

It took Telep a moment to realize Ep Brody knew about his distaste for Chandradaul's company, but when he did, he smiled. Ep Brody went back to sewing his trousers, then said, "It will be us and Vercillian."

Chapter 16

A mountain wrapped in shadow
Peak in golden cloud
A dark and empty hollow
Light and dark abound

Brittle rock, death, decay
Oh my Love I must obey
To the top, I'm dead undying
In my chest, a hand is prying

Broken stone atop the giant
The end of land, so defiant
I'm scared, I'm scared, though must be me
Through the darkness, I'll drink my tea

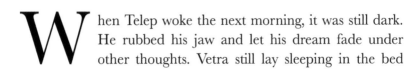hen Telep woke the next morning, it was still dark. He rubbed his jaw and let his dream fade under other thoughts. Vetra still lay sleeping in the bed

next to his. A sadness passed through him. He didn't want her to feel like he was abandoning her. He wanted to hug her and express how much he appreciated her.

At breakfast, he broke bread with Caleb. Having risen so early, the two of them ate in relative peace as the sky behind the ridge birthed the dawn's light. Not much was said, but much was felt.

When he got back to the cave, Vetra was gone. He took his time packing up his satchel, hoping she would return, but she didn't. He looked for her, but when the sun rose in the eastern sky, he was forced to meet Ep Brody.

When he arrived, Ep Brody was leaning against the side of the bridge, a wet towel draped over his head. Vercillian, adorning his usual garb, stood upright next to him, as if trying to see over an invisible wall. Telep bit the inside of his lip.

Vercillian saw him from a ways off and vehemently waved him over, as if they were already behind schedule. Telep turned around one last time and was overjoyed to see Vetra climbing over the top of the ridge. He broke off the narrow path and raced up to meet her. Vercillian called something after him, but he ignored it.

Telep couldn't help but smile as he climbed the ridge. When he reached her, the soft reticence on her face made him feel self-conscious. For a moment he didn't know what to say.

"We're a good team." The words sounded cold and distant, the opposite of what he wanted to convey.

"Yeah, you do good job."

Suddenly, there seemed nothing left to say, and everything he'd meant to say remained unsaid.

Awkwardly, he approached her for a hug, and she leaned her shoulders forward to receive him. He felt her breasts on his chest, her hands light on his back. Vercillian's growl could be heard down the ridge.

"You go now," Vetra urged, tapping his back.

"No." He continued hugging her.

Vercillian shouted again.

"Com, you go now."

"I'm going to come back."

Silence. Then she stepped into him and pressed her hands into his back. Telep smiled but feeling her body against his made him think of Ell. When Vetra told him again to go, he went.

He smiled back at her. She offered him a laden smirk.

Vercillian did not wait for him to reach the bridge before unleashing a tirade about respecting time. Telep would have suffered through a lot more of it had Ep Brody not cut it short. Telep tried to meet Ep Brody's gaze, but his face remained shrouded by the towel draped over his head. He apologized for making them wait, and Ep Brody made him think nothing of it as they stepped over the sea, back toward the Mainland.

Vercillian's anger continued. He kept glaring over at Ep Brody, almost expectantly. After a while, Telep got the idea that there may have been a prior arrangement between them to which Ep Brody was failing to adhere. Vercillian walked in long strides with his jaw clenched and lips pursed. His vermillion tunic was like a separate entity whipping around in the wind, so violently at times that it seemed ridiculous for him to be wearing such apparel. Ep Brody looked relaxed, digging around with his tongue for fragments of food between his teeth and spitting them into the sea.

Howling gusts whisked the sun's warmth from their skin. The air was clear and Telep could see the terrain change beneath them as they walked. Away from the bridge, the sea started off deep and blue with large rolling waves. Close to the bridge, the water calmed, its color lighter with glimmers of brown—the tops of jagged rocks. As they walked, the brown patches became more frequent and distinct. When waves swelled over them, they crested with small white wisps, then big ones.

It was just past mid-sun when they neared the third seacliff.

Dark smoke rose from the high platform where, on the trip out, they had built a fire and gazed at the points of light. Telep shook his head, the memory seeming so distant. His perspective had grown so much since then. One moon cycle had passed, but it felt like three. The things he'd seen, felt, learned, and done now seemed vital to his person.

While they walked, a large bird soaring in the distance caught Telep's eye, though he paid it little mind. When he looked to the cliff ahead, he saw small white tents peppering the lower platform, and one large tent on the higher platform behind the smoke. Telep wanted to ask who was staying there but decided not to.

He scanned the side of the cliff for a climbing route and found one without much difficulty. When they reached the cliff, he saw that the workers from before whom he'd broken bread with were gone. In their place, congregated among the tents, stood men laden in armor, their bodies covered in metal plating from helm to ankle. The armor looked heavy and uncomfortable, and the sight of it unnerved Telep. Somehow the calm look on Ep Brody's face made Telep breathe easier. When they had a short moment to themselves, he asked Ep Brody about the tents and armored men.

"That's just the kind of company my brother likes to keep."

The wind howled as they climbed up the ladders to the top platform. Next to the large tent stood a small open-roofed tent built around the fire, and smoke billowed out. Telep recognized the strong aroma. They were burning merce wood, typically used for smoking meats.

Then he remembered what Ep Brody said about his brother and the story of the found body. A sting of nerves hit him as Vercillian stepped through the tent's flap with Ep Brody, and he was expected to follow.

Inside was another world. When the tent's flap was pulled tight behind him, the swirling wind immediately ceased. A strange, sweet smell filled the tent along with a diffuse smoke putting a haze in the air. The lavish furniture and dark paintings hanging on the walls almost made Telep forget they were in a tent on top of a seacliff. A short and narrow corridor led them from the opening space to another large room. Passing through it, Telep thought he heard a strained female voice. Vercillian stopped them a moment. A flap of leather was heard and Vercillian continued ushering them forward.

An enormous man sat in a large, throne-like chair. He had long, silky, black hair and shoulders even broader than Caleb's. This man, Ep Salo, was a giant. Sitting down, he could still look at Vercillian straight in the eye. His massive physique radiated strength and power.

Silence gripped the tent as Ep Brody stepped in front of him, then his mouth slowly curled.

"Sal!" Ep Brody hopped forward, arms outstretched.

"Brody!" Ep Salo shouted in a deep commanding voice as he rose from his chair and wrapped his brother in his enormous arms. Though they seemed excited, something seemed forced about their interaction; there was a necessity to it, like each one was trying to out-excite the other.

Telep had experienced something similar with his mother after Areto's death. The loss of her first child twisted the way she treated him. The way she expressed love started to feel forced, energized by a painful void.

When the embrace ended, Ep Salo barked an order for chairs. A tall, bald boy who Telep hadn't noticed, slipped through a concealed flap in the tent and brought in two chairs. The boy wore baggy black pantaloons and a tight red vest, the same color as Vercillian's tunic but not quite as vibrant. When Ep Salo peered around the room his eyes passed over Telep but landed on Vercillian who knelt before him and then sat in the chair next to his, which was half the size. Telep wondered why they had brought him in here. Even when Ep Brody introduced him, Ep Salo hardly paid any mind; he simply nodded and took a drink from his golden goblet, a light red drip escaping his mouth and rolling down his chin.

"Fe Beli, good to see you again," Ep Brody said to the bald boy as he sat in the chair placed before him. Ep Salo flicked his eyes to the flap of the tent and Beli bowed his head and left.

Ep Salo settled back into his throne, and suddenly his gaze stiffened.

"What can you tell me?" Ep Salo's voice sliced through the air. The question, along with his stare, was directed at Ep Brody, who leaned forward in his chair, resting his elbows on his knees and folding his hands under his chin. His face remained placid for just a moment before he rocked back and enthusiastically answered.

"All is well, my brother. Progress is being made. We are performing tests on the platform of the bay cliff. Our rowboats are finished and ready. Things are progressing. How have you been?"

"What tests? We should have blown that fucking rock to a stump by now," Ep Salo sneered, turning a malicious eye toward Vercillian.

"No, really, we are much farther along than when last we spoke," Ep Brody began.

"Yes, I expect that much. With the resources you're managing, I think progress should be a given. I want to be farther. I want to be surprised. When are my expectations going to be exceeded?"

"Never."

Ep Salo stared at his brother. Vercillian swallowed.

"I want the final seacliff this solar."

"I know, you've said that. I don't know what else I can tell you. We are doing what we can, but we can't have careless loss of life turning people off of this endeavor. Too much risk—"

"They *will* take risk! They're getting paid five times what they could make anywhere else."

"And the more people who die, the more that figure will rise."

Silence. A thick apprehension permeated the space between them.

"Outside," Ep Salo said, the tension in his jaw holding back an ocean of anger.

Telep noticed Vercillian glaring at him and tilting his head toward the flap of the tent. Telep bustled out of the tent, curious why he had gone in at all. Ep Salo certainly showed no interest in his being there.

Once outside, Telep walked around the top of the cliff. He peered down at the geometric array of white tents on the lower platform, then made his way to the backside of the cliff and sat on the edge, dangling his feet over the black sea below. Feeling a shiver from the strong wind, he tucked his shirt into his trousers. Then he reached into his satchel and pulled out the pale blue and orange stone that he'd seen between his feet while talking to Caleb. It fit perfectly in his hand. He stared at the stone, letting his consciousness stream into it while rolling it in his palm.

A harsh voice carried through the wind from inside the tent.

Ep Salo clearly had a lot of authority. The way he spoke of the workers' compensation and his voracious desire for immediate progress left little doubt that he was a major financier of the project. Probably the chief benefactor. Ep Salo looked older than Ep Brody, which made sense because Telep knew the wealth of Nexus's major houses typically passed to the eldest offspring. But Ep Brody certainly helmed a lot of power as well. Looking into Ep Salo's eyes while he argued about the project's progress was like looking into a deep yawning chasm of insatiable desire. For him, progress was a need. If there were someone other than Ep Brody who could make the project move faster, he doubted fraternal ties would deter Ep Salo from replacing him. He needed Ep Brody. There was something about him that couldn't be replaced, something that made him indispensable.

Judging from Ep Salo's callous demeanor and hardnosed expectations, there was no way he could manage the workers himself, even with the silver to pay them five times their usual wage. Ep Brody had bonded with the workers, learned their names, their crafts, spent time with their families. They loved, feared, and respected him.

Just as Ep Brody had done with him, he sold the workers on the project's altruism. He made them believe that their work was the destiny of humanity by its very nature, and many people responded. They took pride in their work and the collective. Hal, the miner from the cave, prided South End to a fault. Ep Brody had created a special feeling for the project and in so doing had made himself essential.

Naturally, many workers dismissed Ep Brody's altruistic pleas, content to simply trade suns for silver, but Ep Brody had inspired enough to secure his active leadership. On this project, he would be the symbol of human progress for as long as he retained the inspiration of the people. *What power that is*, Telep thought with a smirk. The frustration that he had witnessed from Ep Salo was making more sense. This was a unique balance of power.

Ep Salo seemed so fixated on progress and so disinterested with the people, the process, or the journey involved . . . Telep wondered what was driving his desire.

Telep thought back to Ep Brody's telling of how the foreign body with strange markings and shells was found and the disease it spread. He mentioned the disease had claimed the life of his nephew.

That was Ep Salo's son . . .

WHOOSH! A white blur whipped over Telep's head. He jerked back, nearly dropping the stone as he shielded his face with his arm. Kicking himself away from the ledge, he looked through his hands to see an enormous bird soaring through the wind toward the back of the tent, clutching a fish in its beak as long as Telep's arm.

Never had he seen a bird so big, and especially not so close up. The sun reflected off its glossy white feathers. Each flap of its powerful wings cut through the wind in a low swoosh until it landed just outside the tent's back flap where it dropped the fish and let out a series of loud *CAW*s that cut through the howling wind. When the mighty bird finally ceased its *CAW*ing, it shook its head violently as if trying to free itself from an invisible confinement, its long, white beak swishing back and forth, its gular skin smacking the top of its long elegant neck.

Telep crept to his knees, unable to take his eyes from the bird. The wind died down and silence hugged the top of the cliff. The creature swung its head over, staring directly at Telep. He froze. The bird's gaze pierced through him, like a mother's stare through a child's deceit.

Somehow, he felt sad, for a moment, trapped.

Another bird shot over the cliff, this one just as big, but pale green in color. A forest murk. The span of its wings stretched farther than Telep's outstretched arms. Pinched in its long white beak was a fish, not as long as the white bird's, but a good deal fatter. The green bird dropped it on top of the first fish as it fluttered down to the cliff, nudging the white bird aside. Then it bellowed a single *CAW* before the white bird snapped at its neck. The attacked creature sprang into a defensive stance, puffing out its chest and spreading its wings. The white bird mirrored its position, and the two massive creatures began dancing around each other, snapping and *CAW*ing.

The back flap of the tent tore open, and Ep Salo stepped out. In a flash he swiped up the birds, holding one under each arm, one facing backwards so they couldn't snap at each other, though they did try. Ep Salo whispered something, and to Telep's surprise, the two beasts calmed down immediately. Seeing the two fish on the ground, Ep Salo called for Beli to take them to the chef. Then he glanced over at Telep, who rose to his feet.

"Telep, come back inside," he called. Vercillian held the flap for him.

That's strange, Telep thought. *He sounded cavalier, almost cheery.* After returning the stone to his satchel, he walked back to the tent.

When Telep sat down in his chair, the birds waddled up to his ankles, their heads extending above his chest. They studied him, their long necks swaying like charmed snakes. He returned their stare. Their beaks were not white, but translucent and tinged green with algae. Their eyes were shimmering obsidian, and their feet were white as a cloud with clear webbing.

"They're the smartest birds in the world," asserted Ep Salo with pride as he settled back into his throne.

Telep thought he was joking, but when he peered up at the man, he found him very serious.

Telep sensed he wanted to elaborate.

"Yeah?"

"My parents endowed them to me when I was seventeen solars. They were so small. I trained them to obey, to hunt, to work together. They can carry messages. You'll never find a smarter bird." Ep Salo spoke not in a braggartly way, but as if stating fact.

"Which one is smarter?"

Ep Salo looked at him quizzically, then began snickering. Soon it was a hearty laugh. Vercillian and Beli laughed with him. Telep smiled. Ep Brody waited. Ep Salo's laughter took as long to stop as it had to start, and by the end, he was the only one laughing.

"Theus was the first to come." Ep Salo gestured to the white bird that looked up upon hearing its name. "But Pomyth was the first to bring me a kill."

"Bring you a kill?" Telep asked.

Ep Brody sighed.

"These are hunting birds, trained to fish. They have retrieved meuler, trifin, weoros, even dragon fish. Deadly hunters . . . Do you think you could defeat them?"

The question took Telep by surprise. He looked into the

birds' shiny black eyes, imagining gripping their thin necks and squeezing, then looked back to Ep Salo.

"In a fight? Yes."

Ep Salo shook his head.

"No, the answer is you could not. See those beaks? They're very sharp. They stab. Imagine those driving through your eyes . . ." Telep leaned away from the pointy beaks. ". . . These birds have always been there for me. They are part of my legacy . . ."

Ep Salo talked and talked until the quality of light in the tent changed. Finally, Ep Brody proclaimed it to be nearly supper-time, saying he wanted to get Telep settled into his quarters before they ate.

Before leaving, Ep Salo made a point of telling Telep they were grateful to have him on the project and they expected great things, fast. Telep nodded, masking his disappointment that they were staying the night here. He wanted to continue on so he could see Ell early in the morning. Staying here, the soonest he could see her would be the following evening. He missed her so much he wondered if he would sleep at all.

On the lower platform, Ep Brody showed Telep to his bed— a thin hay mat similar to what he'd been sleeping on in the tunneled cave. Ep Brody was to return to Ep Salo's tent for supper, but after showing Telep his bed, Ep Brody did not return. Instead he gazed out to the horizon. Telep approached with soft steps.

"Are you alright?" Telep asked, even though he hated when that question was asked of him.

"What do you think of my brother?"

"He seems very driven. He seems to really know what he wants."

"You don't know him."

"No, I don't know him."

"You *can't* know him. You could end out your suns with him

and I fear it wouldn't matter. He is so far removed from the man he used to be . . . I wonder what he'd think of himself."

Silence.

"Why is he in such a hurry?"

Ep Brody remained still for a long time.

"We will leave at first light." He dropped his gaze, turned, and climbed the ladders toward Ep Salo's tent.

Chapter 17

As expected, the night crawled by. Telep gazed up at the points of light. The cool night air blew steadily over him, stealing his warmth as it channeled along the wall of the cliff. His body shivered, but inwardly, he was ignited by the excitement of seeing Ell the next sun. Anticipation flooded his mind and churned his chest, a similar feeling to when he first set out on the bridge.

Lying awake for much of the night, he watched the nearly full moon drift across the sky. Then he noticed something different. When he broadened his area of focus and took in the whole view of the night sky, he became aware of a large halo surrounding the moon. It was too faint to notice unless he looked at the sky's entire expanse. He wondered if it had always been there and he just never noticed or if it was something new. He looked directly at the moon, and the halo disappeared; he broadened his view, and it came back. Soon his eyes wandered to other parts of the sky; every point of light twinkled except the moon, which remained constant.

Staring at one faint point, he wondered if it could be affected by his gaze. Perhaps if Ell looked up at the sky, which he often imagined her doing, her eye would be drawn to the same point he was looking at and having their focus on the same thing would connect them in a way.

Telep awoke to the sound of armor clanging as the soldiers all around dressed for a battle that wasn't there. It did not take long for the sun to burn away the clouds leaving the clearest sky Telep had seen since leaving Eveloce. He could see far into the distance in every direction.

Excitement gripped him as he looked around for Ep Brody. He wouldn't have even minded seeing Vercillian, but neither could be found. He assumed they were still on the higher platform with Ep Salo, the ladder to which was blocked by armed guards. Telep took a breath and made his way to the breakfast table where he partook of oat bread and dried meat.

While he waited, keeping a keen eye on the ladder coming from the top platform, he couldn't help but wonder why armed men were present at all. Their number certainly seemed to exceed the supposed purpose of Ep Salo's security. It was true that he was an extremely wealthy and important man but never had Telep seen so many wielders of weapon amassed. He found himself becoming increasingly claustrophobic as more and more soldiers emerged from their tents. They swarmed the breakfast tables, filling the air with brash jokes and loutish laughter. These were not like the soldiers of Eveloce who were always stoic in presentation.

After hurrying through breakfast, Telep retreated to the bridge and to thoughts of Ell. This sun he would see her, embrace her, kiss her, press his being into that which he'd so sorely missed. It excited him that he was now entrenched in the bridge project, and he could tell her he was staying near South End where they could be together.

He imagined her smitten smile. He would arrive at her refinery just as she retired and sneak up and startle her, and her eyes would brighten, and they would kiss. The back of his shirt would stretch in her hands, the back of her shirt in his. They would hold each other as the sun's light softened.

"I told you we'd see each other," he would say. She would stammer questions trying to understand how he could possibly be here, and he would interject all the answers, smiling with a loving gaze. Then there would be a silence and her eyes would moisten.

"I tried so hard to believe you," she would say, and he would comfort her and tell her he had a job on the bridge project with Caleb's blessing. She would cry with joy, and he would ask about her work and how she'd been, and he would listen until she couldn't talk anymore. Then they would have each other and nothing and nobody would come between them.

Telep felt the gentle sway of the bridge as he relished the intoxicating anticipation swelling in his chest. His eyes floated around the horizon and the rolling waters but saw nothing, his consciousness far away.

A man passing behind pulled Telep from his trance, walking with a wobble as if his leg was twisted sideways. Pulling his cloak tight and keeping his head down, the man passed by without a word. Telep gave him but a glance, opting to look past him down the length of the bridge where he feverishly wanted to go. Then he looked to the wooden planks and the images of the man killed on the bridge sprang to his mind. The blood, the husk, the teeth, the stripe.

A loud *crack* shattered the silence behind him. Turning, he saw Ep Brody holding a freshly cracked fóm nut.

"Fe, friend. You ready?" asked Ep Brody as he walked by scooping out a piece of the nut and popping it in his mouth.

"Fe fe," affirmed Telep, adjusting the strap of his satchel and stepping up to match pace. "Is Vercillian coming?"

"Do you want him to? No, he stays with Sal."

Telep breathed a sigh of relief.

The conversation shifted frequently as they walked, Telep more talkative than usual as it distracted him from the nerves dancing in his stomach. He asked Ep Brody if he had received any animals when his brother was given the birds. Silence followed.

"I released them to the wild."

The sun was past mid-sky when they reached the second seacliff, and by the time they passed the first cliff, it was saturating the western horizon a yellowish orange. As South End came into view Telep began digging his thumbnails into the crooks of his fingers. He could see the buildings, the courtyard, the grassy hill extending above the seawall. Taking a deep breath, he peered back at the bridge stretching toward the end of the known world, and a peculiar smile crept across his face.

Looking back to South End, his gaze was drawn to the grassy hill on the far side of the city square. In a haunting silence, a plume of black smoke erupted on the hill.

Bang.

The sound cracked past them like a roll of thunder, echoing across the entire sky.

That's an explosion . . .

Telep remembered walking along that grassy hill on his way into South End's city square. He remembered the lone building. He remembered demanding to see Ell and being taken there. His lips peeled apart. He turned to Ep Brody whose face was white, eyes arrested on the hill. Time stopped. When Ep Brody finally turned and looked into Telep's eyes, it lasted only an instant, but in that instant lived an idea . . . an idea hatefully asserting itself as a truth that Telep couldn't hide from. Thoughts stabbed through his mind—*The grassy hill . . . that's the dark powder refinery . . .* The truth leapt from the depths of Ep Brody's eyes and clawed into Telep's mind unleashing an ineffable sting of pain as everything that wasn't fair in the world, in one breath, flooded into his chest like a swarm of carnivorous insects. And in that instant, he knew. He *knew.* A glaze came over his eyes.

Ep Brody began running full out toward South End. Telep felt the hateful idea crushing and smothering him like an anvil on an egg. He desperately tried to shake it off, but the most denial he could muster was sprinting after Ep Brody, wishing to believe, if only for a moment, that there was something that could physically be done. The world quaked under his feet as he tore toward the city; his neck stiff as rock, his gaze rigid as iron. He passed Ep Brody, the wood planks shuddering under his feet. The black cloud over the grassy hill sped toward him. He wanted his muscles to throb and his lungs to catch fire, but no such distraction came. At the end of the bridge, all he felt was the throng in his chest screaming the unexplainable, inexorable truth that his Love was no longer in this world.

This is not a dream. This is not a dream. This is really happening.

Chapter 18

We lie in bed masking slumber
So enthralled am I, but is it shared?
Faced away, I wait, I wait
Does her heart feel like mine?
Do her eyes remain so wide?
So long must pass, just let it be
Lie here breathing consumed in she

My breath halts as I hear a stir
My heart quickens in idle body

Slight touch on my back, my shoulder
I hear her breath, she's fully mindful!
Oh, what boldness enables the beholder
All I've done has led to this moment!

She wraps her arm around me
Her skin a fiery bliss
Comfort and affirmation and thrill
Everything I wanted slung over me
To grip my hand with driven purpose

Oh my God, this moment is perfect!
A comfort I feel through I and she
But with the calm, a lasting toil inside of me

———

Telep's eyes opened, a glorious physical comfort entrenching his body, reaping all it could from the dream of lying with Ell for the first time. His eyes volleyed a squint until they found enough clarity to recognize the contents of his satchel strewn about the small room lit with the earliest wisps of dawn. His dream was so real, so happy, so long. Now it was all fake—taunting musings of the mind. Reality descended on him like an axe.

The reality he'd known since the explosion on the grassy hill was a haze of pain almost unknowable. The kind of pain that cuts deeper than any emotion the mind can concoct. The kind of pain that alters the past, arrests the present, and destroys the future.

The haze left his face blank, incapable of expressing one iota how he felt. His eyes remained glazed like death. Tears would be drops in the sea. The excitement in his chest became a void, a lack of feeling or future.

Ell was his root. Without her, he couldn't feel the ground.

Sun after sun, he sat in his room, lost. When he felt the void swallowing him, he forced his body to feel something. Staring at the ceiling, he reached under his shirt and brought his fingers to his chest, tracing the ridge of dried blood he'd etched the night before with dull cutlery. Then he traced the six other ridges on his chest.

Time since the refinery exploded became a blur. Six injured, two killed, though no bodies. Just fragments and red paint. The destruction was too complete to recognize either of the fallen. Shortly after it happened, their ceremonial departure from the Mainland took place—a traditional South Endian ceremony where the body of the deceased is cast into the sea. Although there was no body to cast, the ceremony continued anyway.

Telep would have favored an Evelocian funeral, which would see the body planted in the Temple of the Garden, where its decay would fertilize the soil and help grow new life. But without a body, it wasn't possible anyway.

The explosion of dark powder had obliterated the refinery, leaving only charred remains and ashen wood. Having happened at the end of the work sun, and based on the size of the blast, it was believed that a full barrel of dark powder had somehow ignited.

The other deceased was a woman older than Ell, and judging from the amount of flesh and blood caking the fragmented walls, she was also larger than Ell. What caused the barrel to ignite remained unknown, despite Ep Brody's scrupulous investigation.

The evening of the blast, Telep scoured the ruins of the destroyed building, his eyes fixed in a glaze. A man possessed, he searched for a piece of Ell that he could identify as being part of her.

"Ell. Ell. Ell." He repeated her name over and over as he crawled through the blood and ash searching for a piece of her body that he could hold and say, *this is my Love.* But he didn't find it.

The fumes stung his eyes and burned his nostrils as he crawled on his knees studying fingers and chunks of flesh until others forced him from the ruins, covered in red and gray, coughing acid through his throat, leaving black splotches on his arm. He walked to the top of the grassy hill and paced back and forth, looking over the city to the sea beyond through stinging tears, and didn't make a sound.

Ep Brody had insisted Telep stay in his home, which was very modest given his family's means. Since entering his quarters, Telep hadn't left. He didn't want to talk to others.

Ep Brody remained with him for long portions of each sun,

just sitting with him, telling stories. He told funny stories, sad stories, stories of loss, love, betrayal, redemption, even sheer nonsense. He never asked Telep anything or presumed to know how to go about recovering from such devastating loss. He just knocked on the door, waited a moment, walked in and started talking. Telep never expressed it but the distraction that Ep Brody provided helped him.

When he was alone, the emptiness in his chest swelled into an all-consuming void that ate away his future hopes one memory at a time.

During the first sun after the incident, Telep lay awake in his bed, his eyes open but seeing nothing. The only time he spoke was asking if word had been sent to Caleb. Suns passed. After a while he began asking questions or making comments during some of Ep Brody's stories.

Now as he lay in bed, he hated the dawn light. This sun stood out from the others because Ep Brody meant to return to the final seacliff. Telep stared blankly at the bluish, orange stone beside the bed; he wished he were back in Eveloce where he could see his mother and father. A burning ache churned through his chest.

A knock on the door. Ep Brody entered. He didn't start in on a story, just walked to the bed and sat down. Silence and stillness held the room save for faint noises from the square outside where merchants set up their tables. Neither of them moved for a long time.

Then a drop fell from Ep Brody's cheek making a dark spot on the lap of his brown trousers. Telep looked at him. Before that moment, he could not have pictured Ep Brody weeping, but seeing his eyes saturated with tears released a dam inside of him. Suddenly a cavalcade of anguish welled up within Telep, and tears sprang from his eyes like rain. A lump quivered his throat, but he smothered it with his chin. They didn't look at each other, just wept silently until the sun reached its full brightness.

When the tears were dry glossy streaks upon their cheeks, Ep

Brody took a breath, rested a hand on Telep's shoulder, and left. Telep knew he would not return any time soon. He was returning to the fourth seacliff, which was at a critical juncture and needed his attention. Telep was alone now.

Later in the sun, Telep left the house for the first time. He ambled around the city square, watching people go about their business. Couples walked hand in hand, mothers hoisted sons, and fathers carried daughters. All around him, strangers laughed and smiled and loved, each one adding to the void radiating in his chest, the strength of it threatening to drag him into its nothingness.

Feeling the need to vomit, he doubled over. On the stone under his face lay a flattened mother snake, presumably crushed by a carriage while birthing a child that circled around the mother's tail. Telep vomited, the act doing nothing to alleviate the vacuity in his chest. He was isolated, alone, stranded. The pounding, the churning, the excitement he'd felt just half a cycle past was gone. He looked at the sun's light reflecting off one of the bridge's support beams, and a thought came to him. He knew what he would do.

Chapter 19

The sun's light faded in the evening sky. Telep strode with purpose back to his room and packed his strewn belongings into his satchel. He included two new pairs of trousers and two new shirts that Ep Brody had given him, his waterskin filled to the hilt, and all his Nexian silver. Lastly, he picked up the pale blue and orange stone and wrapped it in one of his shirts so it wouldn't scuff the leather.

When Telep approached the base of the ladder leading up to the bridge, he saw two guards talking. He ignored them and stepped past. The guards' conversation abruptly ceased when he walked by, their eyes following him. When he grabbed hold of a rung, one of the guards spoke.

"Where you going there?"

Telep peered over at the guard who was thumbing the top of the axe hanging from his belt. He released the ladder and faced them. "I am going to the last seacliff, where I work." The guard put his hands on his hips.

"And what do ya do there?"

"I'm a climber."

The other guard slapped his thigh. "*That's* where—" he started.

168

"Oh yeah?" the first guard said.

The other guard whispered in his ear, and his demeanor changed. After a moment, the first guard looked back at Telep, his eyes narrow.

"You the pon who risen the beam couple cycles past n' saved ol' Rody?"

The incident seemed a lifetime past to Telep. He slowly nodded, which elicited great excitement from the two guards.

"Oh pon, boy! Eh, ol' Rody the loady! You saved him. Haha!" they laughed. Telep remained still, just waiting. Then one of the guards said, "Fe then, you risen the cliffs now?" Telep nodded again. "Alright, alright, nice place for ya, yeah? Well why you going so late? It's almost dark. You be lucky reaching the first rock."

"That's alright. I'd rather get started than wait until tomorrow," replied Telep with a seriousness that seemed to suck the excitement away from the guards.

"Alright then, safe travels there."

Telep grabbed the ladder and began his ascent. When he was a couple body lengths off the ground, he stopped and looked down at the guards.

"How is he?"

The guards peered up at him. "How's that?"

"How is Roda? Is he still loading pallets?"

The guards looked at each other.

"Oh no, his back was broke. He don't work no more . . . but he okay. His wife takes care of him."

Telep remained still for a long moment, the glaze in his eyes thickening. Slowly he rested his forehead against a rung.

"You alright there, pon?"

Telep rolled his forehead back and forth on the rung, feeling the smooth wood on his skin.

———

Darkness descended quickly, though Telep saw it only from the dimming planks passing beneath his feet. He did not think at all about the fading light. His pace slowed when he could no longer distinguish the iron nails hammered through the top of each plank, but he didn't stop. The night was nearly pitch black, the moon an emaciated sickle hardly visible behind the blotches of wispy clouds floating across the sky. Only a faint glimmer reflected off the calm waters, separating it from the blackness of the bridge. Small waves lapped at the support beams below making soft trickling sounds that accentuated the silence of the night.

Telep kept walking. The sickle of the moon appeared from behind the clouds for a moment, and he stopped and stared at it, its light filling his eyes. When the clouds covered it again, Telep found himself disoriented in blackness. Everything was in shroud. He had no bearing save the force pulling him down and the coastal breeze steadily pushing against his face, robbing his skin of warmth. His muscles shivered, and his teeth chattered, but he paid no mind. He kept walking, feeling his other senses swell in the blackness. The cool salty air burned through his nose and burrowed into the cracks in his lips. His hands lost their feeling, and he tucked them under his arms. He kept going, one foot after the other.

His ankle bent as half his foot stepped off the side of the bridge. He fell forward settling on the very edge with one leg hanging off the side. He stayed there, gripping the wood planks before pulling up his leg and rolling away from the edge. Steady breaths flowed through his nose, each one the same as the last. He lay there a long time. Then, slowly he slid the satchel from his shoulder, drew out a pair of trousers, and put his feet inside, folding the cuffs under his legs. Reaching back in, he unwrapped the stone from the extra shirt and pulled it on over the one he already wore. He set the stone on the edge of the bridge and slid the satchel under his head.

A soft scale of pale brown hazel loomed overhead with the earliest notes of light reflecting off the sky. Telep woke up facing the edge of the bridge. He packed up the satchel and continued on his way, keeping the same docile pace. It wasn't long before he reached the first seacliff. He saw a few people but talked to none of them. It was just past mid-sun when he came upon the second seacliff—again, speaking to no one—and by dusk's graying light, he approached the third seacliff where he had slept by the fire, and where he had met Ep Salo.

Telep stayed back, watching the cliff from afar. It looked the same, still bustling with guards finishing their suppers and getting ready for slumber. Telep wanted no interaction with them. He knew they would not let him pass so easily. They'd probably fetch Ep Salo to see if he was permitted to pass, and Telep did not want to encounter that man without Ep Brody. He found something troubling about him.

So Telep waited, watching the light drain from the sky. He waited out on the bridge until the rumblings of rowdy laughter and raucous conversation ceased, and all that could be heard was the wind and the waves. It was brighter this night. The waxing moon had very little cloud cover. He could see where the bridge met the cliff. It was unguarded. If the clouds remained absent, there was enough light for him to continue on through the night. He continued forward, silently rolling his sandals on the planks.

As he neared the cliff, he heard a familiar sound and froze. It was the scrape and crackle of a fire stick striking against rock. A small flame appeared on the edge of the cliff. It swung up and then faded into a glowing ember soon made hazy by a puff of smoke. A guard sat there leaning against one of the girders.

Telep had no idea what the guards' orders were if they happened upon an unexpected trespasser attempting to sneak by. He had no reasonable explanation for being there so late, and the only people who would recognize him were likely already asleep in the large tent atop the cliff's higher plane. Somehow, he doubted that the guards had many scruples in dealing with such matters. They did not exude the heroism or valor of the Evelocian soldiers he'd read about in the Temple of War who fought to preserve the way of life of their people. The guards of Ep Salo adorned similar armor and weaponry, but they were not the same. They were assuredly privatized mercenaries.

Telep knelt and folded his hand over the side of the bridge. He figured the guard's ability to see in the dark would be hampered for the next few moments as he'd just lit a fire stick near his face.

Slowly, he tightened the strap of his satchel so it pressed tightly to his body. Then he eased himself over the side of the bridge and hung. On the underside, there were diagonal cross-beams supporting the wooden planks. He tried to grab one but couldn't reach. An image of the man who died on the bridge flashed in his mind. He wondered if he, while hanging off the edge in his attempt to hide from Ep Brody, had tried to reach one of these crossbeams but failed. Telep reached again. His fingertips brushed it but couldn't get a firm grip.

He began swinging. For an instant his gaze strayed down to the dark waves tossing and tumbling over the jagged rocks below. As soon as he had the momentum he needed, he swung forward and released his hold. His head struck the underside of the truss, but he hardly felt it as his mind lived in his outstretched hand, which gripped the iron crossbeam like a vice. He swung back and forth, suddenly feeling a throbbing in his head where it had struck metal. He waited for it to subside. Once lucid, he swung from beam to beam along the underside of the bridge moving closer to the cliff. His forearms ached by the time he reached it. He remained as quiet as he could, even curbing his breathing, as he heard the puffs of the smoking guard directly above him.

Telep felt much more comfortable when he released the iron beam and found a firm hold in the rock of the seacliff. He climbed down, the water thrashing and sucking in the hollows of rock below. From one hold to another he moved, trusting his body, trusting the rock. He scaled around the backside of the cliff away from the lower platform; the side facing the mounting moon. At a point, the backside of the cliff became very smooth, and he knew he couldn't get around to the other side without chiseling new holds and steps. His best chance of reaching the other side undetected was to climb up to the top platform, sneak across, and descend the cliff on the far side. Telep remembered scoping out a climbing route on that side when he approached it from the fourth cliff with Ep Brody and Vercillian.

His hand slid up the cool rock face and gripped a hold. He pulled his body up. The waves below called to him louder and louder as he rose above the bridge, then higher, not stopping until his fingers gripped the top platform.

His eyes peeked over. Ep Salo's large tent glowed in an orange light.

Strange labored breaths came from inside . . . rhythmic . . . strained.

Telep drew himself up onto the platform not making a sound.

The labored breaths intensified.

Telep rolled to his feet, crouching low, not taking his eyes off the glowing tent as he crept along the back edge of the platform. When the back wall of the tent came into view, it shone brighter with the rosy glow of fire on the other side. Suddenly figures emerged in shadow on the back wall, fuzzy and elongated. A shriek came from inside. Then a slap, and one of the figures stumbled into the silhouette of a naked woman, her petite body rigid in freight.

"Quiet!" came a shout from inside. The other figure stormed into focus next to her, his massive frame and long hair identifying him as Ep Salo. He seized her shoulders, her body shuddering in the power of his grip.

Telep looked at the figures, then at the far end of the platform, then back at the figures.

His face remained blank.

Ep Salo swung the woman to the ground, and the silhouettes fell into a heap on the floor. The labored breaths resumed, much louder now. Telep looked to the flap in the back wall of the tent and saw it pulled back a crack. Taking a slow breath, he crept toward the opening, silently gliding his sandals over the rock with each step. When he reached the tent, he rested on his knees and leaned to the opening. He could see only part of their bodies—she on her back with him thrusting on top of her. What he saw of her looked bizarre, almost alien. Blue markings covered her body, like a complex design had been painted on her skin, which glowed dark bronze in the iridescent firelight. Triangular silver piercings curved around her hip to the top of her ass. Hanging off her neck was a string of strange shells unlike any he'd seen before. They were shaped like a crab's pincers, and they clicked in rhythm with Ep Salo's thrusts.

The woman's voice cried out, but it was strange. She wasn't saying words. It was like a made-up language. Gibberish. Nothing understandable except the distressed tone in a hillspeople accent.

Ep Salo's hands stretched toward her neck, turning the gibberish into sounds of choking. She squirmed. She slapped and hit at his chest, but her resistance looked futile under his gargantuan frame.

Telep noticed a battle-axe leaning against wall of the tent right next to his face. He took a breath.

Ep Salo pulled back his hand and gripped her hip, straining the piercings. She gasped and screamed. He gripped her harder.

"Stop!" she cried.

Telep moved closer, his head now inside the tent, and again glanced at the axe.

Ep Salo reached past her head to a leather bag on the floor where he pulled out two pieces of silver. He shoved the silver into her mouth and pushed her jaw shut.

"Don't you talk."

He thrust harder.

Telep cocked his head. Then he noticed her feet. They were still. Her arms and upper body writhed, but her feet didn't move.

He's paying her . . . to fight him. This isn't real. This isn't real.

Telep looked to the ground, the firelight dancing on the back of his hand. He pulled his head from the tent and crept back to the edge of the cliff. The labored moans and groans faded behind him. When he reached the far side, he peered down to the bridge below. There was no guard.

Just enough moonlight lit the cliff for him to pick out steps and holds leading down to the lower platform. He found his first step and swung his leg down.

A sound—*clip clup, clip clup, clip clup, clip*. He looked up and saw the enormous white bird waddling up to him; its silky feathers glowing in the moonlight, its webbed feet *clip clup*ping across the rock until its long, sharp beak nearly poked his nose. Telep remained still, staring into its small obsidian eyes. They were both still for a moment. Then the bird puffed its chest, tilted back its head, opened its beak, and let out a loud: *CA—*

Like a coiled snake, Telep's arm sprang out and seized the bird's long neck, catching the warning *CAW* in its throat behind his powerful grip. Large wings exploded off the bird as it flailed about. It stabbed at Telep's face with its beak, but he lurched out of the way and grabbed the bird's neck with his other hand. In a swift jerk, Telep twisted his hands opposite ways—*crack*—and the great white bird fell limp around his hands.

The air became still. Telep looked to the tent—no movement. Slowly, he released his grip on the bird's neck, and a final breath escaped its beak. He flung the bird off the cliff, its lifeless body listing through the air like wilted lettuce to the dark sea below.

Telep peered down to the lower platform—still no guard. He climbed down and continued on the bridge toward the fourth seacliff.

Chapter 20

As the morning light bled across the sky, the twisting spine of rock mounted in Telep's view. He had travelled slowly through the night pondering what he had seen in the tent. He thought about what Ep Brody said to him about humanity pushing forward and striving for the best in itself as a living entity. The idea elicited less inspiration. But looking out over the horizon, he couldn't help but feel a responsibility, even if only to himself. The feeling angered him.

When Telep reached the fourth cliff, he found Caleb sitting on a ledge staring out over the sea. He looked like a statue chiseled at the moment of emotional death. They hugged. They talked for a short while, and then Telep made an excuse to leave. He knew he was hurting Caleb by walking away, but the pain he was avoiding outweighed the guilt.

Telep found Ep Brody on the highest ridge. They looked at each other for a long moment, Ep Brody reading Telep's eyes.

"Okay," Ep Brody said.

Telep nodded, then looked out at the dark cliff in the distance.

Telep idly watched the boat ease down the ramp and splash into the calm water of the bay. The sun had not yet broken the horizon, and the light was soft amid the cool morning air. Resting his chin on his knuckles, his head swayed with the boat as it glided toward the mouth of the bay. Ep Brody sat next to him. Behind them sat two rowers who synchronized their strokes. Chandradaul yelled something to him from shore, but he paid no mind.

When the boat reached the mouth of the bay, it started rocking with the rolling waves of the open sea. Telep kept his eyes on a tiny brown leaf floating in a small pool of water in the bottom of the boat. The saliva thickened in his mouth. He looked up at the horizon straight ahead, and as the boat turned, the dark seacliff came into view. An orange glow of sunlight struck the top of the cliff and crept down toward the water, like a blanket of light revealing the precise shape and contour of the rock's form. The sun's rays warmed them, but the air became cold when they fell under the cliff's shadow.

Ep Brody leaned back against the side of the boat, staring up at the towering mountain. Telep peered over at him, noticing a rhythmic quiver in his shirt over his left breast. Waves crashed into the front of the cliff with a thunderous roar, and the water careened around the sides. The boat rocked until it rounded the back of the cliff where the water calmed. As they neared, Telep scanned for a climbing route.

The rowers asked where to go, but Ep Brody silenced them with half a glance.

Telep pointed to a spot on the wall, and the rowers started toward it. When they were a few boat lengths away, the water became more volatile. Dark green moss appeared and disappeared as the water rose and fell along the base of the cliff. As soon as the rowers stopped, Telep slung the coiled rope over his shoulder along with his wrapped bag of tools and jumped over the side of the boat.

Cold stabbed all over his body. The tool bag pulled him

under the surface and water gushed into his eyes and mouth. He kicked harder to make up for the extra weight and wiped his hand across his burning eyes, peering up at the dancing black cliff ahead. He trained his eyes on the mossy wall in front of him trying to find the hold he'd picked out. Voices shouted behind him, but he paid no mind.

He spotted another hold. It was higher. The momentum of the waves coming from either side made the water right next to the wall especially volatile. When he was a few body lengths away, he stopped and tried to find a way to reach the hold. It would take a big wave to get him that high. Watching the waves, he looked for a pattern in their frequency, but there was none. He felt the cold water leaching away the control he had of his body. Soon he would begin to shake and climbing would be impossible.

Taking a deep breath, he kicked toward the dark green algae directly under the hold. When he reached out to touch the cliff, the water dropped, and his hand slid far down the slimy green wall. For an instant, it felt like the floor had been taken away under the sea. He shot a look left and saw an enormous wave barreling toward him. To his right, another large wave approached. The rolling waves converged, shooting him up. Something slimy licked his forehead and then bit his brow.

In front of him, the wall was different. A crack. He jammed his hands into it. The water fell away leaving him hanging. The crack ran diagonally, and his fingers started to slide, grating over the coarse rock. He gripped as tight as he could, but his wet skin wouldn't stop. He kicked and scraped for a step, anything that would relieve the stress on his hands. His fingers slid until they reached the bottom of the crack and wedged to a stop. He hung still for a brief moment, water raining from his clothes and supplies. His foot found a small lip, enabling him to reposition his hands.

When he looked down, his height off the water shocked him. The merging waves had thrown him a full body length higher than the hold he'd picked out. He grabbed another hold where he could hang more comfortably and took a breath. His right eye felt heavy . . . sticky. He nuzzled it against his shoulder, and it left a dark red splotch. He flicked his head to the side, sending red droplets down to be lost in the turbulent waters below.

As the waves rose and fell on the wall, they made a slew of gurgling and sloshing sounds including a repetitious snort that sounded like a giant horse.

The next hold Telep reached for broke off as soon as he grabbed it. Looking around, there were no other holds within reach. Tightening his grip in the crack, he used his other hand to draw a small pickaxe from his pack of tools. It was usually reserved for climbing walls of ice, but the softness of this rock made Telep think it would be a valuable tool. Sliding his hand through the loop of rope attached to the handle, he seized the wooden grip and drove it into the rock above him. The iron spike penetrated deep but too much soft rock broke away and the spike dislodged. Bits of rock rained down on him, and again, he flicked his head sending more red drops down with the fragments.

Again and again, he struck the pickaxe against the rock until finally it stuck. He pulled himself up, slid his other hand higher in the diagonal crack, and found a higher step for his foot. He continued up this way, sometimes using the pickaxe to chisel out a usable hold in the crack where there was none. When he reached the top of the crack, he found a strong, broad step where he stopped to rest. Standing there, he slid his fingers over the face of the cliff as if closing the eyes of a corpse, and watched bits of rock fall between his fingers. He felt the decay of the mountain, just like the cliff in the bay.

Telep looked at his wet hands and shook them through the air trying to dry them.

The sun shone brightly on the dark cliff, though it remained cold to the touch. Grasping a hold felt like squeezing the hand of a feeble, old man.

He thought of the man from the bridge, pictured his limp body snagged between two jagged rocks swaying with the waves —the tongue of the beast rolling him around in its mouth. He thought of Ell—her face, her hands, her fingers. The plume of black smoke.

He felt the stillness around him. Here he was on the last known cliff climbing for his people, climbing for exploration, his height beyond the threshold of survivability, and still the void churned in his chest. It was inescapable.

His hands clenched the wall, and he pressed his forehead into the rough, cold stone; his clothes flapping in a strong wind. He imagined falling.

After a moment, he pressed his eyes shut. His body was steady. The wind whipped around him but didn't move him; he remained still. When he opened his eyes, the sticky blood on his right lashes stuck them together so he pried his eye open against his shoulder. Looking up, there was an overhang that made the top of the cliff impossible to see. He looked back down at the water. The boat looked so small now. The rowers gestured and waved their arms at Ep Brody who sat still. Telep imagined they were pleading that the waves were getting too large and they needed to return to the bay, but Ep Brody was refusing.

Using the pickaxe, Telep maneuvered to the side, out from under the overhang.

His pickaxe ravaged the wall. Black shards of grating stone rained down on him, speckling his hair and sticking to the sweat on his face and back, rubbing between his shirt and skin. All the holds he came upon, he gripped forcefully expecting them to break off, and many did. He used the ones that survived to lift himself higher. His body was a lissome machine, lithe and agile. His weight became of little consequence. Higher and higher he rose.

He came to a crevasse slanting down the rock above him. It looked like a mythical snake had constricted its body around the mountain, leaving half a tunnel burrowed into the rock. Pulling himself onto the slanted edge of the half tunnel, he struck the axe into the back wall, giving himself a hold. Immediately he sat up and looked at the wall behind him seeing that it became very frail and fragmented not far ahead. The wall on the opposite side of the crevasse looked stronger. There was a hold shaped like a horn, but it was more than a body length away. Telep reached for it with a soft hand, his fingers descending like a staircase. He didn't lean forward. He just held his hand out staring listlessly through his fingers as if reaching for something else, something that couldn't be grabbed, something haunting the path in front of him.

Telep leaned his head against the rock and a warm breeze flowed up the crevasse, rotten, like the throat of a giant beast. The hair on his knuckles fluttered, and his eyes drifted shut with an unremitting weight. A trenchant darkness blocking out all light drew him close, and through decaying lips, whispered to him. *Nothing . . . nothing . . . nothing . . .*

He imagined himself up on a cloud, so high that everything below appeared flat—like a painting of wondrous finality waiting for him to etch his being on its canvas forever. The cloud scratched his skin. A collective of voices from below sang alluring songs of love and peace and harmonious finality.

As he started to lean over the edge, something inside of him pried open his eyes. All he saw was the hold across the gap, nothing else.

Telep pressed his lips together and rose to a crouch where again, he reached out, this time with purpose, but the horn-shaped jut in the rock still escaped his reach. He stood. Leaping from the crevasse out over the open sea, he seized the hold with his left hand and drove the pickaxe into the rock with his right. He jerked to a halt on the adjacent wall. The hold held firm, and the axe drove deep into the rock. A slow breath leaked from his lips. He tilted his head to the side and rubbed his ear on his shoulder. Then, trusting the horn over the axe, he reached for the crack above him. Soon, he was far above the crevasse.

A burn formed in Telep's chest and drove him higher and higher. He didn't slow and didn't look down. No trenchant darkness diverted his gaze. He rose and rose and rose.

Upon striking the axe into the final tier of the cliff before it leveled into a plateau, a speck of grating rock shot into Telep's eye, and he flinched. His rapid blinking slowed by the congealed blood around his brow. A dried stream of red led down the side of his face and neck where it ended in a crimson splotch on his shirt.

The rock of the last tier angled forward at the start, making it easier to lean over the mountain, but it was still steep enough to send anything without a firm hold sliding down and over the side where the cliff dropped straight down. Rubbing the speck from his eye, Telep pulled himself up onto the slanted portion. He looked down at the web of white foam spread over the deep blue sea, hardly seeming to move at all now. Returning his gaze to what lay ahead, he saw that he had pulled himself into a curved trench slanting toward the top of the cliff. It was high on both sides and severely cracked and fragile on the back, which looked to be the only viable path. It was another impression of the mythic snake, the bottom half of a tunnel reaching up toward the sky. And it curved forward so it would get more supine the higher he rose, that is until it ran into the final vertical wall hoisting the cliff's summit plateau.

Telep reached forward to the cracked rock at the back of the trench. When a hold broke off in his palm, he clenched his hand, and the rock crumbled into a mealy dust that soon blew away in the wind, leaving only a splotchy blackness stuck to the sweat of his palm. When he grabbed at another hold, he felt a sting as it too broke off, this one splitting into a thin shale-like rock that was brittle but sharp at the edges. A bead of red stretched into a line down his wrist as he pulled a shard of glossy gray from his palm.

Pulling out his pickaxe, he drove it hard and strong into the back of the trench. It sank deep into the soft rock. He pulled his chin above his two-handed grip on the axe and braced his legs on the sides, just narrow enough for him to support his weight while he broke the axe free and drove it higher into the rock. This time when he pulled himself up, he felt a sting in his torso at the base of his ribs. Bracing himself with his legs, he pulled up his shirt and peered down. A cluster of faint scratches marked the skin on his abdomen, but it felt worse. He pulled the skin next to it, and the scratches slid apart revealing deep cuts as if done with a surgical blade. Blood rushed up through the scores, and Telep lowered his shirt.

Looking at the rock face where he had felt the sting, there was a patch of glossy gray rock. He took a breath, then looked up the trench at the numerous similar patches glinting in the sunlight. With a breath, he swung the axe higher. Pulling himself up, he practiced reducing the weight of his body pressing against the back of the trench. In an instant, the tension in his arms broke as the axe gave way. His feet shot across the rift trying to brace himself. He clutched at anything and everything. A mess of rock broke apart in his arms, but his legs braced the sides and caught him before he fell out the bottom of the slanted gorge.

For a moment, he felt nothing but still. Then slowly a breath passed between his lips and sharp stings emerged all over his rigidly contorted body. Biting his lip with a grimace, he drove the axe back into the rock and adjusted his feet on the sides of the trench. The stinging pangs all over his thighs and torso ached deeply when he moved. The large coil of rope draped over him protected a portion of his chest and stomach. Still, his shirt was scored in several places, and so were his trousers. Painful patterns of precise slits.

After thinking for a moment, he pulled his bag of supplies from his back to his front and tied it to the rope. It hung down from his chest covering most of his torso while also protecting the rope.

Telep lifted his gaze to the plateau above, his face staid and unchanging. Then he looked to the trench in front of him. A strike of the axe resounded purposeful intent as it sank deep into the wall; a resolute stare affixed his face as he dredged his body over the sharp rock. A nimble bracing with his knee, hip, and foot held him up. He gouged the axe from the wall almost with malice.

In this maelstrom of ferocity, his eyes turned to stone, and he methodically rose up the gorge. One stab, one pull, one brace at a time; his mind trapped inside his actions. The grace that Telep usually exhibited when climbing eluded him in the embrace of nature's primal violence churning in his chest; lacking all refinement and elegance, subject to the natural order of survival and endurance flowing through his hardened gaze.

Stinging pains accompanied every pull upward as he dragged his body up the gorge. He fought to stay focused and ignore the throbbing stings and aches. A couple times when he strained in an awkward position, the pain became so strong that he had to acknowledge it in a horrid moan and clenched teeth. Tears leaked from his eyes, but he shook them away. The gorge became more supine, and the pressure between his body and the wall increased with every pull. He saw the vertical wall ahead of him.

It was just a few pulls away, the last obstacle before standing atop this gargantuan corpse of nature. He started pressing his feet against the wall to alleviate some of his weight from his thighs and torso but could only do it little by little for fear of pulling the axe out of the wall. His skin felt wet and sticky, his muscles tired and weak. The strength in his hands faded with every pull.

He kept his gaze forward and upward, always moving, never stopping. He refused to recognize the voice inside screaming that he didn't have the strength to make it to the top, that this entire project was tainted in the procured rape of an unknown beauty, that everything was for a flawed ideal, that he was selfish for turning his back on everyone who cared about him, that he had chosen the way easiest and most self-regarding.

Telep shook his head. With a clenched jaw and weakening glazed eyes, he ignored the voice and everything it said to him.

The final pull in the gorge was riddled with glossy gray patches. He dragged his torn body over them, found a firm brace with his knee and foot, and swung the axe toward the final vertical wall, which was darker and denser. The axe glanced off of it, wobbling in his feeble hand. He adjusted his grip and struck again. This time it stuck. Pulling himself up, he reached for a natural hold in the rock and gripped it. He slung the bag of tools around to his back and reached for the next hold, leaving the axe sticking out of the cliff and using it as his next step. When he pressed his foot against the wall, he felt it slide wetly in his sandal. The acuity of his vision began to fade. It took him longer and longer to discern holds and steps. When he looked to the sky, the blue expanse was littered with black spots. Darkness closed in. He continued on. Hold by hold, he rose up the cliff, moving slower and slower, the spot of deep blue sky fading into blackness.

A step cracked under his foot, bounced down the trench below, and tumbled out over the vertical drop, never to be heard again, ushered to a long and free fall from the clouds into the gentle blue canvas below. Telep stopped. He hung from the wall like a damp rag, his foot scratching at the rock for a step that wasn't there. The grip of his hands holding him to the side of the cliff baffled him as he didn't feel strong enough to lift a cup of water. It was a strength he couldn't feel or control, somehow stored in his fingers. He knew it wouldn't last. His muscles were jelly, his might disappeared, his vision black. He felt all strength leave his body, his drive evaporating into the weight of hopelessness pulling him down.

A warmth spread through his body. He thought of his parents and his home on tier three. He thought of Ell, the way she smiled at him. He thought of Caleb, of Ep Brody and Vetra. He felt the scratchiness of the rock against his skin and the cool breeze whisking through his hair.

He tilted his head back, eyes wide but seeing nothing, feeling the warm sun on his face as his body loosened and swayed. Then something emerged in his vision. A ray of gold burned through the blackness covering his eyes. He turned his head and saw a splotch of blue. He pointed his spot of tunneled sight to the cliff above, but it was hardly there. He was at the top. The lip of the plateau was within reach.

Prying his hand from the hold, he reached up and folded his fingers over the firm lip. His body ached like he had never felt, but he pulled one last time. He pulled with everything he could muster. He imagined himself far away in a distant land with the strength of the world coursing through his muscles. Slowly, he felt his body rise. With everything he had, he churned his body onto the plateau where he rolled onto his back and gasped for air. His chest rose and fell as he looked up at the small hazy circle of blue. And that luminescent spot of sky shone through his tattered and bloody shirt, through the rips in his skin, and into the void, sucking every feeling from his chest.

———

When Telep awoke, his joints ached, and his skin throbbed. Closing his eyes, he focused on nothing. He pushed every thought from his head. Gradually his heart slowed, and his breathing normalized. In a hazy abyss of blackness, he lay there.

The sun hung well below mid-sky, but plenty of light remained. Slowly, Telep loosened the knot keeping the sack of tools closed, moving only his arms and fingers. The rest of his body lay prostrate like a corpse. Reaching in, he pulled out his worn leather waterskin and drank until he coughed. Setting the skin aside, he reached to the bottom of the bag until his fingers found a small tin, which he removed.

Gently, he pulled the coiled rope with the sack attached over his head and laid it next to him. He pulled off his shirt, slowly peeling the tattered fabric soaked in red from his skin. Then he pushed his pants down and kicked them off, arranging his clothes under him to soften the rock. When he looked down at his naked body, it was covered in blood. Deep gashes and scrapes littered his skin. No expression came to his face; he felt between his legs and eased a breath. Picking up the tin, he pried off the lid and smeared his fingers into the pale purple balm and rubbed it into his skin. When the balm touched his cuts, a painful breath quivered from his nose, but he did not stop until every scrape on his body was sheathed in the lavender ointment.

When he felt able, he stood, wobbling at first but catching his balance. He peered over the edge. The height shocked him. The water looked calm from here.

Slowly, he limped over to the other side of the plateau and looked down at the fourth seacliff far below where tiny specks of people rested around the placid blue circle of the bay. It amazed him how far he could see, the vantage point reminiscent of the fifth tier of Eveloce. Stepping to the edge, he rested his hands atop his head and breathed.

One of the specks from around the bay jumped up, arms waving. Then other specks began congregating and jumping. The wind stilled, and Telep thought he heard the faintest whisper of their collected cries and cheers. Though his eyes swelled with tears and a lump arrested his throat, his face remained rigid, and he didn't make a sound.

———

When the collected workers around the bay looked up at him, they saw a silhouetted speck of a hero standing atop the farthest, highest, and most treacherous seacliff; they saw him as an extension of themselves and their efforts to expand and explore. They didn't see into the silhouette, into the blackness to the naked, broken man with tears streaming down his cheeks. They didn't feel his turmoil or conflict. He was their triumph. He was the credence to everything inspiring from Ep Brody's lips.

———

Telep looked down to the tiny waves patting the base of the mountain. They seemed so peaceful from this height. Everything seemed peaceful. Suddenly, a wave of doubt rippled through him, and he backed away from the ledge, the whisper of cheers disappearing behind him.

Doubt . . . What was he doubting? Everything. The project. The power behind it. Everything.

Anger stirred in a thought of Ep Salo. *He has a hatred in him. His drive is a hatred for the plagued body that took his son.* The pride he'd felt for the collective felt different. The feeling weighed on him, gnawed at him. He thought for a long time. He thought about the workers of the project and what drove them. He thought until his mind was reduced to simple credos and proverbs, one of which stuck in his mind above all others.

People can be a means to an end as much as the end serves people.

Telep ambled over the rock toward the supplies at the other end of the plateau, the wind drying his eyes. Looking down at the huge coiled rope and sack of tools, he paused. When he lifted his gaze, he froze. The lump in his throat disappeared. He blinked hard and squinted. His eyes shimmering as they fixed on one speck in the distance where, in front of the bright twilight sky, the horizon was not perfectly flat, where an extremely distant but unmistakable landmass rose out of the sea.

Chapter 21

Wind rushing through his hair
All his troubles left above
He was falling into the sea
A sea of people
Everyone on the Mainland
Their eyes trained on him
He floated in the air
Pushed up by their collective stare
Every instant was just after he . . .
Did I jump or did I fall?
He could not climb up
Could not crash down
Could not be one in the crowd
Suspended, arrested, isolated, alone
In limbo the sun shone

Telep awoke from his dream feeling an emptiness in his chest. Lying on his back in the tunneled cave of the fourth seacliff, his gaze drifted around the textured rock overhead. He lay in a nook, which jutted off from the sleeping section of the cave, so it had some privacy. The pale blue eyes of an older woman moved over him as her cracked hands rubbed purple balm into his wounds. He couldn't remember seeing her before. Her hands glided over his skin, soothing him, healing him.

For the next few suns, consciousness washed back and forth over Telep like waves on the shore. He let his body heal. People came to visit him, Ep Brody, Caleb, Vetra. Only Ep Brody stayed for extended periods of time, and Telep knew it was because Vetra and Caleb were busy working. Now that a stake was fixed in the top of the cliff with a stable rope and pulley system, people and supplies were hoisted easily to the top, and the cliff bustled with new work. Like a bursting dam, the pent-up energy flowed through the collective as if to make up for time lost.

After Telep had set the anchor and rope, Ep Brody was the first one up the final seacliff, though that was the following sun. So, when Ep Brody returned and visited him, Telep expected him to talk about the mass of land off in the distance. He didn't. He just gave him a reassuring grin and it occurred to Telep that he didn't know. Ep Brody hadn't seen it.

Telep peered out at the smooth even light entering the mouth of the cave, the kind of light consistent with an overcast sky. *The horizon was shrouded by cloud. He couldn't see it. No one knows.*

When he looked into Ep Brody's eyes, something kept him from revealing the discovery. He lay quietly and listened for a long time to Ep Brody talk about how benefitted the future would be thanks to his historic climb. Telep felt no such triumph.

He wanted to feel proud. He yearned for it. Even hubris would have been preferable to the void he felt.

Telep lay in the nook for suns. Each morning, he looked to

the light entering the cave and saw it cool and smooth, but he knew the overcast veil wouldn't last forever.

Sun after sun, night after night, he lay there, the stillness leaving him with the pain he wished to ignore. The torturous calm left him alone with himself. His core ached and ached, building up a pressure in his chest until a single idea snapped the stillness. The idea became a decision, and he embraced it, though part of him hated it. Everything he knew was tainted in Ell's death. He couldn't stay here anymore. He needed the unknown.

When he awoke the following morning, the sky was cloudy once again, and he felt stronger. The scrapes had faded, and he could move without intense pain. He sat up and made his way down to the breakfast table, which was abandoned after the morning rush. He emptied the bowl of the pale purple spread, first with bread, then with his fingers. When he'd had his fill, he loaded all the remaining food into a burlap sack, which he brought back to the cave and hid under his mattress of hay.

The idea from the night before danced in his mind like dark smoke, and suddenly he felt the pressure of time it put on him. Deep down, he knew seeing someone he loved could mar his plans, so he kept out of sight.

Before mid-sun—when the old woman would visit—he took his bag of food and satchel, now filled with supplies, to the jagged shore where Vetra had taught him to use dark powder. That section of the cliff was almost always deserted because of the sharp rocks and volatile waves. He stashed his bags behind a large rock.

Slinking up the ridge on the way back, Telep felt the strain on his mending skin. He knew it was too soon to be climbing, but he wasn't going to stop. When he reached the top of the ridge, he looked out over the bay where the small cliff had been. Now it was just a nub straining to stay above the tide. From the ridge, Telep could see atop the ramp leading down into the bay where a small rowboat rested. Several small boats had been constructed now, all of them used to transport people and supplies to the final cliff.

Telep eased his way down the cliff and studied the boat. There were no holes, no apparent reason for its lack of use. When he looked back out to the sea, he saw a boat rounding the crest of the bay with both Caleb and Vetra aboard. He ducked behind the boat and stealthily made his way back to the nook in the cave where he closed his eyes and tried to empty his mind. It worked for a very short time.

The old woman arrived as expected, ready to rebalm and rebandage his wounds. Telep was grateful. When she asked him if he had moved around, he found himself not wanting to lie.

He remained still for a long time, even after the woman left. The jittering light of the oil torch beside him painted unease on the roof of the cave. An emptiness gripped him as people settled into their beds for the night's slumber. He waited for the calm of darkness, but still he dreaded its arrival. He wanted to speak to everyone and no one. He wanted to embrace all those who had filled him with love, but the gnawing emptiness in his core hated that love and what it had cost him.

Vetra's black hair hung in front of her face as she nimbly bowed under the arch at the nook's entrance. A heavy breath fled Telep's lungs. All the things he had imagined saying to her now didn't seem possible. Kneeling beside him, she brushed the hair from her pale face revealing her blue eyes, bottomless in the glow of the oil torch.

"You really milking this vacation."

"What?"

"This pity vacation you use to not work. You really milking it. Now I have to hold hand of sorry replacement. He even worse than you, ya know. You really slow things down."

Telep started to sit up, but Vetra stopped him, putting her hands on his shoulders and easing him back down. "Oh no, you stay lying down. If people see you up 'n about, they gon' put you to work. You want to milk these little scrapes, so you stay lying here." She patted his shoulders and gently pulled his blanket up to his neck. "There, now no one see how healed you are." She patted his chest and her hand stayed there.

The heat from her hand seeped through the blanket, and in that moment Telep felt his emotional veil weaken. He wanted her to leave. He wanted her to stay. He wanted to share what he was feeling. He wanted to acknowledge her playful badgering. Feeling the warmth on his chest, he felt the possibility in her openness. He felt he could seize her hand and start crying, and it would be okay. Her reaction would be the right one. He felt he could talk to her all night about Ell and the gnawing void churning in his chest. He felt her enduring comfort. He felt her friendship. He felt the possibility of abandoning his plan.

He took a deep breath and looked into her eyes.

"I'm tired. I need to sleep."

When she pulled her hand away, the possibilities were gone.

———

When everyone was asleep, Telep slipped from the cave and made his way up to the ridge overlooking the bay, the moon lighting his way. He expected a sentry of some kind but saw none. The boats sat in a row, dimly painted orange by the flicker of an oil torch. He scaled the ridge down to the stony shore and retrieved his stash of supplies. Though lifting the burlap sack strained his sore muscles, he wasted no time. He climbed around the cliff wall and onto the near corner of the bay shore, slowing when the glow next to the boats came into view. Still, no one was there. He crept along, thinking of what he'd say if confronted.

When he reached the boats, he placed his supplies inside the one nearest, scanning the surroundings for outliers. He spotted a bucket filled with water. Though confident he had packed enough, he grabbed the bucket and set it next to his supplies. Everything seemed still save his thumping heart, which he could almost hear. When he pushed the back of the boat, the hull made a loud scraping sound on the rock. It was much louder now than in the sun, but he kept going. He pushed the boat hard down the slope as if tearing a bandage from a wound. The boat slid much easier once its hull reached the algae slick gulch carved into the ramp.

With a splash, the vessel floated freely in the water. He waded out past his knees and stopped. He slid off his sandal and felt the coarse rock on his foot. With a breath, he jumped into the vessel.

The chosen boat was designed for a single rower. Each wooden oar hinged on a pivoting pin attached to the side rails such that Telep faced away from the craft's vector. The smooth wood felt comfortable in his hands as he rowed toward the mouth of the bay, watching the orange light dim from the top of the slope. Still no one could be seen. As he passed the nub of the small cliff, tepid waves filled and drew from a hollow in the rock and he listened to its sound, a dying animal struggling for breath.

He passed through the mouth of the bay, and the boat rocked in the added texture of the open sea. As he looked back, the fourth cliff appeared eerily stagnant. Slowly, it would shrink. He was away from its haunting stillness.

The glow of the torch disappeared from view. No one had seen him.

The ease of his departure weighed on his mind. Part of him had almost expected to get caught . . . expected a sentry to apprehend him and usher him back to his nook where the entrance would be guarded from then on.

A deep breath filled his lungs. He was alone, but this circumstance was completely unknown, and it generated a resonance that filled the hollowness inside of him. He relished the feeling as it burgeoned in his chest. The setting comforted him—the rolling power of the waves, the rhythmic slosh of the oars, the dark shore fading in the distance.

He rowed a long time, looking back at the Mainland, shrinking it with each stroke.

Chapter 22

Telep rowed through the night, using the constant point of light to keep his bearing. He kept rowing as the encroaching dawn swallowed the brightest point in the sky.

Telep tried to distract himself from his aching muscles and throbbing skin. His head swayed with fatigue, but his eyes remained wide and rigid. The cuts covering his body were still very sensitive, and the continual movement of his shoulders, arms, and back added considerable strain. Whenever a stroke stretched his skin too much, a sharp twinge of pain shot through him. He tried to be careful and limit the broadening of his torso so as not to reopen any wounds.

With that in mind, Telep knew this was a sprint. He only had food and supplies to last so long. He did not know exactly how far away the landmass on the horizon was or how many suns it would take to get there, though he had made some calculations. The natural pull of the sea seemed to add to his speed.

When the dawn broke, Telep stopped rowing, detached the oars, and placed them inside the boat. He opened the burlap sack and pulled out a long coil of rope attached to a bulbous gray and white stone. He yanked on it to test the knot—solid.

Then he tied the other end of the rope to the docking hold at the front of the boat and threw the stone overboard. The rope began to uncoil and disappear over the bow.

Reaching into his bag of supplies, Telep took a small sip from a large waterskin, making sure to secure the cork in the nozzle when he finished. Reaching back inside the burlap sack, he pulled out a coil of twine and rolled up brown cloth, which he unrolled to reveal a silver knife. Its blade made up two-thirds of its length, and its wooden handle fit well in his hand. It was meant for slicing meats but cut the twine with ease. Turning back to the anchored rope, which had stopped disappearing over the bow, he leaned over and started drawing it up from the water until he felt the weight of the stone tug on the other end. Pinching the rope where it met the water, he tied on a loop of twine to mark the sea's depth.

A deep breath of the salty air burned Telep's nose as he knelt on the floor of the boat and emptied the burlap sack, spreading his provisions in front of him. He had five large waterskins filled to bursting, plus his smaller waterskin that he'd brought from Eveloce. Under normal conditions, a large skin could sustain him for five suns but with the added energy output of rowing, he figured less. There was a smaller sack inside the big one that had all the food. He set that in the back of the boat next to the water bucket he'd grabbed before pushing off. Looking inside, now in the light, he saw a rag floating in its murky brown water laden with mushy organic chunks. He figured it must be the pail that the chef's assistant used to wash the dinner bowls the night before.

He continued organizing the supplies. A lot of the items he'd brought were wrapped in rags or extra clothes so when he unrolled them across the bottom of the boat, it looked like a tattered patch quilt. On one patch shone two hooks, one small and one large; on another patch lay a small rock hammer and chisel; another had two rolled up shirts and one pair of trousers. On another patch lay a slew of fire sticks. On yet another patch was a new tin of purple balm. He put the twine with the hooks and rolled them up together. Then he rolled up the others. The last item he rolled up was the pale blue and orange stone, his eyes lingering on it as he did so. When everything was packed away, he tied the burlap sack to the seat at the bow.

When he was done, Telep lay down in the bottom of the vessel, shading his head under the seat. His muscles were weak from the night of rowing and his skin ached.

The sun peaked over the horizon, shining its harsh golden rays across the surface of the water. Only a few clouds hung in the sky, and Telep knew it would not take the sun long to burn them away. It would be a clear sun with high visibility, the first one since he'd climbed the final cliff.

Telep closed his eyes and took a deep breath, the scent of salt and freshly cut wood filling his nostrils. He waited a moment, every muscle relaxed, feeling the sway of the sea. Total tranquility. Then his eyes locked wide, and he climbed back into his rowing seat where he mechanically rowed until the pain of it was all he could think about. Still, he kept going.

———

Telep's neck bent awkwardly as he slept on the floor of the vessel, which wasn't a great distance longer than his supine body. His skin was red and bronze and leathery from the relentless sun. A new beard covered his face, long enough to shield the sun but short enough to turn any makeshift pillow into a scouring pad. His head rested on a few folded rags, his forehead bumping the side of the boat whenever a wave came along with enough jostle. His lips were open, but no saliva stained the rag. His mouth was dry. Two large waterskins lay empty at the stern of the boat, and he wouldn't let himself open the third until morning despite not taking a sip in over half a sun.

The growth of his beard added five solars to his face, and his weathered stare added another five. His eyes were yellow and

bloodshot, his hands raw and blistered. Half of his food provisions were gone, though he worried more about his water supply.
He had managed to catch three fish. Two were fat and gray with
giant mouths, and one was long like an eel and had nine sets of
fins along its body. Never had he seen water-life of the like, and
he was enthralled at its newness and diversity.

When Telep awoke, he coughed a dry, raspy cough. His arm
shielded his dry eyes as they shriveled in the morning light. He
licked his cracked lips, but they remained just as dry. He crawled
over to the burgeoning waterskin and carefully uncorked it. His
dry lips wrapped around the nozzle, and he took three gulps. On
the last gulp he almost choked but covered his mouth to retain
the fluid.

He reached for his pillow rag, covered his mouth, and took a
deep breath. He'd found that the salty air didn't burn his nose or
throat as much when it passed through cloth. Peering over the
side of the boat, he tugged up on the rope tied to the stone,
feeling that it was taut. It had been nine suns since the bottom of
the sea had vanished below the length of the rope. After pulling
up the stone and stowing it with the coiled rope in the bow, he
stepped to the stern. It took him a moment to relax, and when
the few drops of dark yellow urine fell into the water, it burned
with a torrid intensity that lingered long after.

When he was done, he waddled over to the seat, sat down
with a sigh, and grabbed a brown towel tied at the top like a
knapsack. Inside rested one roll of bread. It was hard to the
touch, so hard he had to press into it with his thumbs to break it
apart. He ate it slowly, savoring every bite as he looked out over
the water. When finished, he packed it away carefully, grabbed
the tin of balm and removed the lid. It was nearly gone now,
enough for two more applications, maybe three if he made them
very light. After pulling his shirt over his head, he slowly and
carefully rubbed a dollop over the scores on his chest and belly,
which harbored the largest concentration of cuts, and also where
rowing caused the most strain.

Applying the balm had become a morning ritual to make his skin more elastic during the labor-intensive rowing. His cuts had healed marginally but still stung in the extensive toil. Every morning, it seemed to take him longer and longer to settle into his seat and make that first stroke. The physicality of the work had become increasingly painful. His muscles grew more adept to the rowing motion, but his lack of water made them burn as if filled with acid.

The purple balm was cool on his skin and cold in the brisk morning breeze, which he relished, knowing what insistent heat the sun would later bring. He rubbed it in meticulously until his fingers wouldn't slide anymore. He took one more long breath through his rag, grabbed the oars, now with rags tied around the grips to protect his blistered palms, and made his first stroke.

———

Telep's hands couldn't help but shake as he held up the third waterskin, letting its final drops fall to his tongue. He held the empty leather skin in the air for a while waiting for one more drop. When it didn't come, he felt foolish leaving his mouth open so long in the salty air. He threw the skin aside with the others and lay down on the bottom of the boat. The sun had already descended, but its glow still persisted on the horizon. Telep usually rowed until he could no longer fix his bearing by the sun, but he feared that if he kept going, he would have another muscle spasm.

When he woke the next morning, his stomach was in knots. The glow of the sunrise just started to saturate the distant sky in front of him. Since he embarked, he had spent the first half of every sun rowing away from that glow and the second half rowing toward it, an agonizing tedium of being surrounded by nothing.

He had done his best calculation of when he would reach the point where he would not have enough provisions to make it back to the Mainland. With a fair amount of luck from fishing, his best estimate fell on this sun. This was the point. He could not overcome the distance of another sun's row.

Up in the sky, the full moon stared down at him with unrelenting attention. He remembered sitting with Ell at the Temple of the Moon, laughing, lying, kissing, feeling her body, sharing a meaningful moment . . . *One more*, Telep thought. And he put his bandaged hands on the oars and rowed, pushing bubbles toward the rising sun.

———

Back on the green hills of Eveloce, before a climb Telep would look up at the cliff and rub his thumb between each of his fingers. Then he would make a fist and feel the strength of the world in his grasp.

A fog descended around him. For suns, he rowed through a white abyss so thick he could hardly use the sun to navigate. His world shrank to a white dome pressing in around him. The fog isolated him, exiled him from hope. All the color had faded from the warm rays of the sun. The cool air labored through Telep's lungs as he took in the unremitting white smothering the unending sea.

He looked down at his hand. It felt so weak, he doubted he could crush an egg. His arms were jelly. Spidered lines of the sun spread across his face from his eyes to his thickening beard. His eyes were dry and glassy and pink and yellow.

Pulling away the protective towel, he looked into the bucket of putrid water he kept in the stern, seeing it was only a quarter filled. He raised the bucket to his mouth and carefully poured a swallow of the brown water between his lips. With eyes closed, he savored it in his mouth, his tongue absorbing it like a sponge. Then he set the bucket down next to the six flaccid skins of water. Turning to his sack of food, he pulled out a quarter roll, cradling it in his palms. Hard, stale, and weightless, it absorbed him completely. The sack of food dropped to his feet, now just a sack, a lifeless piece of fabric. He remembered back on the Mainland, eating was a social activity.

Since setting out to sea, food and water had become fuel for his muscles to carry him farther into this endless navy abyss. The fact that everything tasted delicious was his mouth lying to him, trying to reinforce the sustenance it so desperately needed.

Sky and sea, sky and sea. He was all that stood out. As the idea of death pressed on his mind, something festered in him, gnawed at him, pleaded with his all but damned circumstance. Desperately, he longed for something to stand out from this flat uniform nightmare, to experience something other than his own slow decay, to actually reach that speck on the horizon where a beautiful land would appear. There would be fresh water and plump, juicy fruits that he'd never seen or touched or tasted before, and he would experience it all to the fullest, and the farther he went, the more things he would discover until he couldn't take any more. He had given himself that chance, but here he was in the middle of nothing and his energy was all but gone, his last morsel of sustenance now embraced in his hand.

He opened up the tin he'd taken of the purple spread. Inside was a smear the size of a pea. He looked from the bread to the tin, and a lump swelled in his throat as he smeared the purple spot gently across the bread, careful not to rub off any crumbs. Staring at it, his face crinkled up and his eyes burned, having no moisture to give. Then it was gone. He held the bread in his mouth, perched atop his tongue, gently sucking on it. Slowly saliva came and softened the rock-hard clump of wheat. The flavor overwhelmed him with bliss, and his eyes burned and burned.

It was gone, the last of it. No more fuel save the moldy brown swill at the bottom of the wash-pail. His fishing line hadn't had a bite in suns, and with no remaining bait, little hope remained in it. He had nothing. His core was numb, detached. He took a breath, resigning himself to rest until the points of light broke through the clouds to guide him further toward his surefire fate.

CRACK.

A sudden jolt knocked Telep from his seat and he heard a sound. Not wood and not water—a real living sound, a loud and gurgled *ROAR*. A new energy filled him. A spray of water jetted up next to the boat, and he sprang to his feet, scanning the water all around for the source but seeing nothing. The boat rocked back and forth. The sea darkened with the shrinking glow of the set sun.

The fog began to lift and when he looked out, he caught sight of white water, the kind he'd seen so often amid the jagged rocks surrounding the Mainland. His jaw dropped. Flying into his seat, he seized the oar handles and feverishly rowed toward the disturbance in the sea, the crests of white slowly dimming in the dwindling light. The boat coursed through the water. His body ached and throbbed, but he felt none of it.

Once closer, he saw that the white surrounded a shiny black surface—rock. It was a platform of rock. He gasped and coughed and strained on, rowing with purpose, each stroke carrying him closer. Hearing the water slosh against the nearing platform of rock, he stood on his seat to look out on it. The rock was flat and had finger-sized holes scattered around it.

CRACK.

The back of the boat surged upward, catapulting him forward over the sea. Time slowed as he watched the boat stand on its nose before falling back to the water in a gush of white. The same gurgled *ROAR* rang out, filling the space all around, instilling in Telep the idea that some kind of water monster had rammed the underside of the boat and was waiting for him in the water below. The boat receded behind him as he continued flying over the water, the glossy black quickly approaching. He landed right at the edge of rock and sea, shielding his face from the lip of the platform as he crashed into the water. He whipped his head around where the side of the boat careened toward him. He braced but the force of the impact pressed him hard into the rock. He shoved the boat back, spun around, and clawed at the rock, but it was smooth and slimy and repelled any grip. His scraping fingers fell into a hole in the rock, and he yanked himself up.

Another *ROAR* and *CRACK* rang out behind him, and the boat lurched forward, ramming into the rock with a crack and a splash, and behind it he saw a shadow disappear into the water. Half the boat now leaned on the platform, and Telep sprang to his feet and tried to pull it up the rest of the way but it was too heavy. He grabbed the rope tied to the docking hold at the bow and dragged out the stone anchor, throwing it inland in an effort to tether the craft.

A silence pulled his gaze to the water where a shadow appeared, darkened, and then exploded in a burst of white water as a large blur of gray sailed into the air with a *ROAR*. It collided with the side of the boat where his sack of supplies hung, and the vessel flipped. The gray blur crashed back into the water, its *ROAR* gurgling down into the depths, leaving behind a haunting stillness.

He ran to the other side of the boat and spotted a large tear in the sack of supplies. Racing to it, he threw its contents up onto the rock, only reaching a few items before the boat lurched forward knocking him back off the edge. The water felt like cold death. Terror seized him. He clawed up at the rock until he found a hole, but it was only big enough to fit two fingers and immediately he felt a sharp sting in his fingertips like an animal was biting them. Gritting his teeth, he dug his fingers deeper and wrenched himself up. When he tore his fingers from the hole, he felt gnawing on his bone. A black claw stabbed out of the hole after him but immediately retreated.

A *ROAR* erupted out of the water next to him. A beast unlike any he had ever seen blasted up through a plume of white water and crashed on the rock in front of him. It was heavy with blubber, and it scooted forward on four strangely stunted limbs before standing up, throwing out its barreled chest, and gaping down at Telep who kicked at the rock in retreat. Its limbs were smeared thin like paddles. Long, thick whiskers stemmed from small patches on its face just above two enormous fangs spilling from its mouth. The beast cocked its head, its gaze burrowing into Telep. Its mouth opened, and a loud *ROAR* poured out through a vast tunnel of razor-sharp teeth. It lunged forward just as Telep scuttled to his feet. He sprang to the side, evading the attack. When he landed, he felt a sharp sting on his ankle where pointy black pincers clipped at his feet. He jumped away again, narrowly escaping another strike and sprinted across the platform thinking of his footing and traction and nothing else.

His ankles bent with the uneven rock, and he splashed through puddles scattered about. He looked over his shoulder and saw the beast galloping after him, its head cocked and mouth wide. Telep was faster, but he could see the end of the platform up ahead. He knew he couldn't corner himself and that he needed to stay out of the water where the creature seemed to be everywhere at once.

Before the end of the platform, there was a break in the rock, a narrow crevasse, beyond which the platform tapered off and disappeared into the sea. Telep felt his space running out. He slid into the crevasse, wiggling and squirming his body down its rough walls to the bottom where he banged his head and scraped his face. Twisting onto his back, he looked up at the gray, hazel sky breaking through the clouds, just dark enough to show three faint points of light. The beast burst into view overhead and ravenously jammed its head into the gulch, snapping its jaws just over Telep's face.

Telep had nowhere to go, the back of his head pressing against rock. Though its thick blubbery body restricted it in the narrow trench, the beast was able to weasel its jaws down surprisingly far. It squirmed and roared, pushing hot breath and saliva on Telep's face. It struggled as if stuck, but then writhed itself free and immediately lunged back in, this time its whiskers grazing Telep's face as it snarled and thrashed.

Telep turned his face away, scraping his cheek on the rough rock beneath him. His body felt like nothing, frozen in a terror so lucid that nothing of who he was or what he'd done could hide from the unblinking eyes of horrific violence and assured death.

The beast let out a pained hiss and sharp squeal before lurching its head back and out of view. Telep listened to its massive body patter away, leaving behind a dreadful quiet. A breath went through him.

He had no awareness of physical strain or fatigue; his body numb in rigidity. A strange comfort came over him, and he felt the walls of the crevasse as Ell's arms wrapping around him. He felt a comfort like he did when Ell would fall asleep with her face nuzzled in his neck and her arm resting on his chest. Delicate sounds of trickling water echoed through the narrow chamber as he scanned the opening above where the points of light shone brighter.

He remained frozen until he felt something move against the back of his neck and he realized it had been there since dropping into the crevasse; he'd just been too petrified to feel it. Then he felt a weight over his shoulder, moving. His eyes shot down to his chest where a long, white worm as thick as his wrist pulsated in slow rhythm, its body slinking over his shoulder and behind his neck. The comfort he had felt turned into a convulsing terror. He tried to rip the monstrous worm away, but as soon as he grabbed it, it constricted around him and his grip slid off its slimy skin. He felt a swarm of hot tentacles lapping at the back of his neck and suddenly a sharp pain, like they were burrowing into him. In a reflex of panic, he gripped the creature again and squeezed, this time feeling the power of the world in his hands. He squeezed until the creature ruptured and hot, sticky fluid gushed over his chest. The torn off piece writhed around as if searching for its other half. Telep reached behind his head and ripped the worm from the back of his neck, feeling a sharp pain as he did so. He threw it out of the gulch and slapped the other writhing deflated piece off of him as he squirmed to his feet.

He poked his head out of the crevasse, his eyes darting around. The front of the boat was still propped up on the platform. The burlap sack with his supplies blew in the wind, and he spotted several items he'd thrown from it scattered around the platform. His gaze whipped around where the beast hunched over at the end of the rock as if sniffing something. Then its head swung toward him, and it let out a *ROAR*. A gust of air shot into Telep's lungs, and he sprang from the trench and began sprinting back toward the boat.

Even if he could turn the craft upright and push off in time, it wouldn't matter. He had recognized something in the creature when he made eye contact with it, a primal intent pulsing in its eyes. This animal was hunting him and would follow him into the water.

His eyes strained in the graying light for a tool; something, anything. The knife had to be one of the wrapped items he threw on the rock; surely it wasn't one of the items that had fallen from the ripped sack and drifted to the bottom of the sea. His hands and feet would do nothing against the animal's thick blubber; he needed something that could penetrate its fat armor.

As he neared the boat, he slowed, trying to spot the outline of the knife in the assortment of wrapped items strewn about. His speed advantage had given him a slight lead on the beast, but he could hear the slapping patter of its gallop getting louder behind him. A glint of light drew his eye to the rock hammer, which had escaped its wrapping not far away. Snatching it up, he whirled around to see the beast only a few body lengths away, still charging full speed.

Holding nothing back, he heaved the rock hammer at the beast, striking it directly in its cockeyed snarling face. A piercing *crack* as the hammer broke off one of the beast's enormous fangs before ricocheting off into the dark water. A *YELP* and a *ROAR* rang out as Telep leapt out of the way of the large mass barreling by him. The animal skidded to a stop at the edge of the platform, its head twisting and reeling. Telep scanned the rock around him for the knife, his legs instinctively scuttling away from the incensed creature turning back toward him. He spotted a rolled up cloth, its shape promising. Bounding over to it, he snatched it up and shook the roll loose, the beast starting another charge. The cloth opened but nothing fell out. It was just a cloth.

Telep scurried back, but when he looked behind him, there was hardly any rock left to retreat to. He had cornered himself. The beast charged him with an electrifying *ROAR*. Telep bolted along the edge, trying to beat its charge into open space, but the animal lunged forward, ramming his side and sending him sprawling onto his back at the edge of the rock, his head dipping into the cold black water. Before he could roll away the weight of the beast mounted his legs. He couldn't move, its massive body pinning him from the waist down, a smothering blanket of death.

The beast snapped at his face but Telep lurched his head back and shielded himself with his arms. Its eyes fumed as it snapped again. This time its remaining fang butted into Telep's open hand, which immediately seized the giant tooth in a firm grip. The beast chomped its jaws, its tunnel of razor teeth churning with desire, but Telep's hand remained safe on the outlying fang. He gripped it with both hands. The animal shook its head violently but Telep felt great power in his hands and kept hold. It lunged forward; its body far too strong for Telep to hold back, but using the fang, he leveraged the glistening teeth away from his face.

The animal squirmed forward, its smothering weight engulfing Telep's stomach. Now the creature had more leverage. When it lunged again, one of Telep's hands slipped off the tooth and his forearm shot into the beast's open mouth, immediately feeling a sting. He yanked it out just as the jaws snapped shut. Streams of red careened down his arm as he tried to regain his dual grip on the fang, but the beast started bucking and snapping wildly. One of the bucks stabbed its fang into Telep's chest to the depth that his fist held it, and he screamed in agony. He pounded his fist against the beast's eye, and his elbow felt a stone move under it. The beast jolted its head back, pulling the fang from Telep's chest. Then it lunged forward again, this time more powerful than Telep could manage. He tried with all his strength, but still he felt the prickly whiskers poking the side of his neck, the ravenous jaws chomping closer and closer, pushing Telep back until his head was underwater.

Telep screamed out in a fury bursting forth like a dam, the water boiling over his mouth. He grabbed the stone from under his elbow and slammed it into the beast's head. The water subdued the *crack*, but a high-pitched squeal erupted when the creature sprang back and pulled Telep's head from the water. The beast continued recoiling, but Telep held on to the fang, his grip becoming iron as he delivered blow after blow with the stone, targeting the eyes and the top of the head where fatty protection was minimal. Telep's unrelenting scream enveloped the space wholly and completely. The animal backed off of his legs, but Telep held firm, eventually being dragged along the rock on his stomach as he bludgeoned the retreating beast. One blow directly on top of its head made its high-pitched squeal die into a low snorting mope, and its frantic retreat become slow, reflexive tremors.

Telep kept his frenzied pace, each strike harder than the last. Soon, the animal hardly moved, but he didn't relent. He struck again and again in an uncontrollable ire, eventually sounding like he was striking wet mud. His arm, shirt, and face all dripped blood. Not until his lungs were completely empty did Telep become aware of the silence surrounding his screams, and the stillness surrounding his blows.

His body collapsed, and he rolled onto his back, his screams becoming sobs shouted up to the points of light. He sobbed hard and long, his head resting against the fallen beast. He sobbed until the black in the sky was pitch.

Finally, his voice gave out, his throat raw, his eyes aching and burning. He became aware of the strain in his arm from clutching the stone, still gripped in his hand. It felt right somehow, almost like it was a part of him. Rolling over, he gazed at the moon, still large on the horizon. He held the stone up in the moonlight, seeing it was covered in red. But it was unique . . . distinct in shape, familiar in weight. He loosened his grip and turned it over in his palm. Where his hand had covered, it was not red but a pale blue and orange.

A calmness settled over Telep. With slow infantile movements, he rose to his feet and anchored the boat to the rock. Then he nestled his head into the soft fat of the fallen beast, pulled his knees to his chest, and closed his eyes. No creature bothered him during the night.

Chapter 23

For Telep, taking his mind back to the morning when he awoke curled into the bloody corpse of the beast seemed ephemeral, like the past two suns had transpired all at once. He had slept through that night with no trouble, a deep, dead sleep, not waking or even stirring until the sun was already perched high and bright in the sky. His throat had been dry and raw, but he felt rejuvenated despite not eating since the single bite of bread and spread the sun before. Something in him had felt new and refreshed, something he did not analyze or argue with.

The cloudy veil that covered the southern horizon the sun before had disappeared, and when he looked in that direction, he froze. His heart swelled and churned. Before him stood a mountain of land. It looked so close, the horizon set apart behind it. The fog and cloud cover had hidden it for the past several suns, but now here it was. The realness of it sank in. The speck he had seen way off in the distance now screamed its presence before him. What was once a dream was now reality.

He'd spent that morning carving up the beast. He had found the knife on the rock near the boat and used it to slice cut after cut from the corpulent corpse. His aching fingers pushed pieces of the raw, fatty tissue into his mouth. He harvested the animal completely.

Surprisingly, when the supplies had been scattered, most had landed on the rock, but a few items had been lost, including one of the oars. When he'd wrapped and packed his food and supplies, he did not wait, but gathered everything immediately and set out that very sun for the landmass before him.

Now the land was still a few suns away, his pace slower with only one oar. His boat was damaged, but the essential hull remained intact. He faced forward as he paddled, alternating sides to keep his vector straight, which was easier with his destination in front of him. During a break from paddling, he looked at his oar closely and spotted the subtle shift in the grain of the wood from when Chandradaul had switched from a plane to a knife in smoothing it. He grinned to himself, then continued on.

His resting periods became shorter as the nourishment from his kill continued to strengthen him. His body was still healing from the injuries sustained on the small rock platform, and he had aggravated some of his old cuts. There was a sizable cut on his middle finger, which he excused from his grip on the oar. The spot on the back of his neck was still very tender, and he touched it compulsively during his paddling breaks, but it did not inhibit his movement like the gash in his chest from the beast's fang, which panged with every stroke.

He could feel the moist, fatty tissue of the beast rejuvenating his body. Consuming it filled him with a sense of responsibility and admiration for his slain foe. While its flesh revitalized Telep physically, it was the life and fight of the beast that did more for him. Being pushed to the brink of death awakened in Telep a new verve, a new tenacity, a new drive. He admired the beast for protecting its territory, for actively engaging its surroundings, for making its own life undeniable to another living thing. He felt a responsibility to the beast to make use of its death, to carry forward the natural force of life gleaned from their struggle, and to foster something with it. He could feel the lifeforce of the beast inside of him completely subject to his will. For *he* had survived. *His* drive lived on. The fallen animal's flesh nourished *him*. He was the victor, the alpha, the conqueror.

————

Over the next two suns, Telep's body continued to mend and bolster. His drive strengthened, spurred by what lay ahead.

When he gazed out at the approaching landmass, an ineffable aura seemed to surround it, as if seeing it in a dream or a memory where its significance and consequence dwarfed all else. The closer he got, the more features emerged. It had dark red cliffs and opulent marine foliage of lemon green, and it was accented with blue and turquoise near the water, and brown and red higher up.

His chest churned with excitement as he planned to arrive shortly after dawn. The sun hung low on the horizon, but its light still illuminated the colorful water surrounding the shore. Most of the landmass touching the water was vertical rock face, but it broke into a sanded area at one section that seemed to be a gradual incline. The bright tan coloring of the sand starkly contrasted the dark red cliffs. The rest of the coastline looked to be thick jungle.

The front of his boat swayed back and forth as he paddled toward the bright patch. Closer to the beach, the rolling waves swelled but did not crest until just before shore. The waves began pushing him, carrying the vessel forward before passing underneath. The waves grew so large that after passing by, his boat became unstable on its downward slope, and he'd rotate away from the beach.

Telep fought to keep his vector, but the backslide of the passing waves made it nearly impossible. Only when he was amid them did the waves reveal their true authority. Watching a wall of water careen past him, Telep realized how massive these rolls were, each one a monument of power. He grabbed his satchel and wrapped it around his arm and over his shoulder. A stab of nerves hit him as a passed wave turned his boat almost parallel to the beach. He fought the bow back toward land. Another colossal wave hoisted him up, surging him toward shore.

A pang shot through him with the thought of coming this close only to be crushed by a wave. How had he not seen this danger? The waves had appeared manageable upon approach. Now they tossed him around like a leaf in a storm. What was just so calm and serene now threatened his life. Why did he think this would be controllable? Leaving the Mainland hadn't been easy . . . why should entering this land be easy? He looked down on the beach from the towering wave.

Telep hacked at the water, paddling backwards. Finally, the giant roll of energy passed by, blocking the entire beach. Somehow, he managed to keep the vessel straight, and he paddled desperately toward land, but something was sucking the boat back. In an instant, the front of the vessel jerked upward, launching Telep into the air. He splashed into the cold water, just missing the boat. He thrashed up to the surface just in time to see the rear of the boat whipping toward him. His arms shot around his head, and immediately the wood hull smacked into him, his body spinning and twisting under the water. Again, he fought to the surface where he saw the boat careening toward the beach on an enormous wave like a piece of driftwood. A giant bird soared motionless above him as he thrashed toward shore, the suction of the sea dragging him back. Another colossal wave hoisted him on its shoulders, curling him in its crest as it careened forward in a fray of helpless abandon.

The dark red rock behind the beach sped toward him. The wave exploded on the sand, all the air vacating Telep's body as he twisted in the violent surf. Water flooded his eyes, nose, and stomach. He hit a wall of rock and pressed a hand against its solid surface as the water receded down the shore. He couldn't see, the burning of sand and salt locked his eyes shut. When he

forcedly pried them open, all he could detect through the excruciating pain was dancing streaks of light and color. He coughed
violently, coarse liquid spewing from his nose and mouth
between gasps for air. He scratched the sand from his eyes,
almost in time to see the wall of water before it slammed his
head into the rock, and all became black.

Chapter 24

The sun blared overhead with no clouds to dampen its rays. The wind blew with turbulent consistency along the coast, strong enough to push rifts of sand along the beach.

Telep awoke with a weight pressing on his stomach and salt-water spewing from his lips. For a moment, the weight felt comforting, but then he discerned it as a hand, and he slapped it off and rolled away in a whirl of sand. He tried to wipe the sand from his eyes, but his hands were sandy as well. He forced his eyes open anyway, feeling the ache of the immense light. The feeling of the hand on his stomach lingered, though he knew it wasn't there. An image of the diseased body Ep Brody had described flashed in his mind. *This land is the origin of that disease.* The air felt contaminated. He backed up further.

A dark figure rose before him. He squinted painfully through the sand peppering his eyes. A familiarity lived in the figure's shape, and as it stepped forward, Telep saw a woman . . . and she was scared. He couldn't help but think of Ell's face the moment she'd learned she and her father were banished from Eveloce. There was that squirm in her eyes, that diffidence, that inability to know with certainty how to proceed. The trepidation thickened like smoke in an enclosed room.

As Telep stood, he brushed the sand from his eyes until he could look without squinting. He stared at the dark skin, narrow eyes, and tiny nose. Her hair was crazy. Long rags clumping together in rolls that hung past her waist. A clump of tangled hair hung over her face, reducing one eye to a speck of reflected light, which studied him with intensity akin to the fanged beast. Her other eye reflected a lively green, still flickering in trepidation.

Her skin was darker than he had ever seen, even more so than the hillspeople. Dark blue patterns decorated her skin. The markings were thin but spanned her entire body. The sight of her immediately made him think of Ep Brody's description of the diseased body as well as the woman in Ep Salo's tent.

Her clothes were barbaric . . . but mesmerizing. They looked to be made of some dark green plant woven into an intricate pattern, but the foliage used was . . . unrecognizable. It had veins like a leaf, but it moved like silk and shimmered like satin. The material hung from her waist, down over her right knee where it cut up in a straight line to her left hip and connected to the back with a thin leather tie. The fabric flowed like water as she adjusted her feet in the sand.

She appeared about his age, maybe slightly older. They stared at each other—studying, analyzing. Her left hand disappeared behind her hip into a leather pouch, and Telep heard the clink of stones. He held up his open palms. She cocked her head and glanced out to sea and then back to him, hesitant to keep her eyes away for too long. She kept looking back and forth between him and the sea as if searching for something.

"Takoia," she spoke, her chin pushing forward and her eyes narrowing.

Telep remained still.

"Takoia," she shot again with the same gesture, her hand dipping deeper into the leather pouch. Telep shook his head.

"Takoia. Takoia."

Telep held up his open palms once again and took a step back.

"Uv . . . aro . . . takoia. Om . . . takoia . . . ayzay," she said, putting her right hand over her chest, then in front of her, then out toward the bulk of the land.

"Aro . . . takoia . . . uv." She gestured toward him.

Telep blinked. From her voice, he gleaned only tonality, but he knew what she was asking. *She wants to know where I came from.* Behind her, he saw what was left of his boat, stranded on the sand behind some brush. He guessed she hadn't seen it.

He pointed out to sea, her gaze following. *Why am I pointing? She can't see where I came from . . . But if I could see this land from the top of the last cliff, then from the top of this land, they should be able to see that cliff as well. It too would be a speck on the horizon. Maybe she will make the connection.*

"I'm . . . from . . . there," he said, pointing out to the horizon. She stepped toward him, and he stepped back in retreat. After a pause it happened again.

Telep remembered Ep Brody's description of the disease and how painful and horrible it was. He felt he needed to keep a distance in case she could infect him, or perhaps they could infect each other.

She tilted her head, confused. He pointed to her with his whole hand the way she had done, then he pointed back and forth to her and himself and coughed.

"Sick," he warned.

Her eyes narrowed. She pointed at him and coughed a fake cough.

"Uv . . . fico," she posed, coughing again for clarity.

"Yes," he nodded. "Me . . . sick." He coughed again, this time doing his best to sell a serious illness.

She studied him for a long moment.

"Yokk."

Her voice was firm and direct, her eyes unblinking. She

repeated it over and over as she backed away, her head tilted, and her fingers interwoven in front of her. Telep remained still, nodding as if he understood. She kept peering back at him as she left, walking down the beach toward the dense outlet of green foliage. She walked past his boat but did not react. Perhaps she had seen it or even pulled it ashore.

Telep remained still until she was out of sight, then he darted down the beach in the opposite direction. He figured that she wanted him to stay there while she retrieved cohorts from her colony, and then he would be subject to their will.

The girl's face lingered in his mind as he ran down the beach. There was something about her . . . He almost felt guilty for leaving. Now was the time to explore this land, to see what no Mainlander had seen, to make new discoveries and fill himself with the unknown.

The thoughts swelled in him as he ran such that when he reached the red cliff at the end of the beach, he slapped his hands over his mouth and screamed and jumped and fell to the sand. *I'm here . . . I'm here!*

When the moment passed, he grabbed the red cliff and began climbing.

———

The foliage at the top of the cliff seemed to connect with Telep. When he looked around, the harmonic sway of the trees, plants, leaves, and ferns hypnotized him with their beauty. The leaves on the trees varied in color from bright yellow to ruby red to deep brown, and they moved like the girl's garments, like water. All of the flora was so thin and silky, a mesmerizing array that harmonized and swayed in the wind's gentle touch as if slowing time for the sake of its own beauty.

Telep moved through the forest in the slow, fluid rhythm observed around him. The forest floated past him like a dream. He flowed through the trees like a winding river. The calmness of the forest allayed his heart, the air intoxicating him with its dense purity. Everything was new.

The sounds beckoned him further. A low wraithlike hum emanated off the ground and filled the void between his lungs— an all-encompassing drone permeating and binding anything and everything amid the trees. High-pitched ethereal chimes shot down from the canopy like strikes of lightning, sounding directional at first, but then turning the forest into an echo chamber and getting lost everywhere at once. The sounds moved in waves, sloshing around a pool of collective harmonies, a living thing with surreal presence.

He could have looked at or listened to any one element of the environment for an entire sun but taking the whole scene in and moving through it gave his mind a feeling of exponential expansion. His core became numb. The wounds of long ago shrank into the infancy of their conception. All of it seemed so passed, a separate time. And this, here, now, was different, set apart, its own entity in time to be experienced pure, clean, unsullied.

But when Telep brushed his hand against the satin sprouts of a fern and felt the extraordinary softness, his mind retreated back to words confided by Ep Brody who dreamed of living in a world of all things new, and Telep knew that this was it.

———

Telep explored the land for many suns, staying in the elevated eastern portion where everything was undisturbed, free of human influence. No clearings or paths had been cut through the forest; it remained as pure as a newborn child.

Though he consumed far less than he did on the Mainland, he tried lots of new things; primarily berries, nuts, a common, fat bug found on brown leaves, and a dark green, pointy fruit that he named lightfruit because its points resembled a bright point of light in the sky. Lightfruit hung high in trees and he enjoyed the climbing. He used large leaves to channel rainwater into his waterskin.

In the evenings, smoke rose over the trees on the lower, western portion of the land where he had not ventured. The smoke was light and isolated, the mark of a controlled fire. But one evening, the smoke was a dark greenish brown. The only smoke he'd ever seen close to that color was on top of the third seacliff with Ep Brody, though even that wasn't as vibrant. He figured whatever peoples inhabiting the land predominantly remained in the lower portion of the landmass where several clearings and passages had been cut from the forest canopy.

He found several vantage points where he could look out over the land and sea. Water surrounded the land on three sides, but the land behind the carved-out settlement extended out of sight. It seemed to narrow farther out in the distance, but it excited Telep that he could not see the whole of it. When viewing the landmass from the sea, it appeared contained to the east and west, but from the high elevation, he could see no end to its extension south.

There did not appear to be a way of venturing there without going through the inhabited portion of the land. In his current location, large cliffs surrounded him on three sides. The only direction to travel was toward the inhabitants. The portion he deemed safe to traverse would take many suns to explore.

New sights, smells, tastes, touches, and experiences filled every sun. One morning he came upon a cave. When he stepped to the entrance a sense of familiarity gripped him. Obviously, he had never been here before but when taking a deep breath, an image of blackness flashed in his mind. He stood confused for a moment, but then remembered the smell. Breathing in deeply, he remembered smelling the same pungent odor in the cave he'd explored on his journey to Nexus. That cave where he had met . . . he couldn't remember their names.

What they were mining, that must be in this cave too, Telep thought as he stepped into the dark burrowing hollow, noticing the untouched walls.

Telep turned his gaze back out of the cave's mouth to the silky fauna glowing in the sun's rays and listened to the ethereal reverberations from the forest echo past him.

Chapter 25

One sun, the dawn's early light found Telep sleeping in his hammock, which he had woven from braided vines and tied between two strong branches a few body lengths off the ground. The morning mist was cool on his face and cold on his nose. When he squinted into the morning light, something felt strange . . . different. There was a quietness.

Something moved in front of him. Rubbing his eyes, he lifted his head and peered toward the trunk of the tree. Stillness. Then he saw something over one of the branches supporting his hammock—the blink of two yellow eyes. Suddenly, the shape of a large mammal popped out, its gaze trained on him. Telep froze, a breath trapped in his throat. Somehow the animal was the same color as the branch, the texture of the wood ingrained on its body.

With a loud snarl, the animal sprang forward bearing a clutter of shiny black quills in its mouth. Telep jerked himself off the far side of the hammock, swinging the near side up in front of the lunging animal. Claws tore into his back. He tried to fall to the ground, but his foot got caught in the vines. The animal also became tangled in the crisscrossed weave of the hammock, screeching and snarling as it violently struggled, only twisting itself further in the web of vines. Hanging upside down, Telep looked up at his ensnared foot. The animal bucked and writhed, shaking the vines and swinging back and forth. Telep eyed his satchel hanging from its knot on the branch below and grabbed for it—just out of reach. He swung closer. The creature writhed its head free and snapped at Telep's leg. Telep used his free foot to kick it in the mouth. As it screeched and bucked in the tangled web, its skin changed color from the brown of the tree to the dark green of the vines. Telep reached again for his satchel, his fingertips grazing the leather.

The hammock's mess of tangles began to unravel, and the creature's front legs fell free. Its head twisted toward Telep, jaw open, black quills glistening. Again, Telep kicked its face, feeling a sharp sting in his ankle. The animal spun around while Telep reached again and snagged the strap of the satchel, gripping and pulling it close so his other hand could reach inside. The mess of vines unraveled further, and the creature slipped lower, Telep feeling its hot breath on his face. It swiped, but Telep swung his head up to his waist, just evading the claws.

Finally, his hand found what it was searching for. He let go of the satchel and swung toward the fury of claws and teeth where he plunged his knife into the creature's neck. Its body lurched and its mouth opened but only a gurgled breath spilled out, followed soon by a stream of dark blood.

Telep cut the animal free and it fell to the ground. After cutting himself free and dropping down, he knelt beside it, watching its torso convulse with each lack of breath. The creature seemed smaller now.

It made no attempt to stop Telep from leaning over it or placing his hand on its neck. It was soft to the touch, and when he looked closely, he noticed the fine hairs covering its body, which he watched change color from the dark green of the vines to the dark brown of the forest floor.

When Telep drew his hand back, now stained a dark red, the hair on the creature's neck had turned the color of Telep's palm.

Taking a breath, he covered the creature's eyes and jammed his knife into its neck, making it tremor one last time. He watched its color fade until it became a pale, white body with fine translucent hair.

Telep sat back against a tree where a ray of light shone through the forest canopy and warmed his face.

———

Telep had avoided making a fire because he didn't want the inhabitants of the land to spot the smoke. But now he accepted the risk and built a small fire. He kept it burning long enough to cook every edible cut of flesh from the slain animal. The meat was tough but had a delicious flavor he'd never tasted. When he couldn't eat any more, he wrapped the remaining meat in leaves and put them in his satchel.

———

Suns later, Telep travelled south and west in search of water, as it had not rained in some time. The streams he'd frequented were now nothing more than trails of glossy mud snaking through the forest. His mouth was dry, but he didn't drink the last of his reserve. Feeling the weight in his waterskin gave him a comfort he wished to retain. Knowing the streams widened as they descended in elevation, he followed one toward the lower portion of the landmass. After passing the furthest point he had gone before, he became very vigilant, unsure how far to the east the inhabitants foraged.

The lack of rain confused Telep. Since arriving, the rain had come almost every sun. It didn't last long but was hard enough to fill his waterskin as well as a reserve well he'd dug in the ground and lined with leaves. But with his well dry, and only a few swallows sloshing around his waterskin, the risk of encountering the potentially contagious inhabitants became necessary.

He walked and walked but found nothing. The trail of glossy mud widened but still offered no collectable moisture. Then the ground became soft, and his feet began sinking in. Looking ahead, he saw a large marsh, far too supple to walk across. He imagined the dark muck swallowing him whole, pulling his body into a place unknowable to the living. Stories of such happenings had circulated back on Eveloce, but never had he seen such terrain. He allowed his battered sandals to slowly sink into the mire as he looked out over the swamp. It was a vast expanse of black muck and dark olive foliage. Strange trees littered the marsh. They were twisted and bulbous with swollen arthritic joints and large root systems beginning their outward expanse far above the muck, making each one look like a warped sandglass.

The thought of traversing the marsh on the roots of the deformed trees crossed his mind, but he opted to go around it to the north and then continue west, figuring that he would not want to drink water trickling directly out of the dark sludge anyway. Yanking his feet from the sucking muck, he started around.

When the edge of the marsh came into view, a scattering of strange bushes also appeared—twisted balls of black thorns harboring bright red berries in their barbs. Running his tongue over dry lips and swallowing an empty swallow, Telep stepped closer. The berries were large enough to flood his mouth with sweet nectar. He removed his sandals and stepped into the muck, which stretched halfway up his calves when he reached the nearest bush. The red berries seemed to glow amid the twisting black thicket, so ripe and juicy. Telep bit his lip in anticipation as he delicately spread apart the thorns and reached his hand in. Just as his fingertips grazed the nearest berry, something struck his head. His body jerked in surprise, and he felt a sting in his hand and wrist from the thorns.

After steadying himself, he looked down at what looked to be a soft-shell nut of some kind, about half the size of his fist.

Peering up, he saw a cluster of them hanging directly overhead from one of the sandglass trees. Taking a breath, he maneuvered his hand back toward the ripe red berry. With two fingers pinching the stem, another nut thumped his head. His body didn't jerk as much this time but still enough for a few more thorns to prod the back of his hand and forearm. The nut settled on the marsh floor more than a body length away. Getting frustrated, Telep bit his lip and again reached for the berry. Again, he felt a *thwack*, this time on the back of his neck. The nut plopped into the muck behind him. Telep cocked his head and clenched his jaw. He scanned the area. Everything was static, not even a stir. Another nut struck him on the shoulder, and he didn't even flinch. Seething, he shoved his arm into the bush and grabbed the berry out. He ignored the stings in his hand and forearm and thrust the plump berry up to his lips.

"Zuk!" called a voice.

Telep was so startled, he nearly fell in the muck. Spinning around, his eyes fell on a figure . . . the girl from the beach standing alarmingly close. He froze. The sheer shock of the moment disarmed him. He'd been alone so many suns. As vigilant and alert as he'd been, how could he be surprised this completely?

The girl wore the same clothes and adorned the same blue body paint. She didn't appear threatening. He saw concern in her eyes, and a soft-shell nut in her hand.

"Zuk."

Her eyes shifted down to his waist where his hand still clutched the red berry. He lifted it to his chest and her eyes followed, growing with alarm.

"Zuk! Zuk! Zuk!" She lurched closer.

"Stop!" Telep blurted, holding out his other hand and lowering the berry to his waist. She stopped. The tone of her voice was so . . . expressive. They stared at each other a moment. Then she pointed with her whole hand to the berry.

"Rünic."

Telep shook his head, though when he looked into her eyes he almost understood.

"Rünic, rünic." She crossed her hands over her throat and made a choking face. She pointed back to his hand and repeated the gesture. Telep glanced down at the blood and red juices dripping off his fingers.

The berries are poison. She's trying to help me.

Telep dropped the berry. The girl's stance softened, and she stepped forward. Telep backed away and gestured for her to stop, then started coughing. She cocked her head quizzically, and he returned the sincerest look of warning he could muster. A wave of shame pulsed through him when her expression reflected a knowing disappointment.

Telep pointed to her then back to himself and shook his head. She stared at him, confused but attentive. He thought for a moment and then pointed to her with his whole hand the way she had done and then pointed back to himself. Then he touched his own hands, mimicking that one of them was hers, and then put his hands over his throat the way she had done to communicate *poison.*

A look of understanding came over her face. She pointed to him then back to herself. "Rünic?"

She understood. Telep stood still, awed with the understanding between them. Their languages were unknown to each other, their inflection patterns wholly different. Her intonation did not rise at the end of the word, but still he understood it as a question.

How? Was it the way her head moved forward while saying the word and then stopped, like the movement signaled uncertainty and holding still signaled her awaiting confirmation that what she said was correct? Had that association been ingrained in Telep's mind back on the Mainland? Was such a thing possible? Could such a gesticulation span the vast sea between them? *Are we perceiving communicative signals inherent in the human species? Or is there a mysterious link living between us?*

Snapping out of his state of awe, Telep eagerly nodded affirming her inquest.

She looked at him a moment, then touched her fingers to her chest. Telep cocked his head. She pointed to him and awkwardly nodded her head, imitating what he had done; then she pointed to herself and again touched her fingers to her chest. For a moment, he waited for her to continue or to try again but she remained still. Then, staring into her eyes, he understood what she was communicating. He pointed to himself and nodded, then pointed to her and touched his fingers to his chest. She smiled and touched her fingers to her chest, then nodded. Two gestures, one meaning.

Telep blinked rapidly, awed with how perceptive this girl was. She had just recognized how he gestured *yes* and subsequently taught him how to do so in her culture.

They shared a delicate smile. Then she tossed him a soft-shell nut and pulled another one from the leather pouch on her hip. She dug her thumb into the thick skin and peeled it back. Holding it above her lips, she squeezed releasing a trickle of clear liquid into her mouth. Dryness sprang back to Telep's throat. He imitated her in haste. Though he didn't catch as much of the liquid as she did, its sweet taste filled his mouth.

When he finished, he looked up at her, suddenly feeling the large distance between them. He pointed to himself and said, "Telep." He repeated it a few times.

"Tele," she tried.

"Telep," he nodded.

"Tele . . . p," her lips struggling to make a "p" sound. He smiled.

"Telep," she said again, this time pointing at him. Seeing her face, he knew she understood. She pointed to herself.

"Xaella."

Chapter 26

Telep and Xaella spent the next few suns together. They ate together and slept in nearby trees. They grew their methods of communication. She showed him streams and different ways to collect water and gather and store food; but they stayed in the uninhabited portion of the land. It was a painstaking process, but Telep made her understand that he would not go to her village. She had led him that way a few times, and he had to stop and convey that if she continued, she would go alone. She didn't seem to give much credence to his idea that they could infect each other.

The more time Telep spent with Xaella, the more he questioned the disease that spawned when these people came in contact with Mainlanders and how it worked. He wondered if he would spread a disease to them, or if it only passed one way. The idea had made sense before because he pictured the people of the body that had been found as being unclean. It was easy to imagine a colony of lepers inhabiting an unknown place somewhere out in the sea, but after seeing Xaella being very clean and healthy, he questioned how she could make him sick. Perhaps it was not the inhabitants as a whole but something specific to the body that was found. Maybe it was the disease that killed them. Still he remained cautious.

One morning, he woke before Xaella and decided to gather food for breakfast. He found lightfruit in a nearby tree. It hung only a couple branches up making it easy to retrieve. While mounting the first branch, he heard a distinct buzzing but paid it little mind. In position to pinch the first lightfruit stem, he saw the source of the sound. In front of the fruit hovered a large insect with a black head, a dark brown body, and a thin green stripe extending all the way to the sharp black tip of its stinger. Its buzzing wings cast a yellow haze around its body. The bug looked familiar somehow. It hovered completely still, fixed in the air. Then it turned and faced Telep. Stillness. With a *buzz*, it vanished, flying so fast he could hardly see which direction it went.

The weight of the lightfruit surprised Telep. Hundreds of them weighed down the surrounding branches. He thought over how many to pick. His food intake had dropped drastically since leaving the Mainland; he'd never eaten more than three lightfruit in a sitting. He picked seven. One he ate on the way back, and the others he packed in his satchel for Xaella and him to share.

When he returned, Xaella still lay motionless in her hammock. Staring up at her body, he thought back on his journey and how unlikely it was to be here, in this moment, standing where no Mainlander had ever stood, savoring a flavor no Mainlander had ever tasted, looking up at this girl's long rolled clumps of hair hanging through her hammock like icicles. The ground comforted his feet as he gazed up at her.

How would Mainlanders look on her?

The image of Ep Salo ravaging the girl on top of the cliff flashed in front of him. With the blue paint and dark skin, it was clear whom she was meant to resemble. Telep felt a throb of hate. The images from the glowing tent elucidated the hard truth of a wounded man fucking his hate into a bought imitation.

A horde of thoughts Telep had tried to forget suddenly pervaded his mind in a wave of overwhelming fatigue—the iron confinements, weapons, armed men, dark powder, Ell. The images sloshed around in his mind. The trees spun in front of him. Dizzy, he stumbled to the base of Xaella's tree and closed his eyes, resting his plump satchel on his lap so she would know he had gathered breakfast.

Images of brutality swarmed his consciousness. The history of oppression came alive before him. People being beaten, starved, killed . . . a vortex of violence he couldn't control.

A hollow state ensconced him. It seemed to go on and on without end, pulling past, present, and future into a black abyss that feasted on his mind. Grisly images stabbed at the void in his chest. He couldn't move.

Helpless. Not alone. Blind in open eyes. Surrounded. Churning through a crowd of lifeless faces. Trapped. Alone. Terror. Strapped to a carriage. Head and limbs jostling like a corpse on a bumpy road. No stop. No stop. A horse in front of the carriage. A carrot in front of the horse. Not a carrot . . . a heart, black as death . . . beating horribly and always out of reach.

———

Boom . . . boom . . . boom. Telep awoke with something cold and hard beating on his forehead like a hammer—boom . . . boom . . . boom—intensifying the pounding ache trapped amid his thoughts. His senses jumbled.

Boom . . . boom . . . boom. His perceptions started trickling together. The surface under him was so flat. Unnaturally flat. He desperately craved sleep, but the pounding on his forehead persisted.

Boom . . . boom . . . boom. More than anything, he wanted it to stop, but it wouldn't. A gurgle sputtered from his throat. A mash of unknowable sounds gnawed in his ears.

Boom . . . boom . . . boom. He tipped his head to the side, but the pounding followed him, beating relentlessly on his forehead. Finally, he found the muscles in his eyes and cracked them open. Dizzying blurs focused into dark faces staring down at him, illuminated only with torchlight. An old woman with a heavily decorated face jabbed two fingers against his forehead.

Tap . . . tap . . . tap. Suddenly, awareness hit him like a boulder.

I'm in the indigenous village. . . . These are the inhabitants!

He tried to shout but could only gurgle. His body was foreign; he fought for control of it. His muscles spasmed lurching him off the table. Hitting the ground seemed to jar his body to attention, and he regained enough control to scuttle back and away from the dark faces looming over him. His head struck a wall. It sounded like wood. This was an enclosed room, and the only way out was behind the group of inhabitants. The fire of their torches danced in their eyes as they stared at him.

"Stay away from me!" He tried to focus his eyes. He pressed his back against the wall as if bracing it up. The faces remained still; their bodies painted with patterns of blue just like . . .

"Xaella!" No one moved or spoke.

"Stay away from me! Xaella!" He shouted her name over and over.

The more he yelled, the clearer his mind became, and the more he recalled. He had fallen asleep by the tree . . . He was waiting for Xaella to wake up . . . Why wasn't she up? She always woke before him. Yes, he was by the tree . . . *How did I get here? They drugged me!*

"Xaella!"

The inhabitants looked at each other, then spoke among themselves.

"Xaella!"

One man stepped in front of Telep, a strong sturdy man with a calm and thoughtful face. His skin didn't have blue markings like the others. His physique reminded him of Caleb. Kneeling down on one knee, he held up a calming hand. Telep watched the flames dance in the man's eyes. He breathed, but his mind remained fixed on Xaella. Where was she? Why wasn't she here? One look from her would tell him so much.

When the strong man left, Telep stumbled to his feet and tried to follow him out, but the other inhabitants cut in front of him.

They did not seem hostile, but he knew getting out of the building would require a physical altercation. His mind and body still felt on different planes. Even if he found enough control of his legs to run into the thick forest, he would first have to fight his way through these people blocking the exit. Curling into a ball, he conceded his mind to the hazy delirium pressing between his thoughts. He broke into a feverish sweat, unable to move, drowning in his clothes.

———

When he woke, Telep's mind pounded in rhythm with his heart, and he thought about Xaella. Why wasn't she there? Was she okay? Were they not allowing her to come?

Telep looked around the room, a single-space structure with a wood floor and stacked logs for walls. The room was empty except for a long table where he'd woken from his state of delirium. The ceiling rose higher on the far side and sloped down toward him and hung over a gap in the top of the back wall where light seeped in. The only other opening was a doorframe on the far wall. Outside appeared to be an open space, perhaps a courtyard. Strange looking buildings and huts lined the other side of the open space.

Peering outside, he noticed a young man staring at him with narrow eyes and pursed lips. With his arms crossed over his bare chest, the man broadly displayed the toned muscles of his short and slender frame. The black pants he wore extended to his knees. The morning sun glinted off his bald head. His dark skin bore blue markings similar to those of Xaella, though his were strikingly more elaborate. The weight of his stare poured through the opening, daring Telep to step near it.

Telep reflected on the amount of physical contact it must have taken to bring him to the village, which was at least a couple suns' walk from where he lost consciousness. He reasoned that if there were a disease to be had, he would already have it. It would serve no purpose to continue avoiding physical contact with the inhabitants.

Telep looked at the man outside and imagined getting in a skirmish with him, but then he saw Xaella across the courtyard. He rushed out of the building but stopped when the man yelled and crouched, ready to tackle him. Telep stopped. The man continued yelling at him, making all sorts of strange gestures. Behind him, Xaella approached.

"Iphito!" Xaella shouted. The man paused, stood up straight, and yelled something over his shoulder. Xaella's face was sullen. Stepping past the glaring guard, she motioned Telep over to the building.

She looked him in the eye, her face sad and frustrated. Telep knew she was the only one who could give him an explanation of what happened. Her expression told him something weighed heavily on her.

He felt a strange connection with her, like the tunnel of their shared gaze was wider than normal, like their minds were synced in a way that enabled communication far deeper than words. He trusted her, and he wanted that trust to continue past this sun.

She pointed at him, coughed a fake cough, and looked at him questioningly so as to ask if he felt sick. He swiped his palm with his fingers, which was her gesture for *no*. She nodded her head, not surprised.

Looking at him with concerned, almost pitying eyes, she reached into her leather pouch and pulled out a lightfruit. She pointed to him, pretended to take a bite, then shook one finger back and forth in front of her. Recognizing he didn't understand, she thought for a moment and pointed to him again, pretended to take a bite, and then shook her head emphatically.

"Rünic," she said.

He understood but was confused because he had eaten light-fruit several times with no ill effects. Then she pulled out another lightfruit and bit into it. He cocked his head. She brought the bitten fruit close to her face, studying it. Then she gestured for him to do the same and tossed over the fruit. He brought it to his face. It was the same pointy, lime green lightfruit he'd been eating. She handed him the first lightfruit and when he studied it, he noticed tiny orange dots speckled across it.

I poisoned myself.

———

Iphito, the bald guard, and a few of his mates ushered Telep down the street. Xaella came as well, but Iphito positioned himself between them. He seemed to be either very protective of her, scornful of Telep, or both.

Telep noticed all the people in the group wore different types of clothing. One wore short pants, one long, and a couple had long kilts. Some were topless, some had tight fitting shirts, and some wore what looked like a fitted blanket with a hole cut out for the head. He saw a few women with triangular, silver piercings along their hips. He also saw several people wearing necklaces of strange shells unknown to the Mainland. The majority had short, dark hair, including the women. Xaella was one of the few outliers whose hair hung past her shoulders. Most people had blue markings on their skin, varying in pattern and intricacy. There was only a few that had none.

Everything in the settlement looked unique and exotic, whether its function was recognizable or not. Telep wished he could analyze and appreciate the arrangement of the buildings and the organization of the village, but Iphito and the others ushered him along with haste.

The buildings were mostly wood, and almost all had slanted roofs like the one where he'd been kept. They sloped away from the street toward the forest. A long, wooden structure ran behind the row of buildings, lining the edge of town where they walked. It was made from trees, sawed in half, and hollowed out. The structure channeled water that would run off the buildings and into a cistern of some kind. Telep hoped to get a closer look at it. Maybe see it in action.

The buildings themselves were very open, lots of doors and windows and overhanging roofs. Most of them, he could see straight through to the other side. He saw people eating at round tables, knitting, washing clothes. Everything seemed to be out in the open. The room where he spent last night was the most closed off building in the village.

People stared at him as he walked by; some stopped what they were doing, others took note and carried on. His light skin was something to be seen. It made Telep uncomfortable.

They arrived at a small hut, completely open save four wooden posts at the corners. The straw of the roof was maroon as if caked in aged blood. It brushed Telep's hair as he ducked under its overhang. The dialogue amongst the group of older men and women standing inside ceased, and everyone's eyes shifted toward Telep as they formed a semicircle around him. Among them stood the tall, strong man with no blue markings from last night; the man who raised a calming hand.

Telep could see him much better in the light. He had a powerful face with thick eyebrows and a strong jaw. He wore a white, fitted sheet and long, black pants. The man stepped forward accentuating his height over Telep, who suddenly felt self-conscious about his behavior the previous night while in the haze of the toxic lightfruit. The man wet his lips; his eyes steady.

It dawned on Telep that he had no idea what these people were about to say or do. He had no idea what they thought, what they believed, how they identified as individuals, or how they identified collectively. Nearly everything he knew of these people, these inhabitants, stemmed from Xaella, a single person whose nature and disposition might only minimally reflect the collective. *And whatever they do will be irrefutable. I am one man and I am alone. They could sacrifice me on an altar, and my last words would be a slur of strange sounds.*

The strong man pointed at Telep with his whole hand, his piercing eyes unrelenting.

"Tele," he posed, his voice deep and smooth.

"Telep," Telep said with a polite nod.

"Tele."

"Telep," Telep confirmed with a smile.

"Tele," the man stated once more with an affirming bob of the head, as if declaring the matter settled. Then he pointed to himself. "Anomache."

"Anomache," Telep repeated, matching the tone and inflection as best he could.

Anomache touched his fingers to his chest and stepped back.

Telep looked around at the other faces. He recognized the older woman who had pounded his forehead the night before. A deep blue garment hugged her body, matching her striking eyes, contrasting her bronze skin and gray hair. Wrinkles circled her calm and wise eyes.

Anomache knelt and spread out a roll of leather on the ground and gestured for Telep to kneel down with him. Drawn on the leather was a map, a representation of the landmass. Telep recognized the beach where he arrived, the high cliffs to the east, and the shape of the present settlement. A wave of exhilaration shot through him as his eyes tracked along the route he had taken to get here. His chest churned as he looked to the south and saw that the landmass was indeed an island. It extended south a ways but eventually curved around on itself to form a finite block of land surrounded by blue sea.

His eyes moved over the drawing, analyzing it, studying it. He forgot about the group of people surrounding him. Using the length of the beach as a recognizable unit of distance, he approximated how long it would take to reach the southern coast. He also noticed that just off the coast of the southern-most tip, there was another small landmass nearly touching the edge of the map.

Anomache pointed around at the people in the hut, then to the village on the map. Then he pointed to Telep and then back at the map like he wanted Telep to point something out. *They want to know where I came from.* He thought for a moment, peering around at the curious faces. Then he got up and walked out of the hut. A couple people started saying something, but Anomache quieted them.

Telep walked a few paces and pointed to the ground. The people followed him out, staring at the ground under his fingers. Telep knelt down and made an outline in the dirt replicating the Mainland, just detailed enough for it to be recognizable as a mass of land. A circle had formed around him by the time he finished. He looked at them, pointed to himself, then at his drawing in the dirt. Some of them looked around, not under-standing, but Telep saw Anomache exchange a glance with the wise-looking woman. They understood.

———

Many questions followed. They wanted to know a lot of things, and Telep did his best to understand and satisfy their curiosities. They wanted to know how he got there, and he took them to the beach and showed them the remains of his boat. He relied heavily on Xaella to interpret and relay. He could communicate with her far easier than anyone else.

There was a distinct benefit to being in a group because only one person needed to understand, then they all would.

It was not long before he relaxed and breathed easier. They were not going to sacrifice him on an altar. They were not going to cast him off the island. They were not going to pit him against a wild beast.

For the rest of the sun's light, he answered questions and walked around the village. In one instance, he stepped away from everyone to relieve himself in the forest. No one thought anything of it. More confident now, he asked for water when he became thirsty, and they gave it to him.

The inhabitants showed him their way of doing things—bathing, washing clothes, collecting water. They showed him their crops. They broke bread together, though not the kind Telep knew. People seemed intent on him eating. They kept offering him more and more. He did not want to be rude, but eventually he had to decline.

Most of the people were friendly, though some remained cautious. Others glared with thick animosity, their silent eyes bearing down as if waiting for a mistake from Telep to justify their true desires.

Chapter 27

Over the next several suns, Telep learned a lot about the inhabitants and their village. Anomache was the leader. His words carried the most weight. Telep guessed that the group from the hut was made up of advisors, each of whom oversaw a different aspect of the community.

The way they lived interested Telep, but after a while, the fascination began to fade, and he found himself wanting to take the map of the island and explore. No such possibility presented itself as the curiosity of the inhabitants filled his time.

He paid special attention to how people perceived him and noticed a stark divergence. Most people seemed to like him. Some people presented him with gifts. One woman gave him a strange looking bone. It came from the jaw of an enormous animal he'd never encountered, and it still had some of its teeth attached. But others looked at him scornfully, like they were waiting for him to do anything wrong so they could use it as grounds for banishment. It wasn't that they had gotten to know him and decided they disliked him. They were naturally disposed. Prejudiced.

This attitude was most evident in Iphito, the slender young man who had kept watch of him the first night. He always seemed to be scrutinizing Telep with an abrasive stare. Telep could feel the eyes on him walking down the street, but having others with him made him feel safer, especially Anomache. No one would go against him. Anomache did not smile at him or even go out of his way to be nice like some of the others, but looking into his eyes brought a calm and secure feeling. A weight hung behind his eyes, a strength.

After a while, the leaders returned to their usual occupations and fewer and fewer people accompanied Telep around the village. The excitement of his presence waned.

One sun, he and Xaella travelled to the westernmost point of the island, which rested up on a cliff. It was not as high as the cliffs in the east, but it took some skill to climb, which felt good as Telep was aching to climb more than a tree.

Xaella watched in awe as he flew up the vertical terrain, stunned at his climbing ability. Though Telep was aware of Xaella's gaze, exercising his skill a little made him feel calm. He was impressed with her climbing skills as well. She climbed with precise moves like she knew the rock face well. He noticed her smiling and it made him smile.

When they reached the top, there was a small clearing where they could see far out to sea to the north and west. To the east and south stretched an amazing view of the island and its colorful trees and rolling hills of forest. At the edge of the cliff, they looked out to the horizon.

Telep scanned the line between sea and sky for a speck, a blip, a dot, but it remained perfectly flat. Unblemished. The final cliff of the Mainland stayed hidden, leaving this island in perfect isolation.

Looking over the western side, Telep's gaze fell upon a cove unlike anything he'd seen before. Towering over the deep blue water was a continuous rim of dark rock. It looked like a giant bowl. On one side of the cove was a dark sand beach leading into the forest. The other side had an opening in the dark rock leading to the open ocean. It was narrow at sea level, but broadened at the top such that it resembled a giant "V." At the top of the "V" on one side, the rock narrowed and then bulged into a large boulder, resembling a scrawny neck holding up a giant head. The water inside reflected a striking pure blue. Set apart from the rolling waves of the open sea, its stillness exuded a calm tranquility. The scene formed a clear image that sank deep into Telep's mind.

A short ways from the clearing at the top of the cliff, Telep came upon a circular marble basin with just enough water to cover the bottom. It reminded him of the Temple of Water back on Eveloce where there too was a marble basin that showed his reflection. Stepping away from Xaella, he leaned over the side and peered into the water; a lean, emaciated face stared back at him in horror. A long gruff beard, drawn cheeks, dark sunken eyes. *That's not me* . . . He felt cold. A clap of thunder rang out, and in a flash, rain poured down on the cliff, his reflection lost in a barrage of jumping droplets. Feeling Xaella's eyes, he buried his face in his hands.

Telep's journey washed over him. That man in the basin . . . *he* didn't row across the sea . . . *he* didn't slay the fanged beast . . . *he* didn't land on the beach of an unknown world . . .

Tears filled his eyes. The image he had of himself shattered. The face in the basin of the Temple of Water was gone. Irrefutably and irretrievably gone. He was so different now. Guilt gripped him like a vice. How had he become this way? How had he abandoned his family and friends and everyone he loved? He wanted to see his mom. He wanted to see his pa. He wanted to be the man Ell loved, not this withered wanderer.

He felt Xaella's hand on his back. It was so warm. He grabbed it, held it, and pressed it to his forehead as the rain slowly dried his eyes.

———

Now that Telep was experiencing the benefits of a community, he felt the need to contribute. He was afraid that having a job would keep him from exploring as much as he would like, but Xaella told Anomache about his climbing skills, and he was assigned the job of Cartographer. Their current maps of the island were generations old and some of the difficult to reach areas were not recorded in any detail. His occupation was to survey the island and create an updated map. He planned his routes so he would consistently pass through the main village, which enabled him to restock supplies and spend time with Xaella—eating meals, taking walks.

One night on a trip out in the forest, he had a dream where beautiful flowers surrounded him. They were the flowers he'd seen many times in the Temple of the Garden. Surrounding the flowers was not the beautiful hillside of Eveloce, but an abyss of black. He tried to step toward it but couldn't move. Looking down, he saw a spiraling weed clutching his ankle. Slowly, it spread out in all directions, overtaking the flowers like a wave. It choked and ravaged the flowers, their beautiful color lost in a fray of carnivorous green. Telep ripped his foot from the ground, but it was immediately seized again and sucked back stronger than before.

After consuming all the flowers, the weeds began growing up, as if climbing the sides of an invisible well. They grew higher and higher until the well was impossibly deep. When he looked down, the weeds had already consumed his legs and were spiraling up his torso. He ripped and tore at them, but they seized his arms and slithered up his neck to caress his face. He felt his body being consumed until he was ripped back into consciousness with something crawling on his face. He crushed it with a slap and wiped the remains from his cheek. The images of the dream burned too deep for him to fall back asleep.

———

In the sun's early light, Telep arrived at a grouping of caves, the sought landmark capping a three sun walk southeast from the inhabitant's main village. They were very different from the cave he'd found on the east side of the island, which had been part of a hot spring, similar to the one he'd seen back on the Mainland. These caves burrowed deep into the ground, reminding him of the one he nearly got lost in before reaching South End, where they were mining ingredients for dark powder. Telep felt a shudder as a swarm of wingfurs swooped from the cave and dispersed among the trees.

Looking into the black mouth of the cave, the image of the plume of black smoke rising over South End flashed in his mind. Ell refined what came out of that darkness. Within lay the ingredients that took her. Telep remembered being drawn into the cave on the Mainland, lured by curiosity. Now, looking into the blackness before him, he felt sick. No part of him wanted to step inside. He wanted it to stay black forever.

———

A few suns later, Telep travelled to the cove he had seen from the western cliffs. Seeing it from the dark sand beach only heightened the scene's majesty. The water was a pure and unblemished blue, the tall surrounding cliffs protecting its beauty. A secluded fortified oasis. The opening on the far side of the encircling cliffs —the "V" in the rock—looked like the curtain surrounding the cove had been torn from top to bottom, allowing minimal influence from the outside world.

Feeling the cool water lap over his feet, Telep realized this would have been a much better mooring location than the treacherous beach. At water level, the bottom of the "V" was wide enough for a vessel to pass through with ease.

Telep looked around at the fine, dark sand under his feet, vividly contrasting the blue water and black rock. This marked the gentlest transition from land to sea he had ever seen. Never before had he been able to walk from soft sand into peaceful waters.

He thought over the extraordinary things the Mainland had to do in order to manufacture a place where they could transition from land to sea. Even on this island, the borders were very fortifying. High cliffs spanned the eastern side, and thick forest slopes covered the north and west. The beach he landed on had smashed his boat to driftwood and left him lucky with his life. He had not explored the entire southern coastline, but if the existing map and the rest of the island was any indication, this cove was the sole outlying exception; the one hospitable entrance of a closed off land.

———

Telep ventured to the southern tip of the island, his pace slowed by the dense forest. He hacked his way through with a stone blade the inhabitants had given him.

Xaella taught him the importance of keeping a blade or walking stick in front of him when walking through the forest. On one of their walks, he felt her hand on the back of his shirt holding him back. When he looked closely, a small black dot stirred in front of his face. Taking a step back, he saw an enormous spider web spanning the path, ready to wrap around his face; the black dot was an eager spider crawling across its creation.

Xaella always impressed Telep when they travelled together. Her eyes flourished in the forest. She could spot things at a distance that Telep struggled to find up close. He often found himself beguiled by her abilities and learned all he could from her.

The southern tip of the island was rich with black sand and dark red rock. Thick, black roots from the edge of the forest wrapped around large red boulders scattered along the coast. This was the farthest south the land would take him. He looked at where he stood on the map, very close to the edge where a light speck disrupted the field of blue. Peering up, he saw the speck's embodiment out on the horizon, a bright seacliff rising in the distance.

When he had asked about the seacliff, the inhabitants responded that there was nothing of importance there, though he got the impression that no one had been there for some time. It seemed like a story passed down from an older generation who had explored and felt the rock under their own feet.

Telep gazed out at the seacliff, his eyes captive to its pull. He wanted to scrape together a raft and paddle to it, to explore it, to stand atop it and gaze beyond. Though the sea was rough and plagued with rocks, and venturing into it would be a great risk, the lingering hollowness in his chest fed the fire of his desire to do just that. But something stopped him. Something inside would not let him.

Telep thought of the Mainland and the bridge project endeavoring to reach this land. He thought about the murder on the bridge. He thought about Ep Brody's words: "Land is power. And power always seeks more power." He thought about Ep Salo having his way with the woman in his tent after dressing her up like the foreign body he held responsible for his son's death. He thought about Ep Brody's passion and leadership. The people of the Mainland had filled their plot of land and now they were expanding. And that was a beautiful thing.

They embodied the progressive ideals he'd learned in Eveloce. The men and women who were inspired by the idea of expanding their people and growing their territory would look at this beautiful land they worked so hard to discover and they would see it as theirs, as the spoils of their labor, as a crowning achievement for the expansion of their species. They would look on it with a feeling of privilege and entitlement. *They* pushed the veiled horizon back. *They* connected two lands. *They* were the best of their kind, those most deserving. And even without the hate driving Ep Salo, without the iron confinements and armor and soldiers; any notion of true cohabitation with a people found on their discovered land would be short-lived. They would take from the inhabitants what they needed and cast them aside as a lesser community, a community incapable of defending or protecting its own land.

Keeping his gaze on the seacliff, Telep took a deep breath. For the first time since leaving the Mainland, he felt needed in a way he couldn't ignore.

Chapter 28

A full season passed. Then another, and another.

Telep stayed busy, continuing his cartography, travelling alone for long periods. He learned about the inhabitants and assimilated some of their cultural norms but maintained a precise detachment. He continued to wear his own clothes, washing them as regularly as he had back on the Mainland, despite the inhabitants doing so with much more frequency. Though always polite, cordial, and accommodating, he remained closed inside. He built a wall around himself, guarding his truest thoughts. Everyone was kept at a certain distance, everyone except Xaella.

The two of them spent a lot of time together. She taught him the basics of the language, though it never felt fluid to him. Telep recognized that the other inhabitants did not like how much time Xaella spent with him, even those who were friendly. He could see distance growing between her and her people. The more time she spent inside his wall, the more detached she became from others.

Sometimes, Telep imagined himself adapting to the culture of the island, making friends and fostering relationships; throwing all of himself into the community. Something inside him wouldn't let it happen. The blanket of the past weighed impossibly opposed.

———

In the early twilight of a cloudless sun, Telep made his way through the village toward the beach, where the boisterous laughs and raucous exclamations of island festivities could faintly be heard through the trees. He chose a back route that was rarely taken, yet something felt strange. Stillness hung in the air of the empty village. But then, he noticed movement inside one of the huts. It was a naked woman sitting atop a man, rocking back and forth. It was Valasca, the head of medicine who had pounded her finger on his forehead the night he arrived. Eyes closed and mouth open, her face reflected torrid rapture. Her hands pressed into the man's chest, her arms pressing her breasts together. Telep looked away, but then he looked back. Something about her face . . .

Her eyes opened and trained on Telep, who froze, too star-tled to look away. Her stare was tepid, unembarrassed. She didn't stop or slow down or cover her body. She remained entrenched in her pleasure.

Telep looked away embarrassed and ambled out of sight.

Like their architecture, the people of the island were very open compared to the Mainlanders, but not so much that they would consent to outside eyes during coitus. The look on her face—something about it rapt Telep. Valasca simply would not interrupt her satisfaction, not for him, seemingly not for anything. She could have looked out and seen the forest raging in fire, and her reaction would have been the same.

When Telep stepped from the forest onto the open beach, he saw bunches of people scattered across the sand, all frozen, all facing the sea. Static. Still.

The smoke from the cooking fire wafted behind the trans-fixed chef, her hands caked in dry blood, the fire-licked ouroko charred black over the flames. Only the children moved, running across the sand with innocent laughter, impervious to the stillness seizing the atmosphere. Waves lapped at the feet of spellbound people. Statues decorating the sand. All were standing. Every single person. All heads faced the same way.

Telep followed their gaze out to sea where a large crimson sail broke the horizon.

A weight dropped in his chest. A gnawing pain stabbed in his stomach. The plans he had made churned in his mind. He took a deep breath.

He spotted Xaella out of the crowd and swallowed hard, his throat constricting. Taking her hand, he ushered her down the beach away from the others. No one noticed. None of the inhabitants had ever seen a sea vessel of this magnitude. Everyone continued staring as if in a trance.

Xaella's eyes trembled. Telep thought of what he needed to say.

In his time on the island, Telep had heard a story that now came to his mind. It was told around social fires as a parable, each telling embracing new details. In the tale, a young girl decided to walk to the highest cliffs in the land. She walked and walked, and in the evening, she could see no land higher. As she sat atop the cliff, enjoying the view of the surrounding sea, she heard a strange sound—a slow quivering hiss. The girl peered over the edge and saw a black fwykurr trapped on a ledge a few body lengths down. A fwykurr was a reptilian animal, comparable to a snake on the Mainland, except that it had tiny legs and webbed feet and three large fangs protruding from its mouth like a trident.

The girl figured that the creature must have fallen and was now stranded on the ledge with no way of getting food or water. It was wasting away. There were different versions of the story, and some had the animal crying out from the pain of consuming its own tail. The girl felt pity, and she climbed down to it. When her foot touched the ledge, three sharp fangs ravenously plunged into her calf. The sickly creature thrashed about, tearing its fangs through the soft flesh. The girl screamed and kicked and tried to pull the serpent away, but it was too strong. It kept biting deeper and deeper, devouring its way inside her leg. Soon, only the whipping tail stuck out from her calf. She pulled at it as hard as she could, but it only squirmed deeper. Then it was gone. The girl lay on the ledge crying. "Why!" she screamed. Then the pain faded and she felt the creature become part of her, its consciousness melding with her own, and in a moment of lucidity, she knew why. Slowly, her body rolled off the ledge and fell into the sea below.

Because of the story, "fwykurr," the name of the snake-like creature, was synonymous with danger.

Telep looked to the red sail in the distance, then back to Xaella.

"Fwykurr," he said, staring into her wide green eyes. She started to smile, but he grabbed her shoulders and repeated the word. Her smile vanished. He pointed to the sail on the horizon and spoke once more.

"Fwykurr."

Her breath shuddered; her eyes trained on his. Swallowing, she touched her fingers to her chest. He squeezed her shoulders, pulled her close, and spoke into her ear.

Her eyes deepened as she listened. His language was broken but his message was clear.

When he finished, he ran toward the forest.

———

That crimson sail on the horizon was the realization of what most of Telep's life had worked toward—progress, expansion, evolution, discovery—saying nothing of the work he did for the project directly. He and the Mainlanders would now become a multi-land people.

Even though Eveloce was not actively involved in the project, its ideals and principles, so near to Telep's heart, manifested so clearly before his eyes as he gazed out at the burgeoning sail approaching the new land. The bridge project was an effort to connect the Mainland with other lands. As an individual, he had done that. He was the only person to see both lands and know both peoples. In a way, he *was* the bridge.

Since leaving the Mainland, Telep often wondered what the Mainlanders thought of him, particularly those involved in the bridge project. He wondered how they remembered him and how they would receive him. Would they remember him for his contributions or would his final note of desertion ring loudest? Would Ep Brody embrace him, or smash his face with a husk?

Telep had not told anyone about the distant landmass he saw as a speck on the horizon; he used it for himself. He could claim that he hadn't seen it, that the only thing compelling his departure was the painful shroud of a shattered heart after Ell's death. He could do that, but Ep Brody would know the truth. The connection they shared would betray him, and Ep Brody would know.

Telep imagined Ep Brody stepping from the ship to this new land.

———

Telep's preparation guided him through his tasks. Once in his hut, he threw supplies in his satchel and headed back the way he came. Deep breaths filled his lungs without recess as he made his way through the forest back toward the beach, though they did nothing to lessen the insistent clawing of nerves in the pit of his chest.

His mind churned.

The ship was here. His past life had tracked him down like a lost sheep.

He knew of only one place the ship could moor—the cove. But he did not know how long it would take them to find it. He needed to be there to meet them. He decided to walk the beach for as long as he could on his way to the cove so that he could monitor the ship.

When he stepped out from the forest onto the sand, people still gazed at the growing vessel. With another deep breath, he started down the beach toward the cove. A voice barked out. Telep turned to see Iphito storming toward him.

"Hajah!" he shouted, his teeth grinding in intensity, his stride spraying sand. Other people began following.

Telep felt their eyes and stepped back.

"Hajah!" Iphito railed again. "Hajah" was the island's term closest in meaning to "visitor." It did not have a negative connotation until it came off Iphito's tongue.

Iphito's strong, bony hands connected with Telep's chest and he pushed hard. Telep stumbled back, almost falling to the sand. He showed his open palms, but Iphito pushed him again. And again. He stabbed his finger out at the ship, then at Telep, then back at the ship. He unleashed a tirade of angry speech, talking too fast for Telep to understand any of it.

He wants to know my connection with the ship. I told them I came from the sea, and this ship comes from the sea. They are scared. They must have wondered what was out there. Maybe their ideas are frightening.

Telep kept his open palms in front of him, trying to calm Iphito before many others congregated. But he wouldn't calm down, and they did gather. They formed a semi-circle around him. Others started speaking as well, but in the swarm, Telep couldn't make out any of it. One young girl in the crowd stared up at him as if he had just drowned a rabbit. One man next to Iphito stood taller than the rest. His eyes bore pure contempt as he jabbed two fingers into Telep's chest. The semicircle constricted around him. Telep thought about running, but he knew he couldn't. Then it would all be over.

"Zuk!" commanded a voice from down the beach loud enough to silence everyone. They all turned to see Anomache parting the crowd. His stern eyes never wavered from Telep as he stepped in front on him with a domineering presence. All the time Telep had been on the island, he had known Anomache to be a fair and honorable man. He had treated Telep well. Now, with a scared and angry mob surrounding him, his life was in Anomache's hands. He had no choice but to divulge his plan and plead for trust.

———

The light seemed to fade with each step as Telep paced westward down the beach toward the cove. Before allowing him to depart, Anomache had searched his satchel and removed the knife. He also assigned two men to accompany Telep and make sure he followed the spoken plan. They were given knives.

Telep's breaths streamed fast and shallow in a mechanical rhythm. The closer the cove drew, the harsher his chest churned. He tried to distract himself by thinking of the sand under his feet and not where those feet were taking him. In the draining light, the ship was still headed straight for them. He remembered gazing upon the island when *he* approached it from the sea. From afar, the bright tan sand looked like a perfect place to land. But when they got closer, he knew they would recognize the prohibitive strength of the crashing waves and seek another place to dock. The question was: Would they go east toward the red cliffs, or west toward the ultra-dense forest? If they turned east and sailed around to the back of the island, they would not reach the cove for several suns, but if they turned west and followed the coast, they could happen upon it during the night. Would they enter the cove in the cover of darkness or wait for the sun's light?

Telep thought back to his lesson in the Temple of History when he learned of The Unseen Act. This was the turning point in the war that ensued after the West Isles proclaimed themselves independent from the Mainland over one hundred solars past. Specifically, it was a massacre. After tactfully removing the sentries, nine Nexian spies killed four hundred West Isle soldiers in one night by sneaking into their tents and slitting their throats. They were able to do this by drawing the West Isle army onto a patch of land where the spies had been training for a full cycle. They knew the land, and they won the war.

Because no one on the ship knew the land, Telep guessed they would dock in the light. That would give their superior weapons and training all the advantage they would need.

The inhabitants were not warriors. It would be a challenge for them to even create the illusion of a formidable fighting force. They had few weapons, hardly even using them to hunt. Most of their animal meat came from nets and set traps. Their weapons consisted of sharpened sticks and small stone knives. They were a people of preparation, and they were not prepared.

The two men struggled to keep up with Telep as the beach ended and they plunged into the dense forest. Though they were far more adept in the forest, Telep moved faster. What should have been a cautious exploit of evading thorns, sharp brush, and dangerous bugs, Telep turned into a tactless gauntlet of punishment.

He stormed through the forest like a force of nature. The two followers tried to keep up while still evading the dangers but couldn't match the speed allowed by Telep's brute appetite for pain. Feeling the cuts and scrapes helped distract him from the deep, yawning chasm in his chest. He tried not to think about it, not to feel it, but it was there, and it stayed there, and it grew.

Small rays of moonlight shone through the thick canopy and speckled the forest floor. The farther west they travelled, the steeper the terrain became, but Telep did not slow; he moved faster and faster. The men behind him wheezed and gasped for breath, but he felt no such need. His lips remained pursed as steady breaths coursed through his nose. Physical exhaustion would not tear his mind from the darkness. He wished his muscles would ache and his lungs would catch fire, but they didn't, and his body whisked up the mountain like an ephemeral machine, feeling no pain.

He shuddered when he thought of the stillness awaiting him once he arrived. A burning feeling erupted inside of him, and he stopped. He glanced down, his chest pulsing rapidly. Seizing the sides of his head, he doubled over, vomiting across the ground. He fell back against a tree, his breath quivering. He peered down at the red stripe of vomit on the forest floor refusing to seep into the dirt. Shoving himself from the tree, he stepped over it and continued on.

Chapter 29

A small lump of rock pressed into Telep's back as he sat at the top of the "V" overlooking the mouth of the cove, the moonlight painting white edges on the blackness around him. He could have found a more comfortable spot or padded the lump with an extra shirt from his satchel, but he didn't. He leaned against the neck of rock that held up the giant boulder sitting atop the gateway to the open sea. From his perch, he could see the calm water of the cove to his left and the rolling ocean waves to his right.

The rock surrounding the cove was a deep matte black, smooth and sturdy, completely unlike the brittle complexion of the Mainland's final seacliff. This rock was elegant, strong, alive. He peered down the slope of the "V" to the inky black water at the cove's entrance.

The two men charged with his company rested below on a wider ledge jutting off the inner wall of the cove. The climb to Telep's vantage point was beyond their skill level.

The night crawled by as slow as the full moon across the sky. He sat there with the lump in his back and thought of Ell, his Root. He thought of their nights together, and the way she smiled and kissed and laughed.

The thoughts of her calmed him for a while, but then saddened him and sent small teardrops falling to his shirt. He pushed his mind elsewhere. He thought of his mother—how comical she looked when she ran, how frenzied she got over small things, how patient she was with him, how important she made him feel. He thought of his father—how they used to wrestle, how he never let him win but made him feel confident anyway, how he chewed his food so loudly, how he conveyed so much without saying a word.

As the night wore on, Telep drifted into a tranquil state, almost as if lured by the natural setting around him. The stillness of the cove comforted him. Sitting there in the silent dark, his gaze glided around the cove and the moon and the water and the rock.

The melodic croon of a songbird pulled him from the dream-like state. He looked around, startled by the increased visibility. He could see texture in the trees behind the cove's shore, the fluttering hair on his white knuckles, color on the water's surface. Dawn was beginning to break.

When he peered over the ridge out to sea, a wave of fear coursed through him, electrifying his nerves like a broken tooth in a windstorm. He blinked hard and squinted, his eyes shuddering as they beheld the ship sailing dead on.

It was unmistakable. It was there. It was here. *This is it.*

The ship was the size of his thumbnail when he stretched his arm out in front of him. Telep's hands began to shake. He squeezed his satchel as hard as he could but couldn't stop them. With a trembling hand, he reached into the leather sack, pulled back, and reached in again. He looked to the ship, then to the cove, then back to the ship. Everything was spastic, nothing still. His eyes sprang to the men watching over him and saw them asleep on their ledge.

His heart was a boot kicking from the inside, sending wave after wave of raw nerves through his body. He tried to breathe but couldn't find enough air. He looked to the shoreline on the inside of the cove, but it was still too dark to see anyone. His hand shot back into the satchel. When he found what he wanted, he gently wrapped his hand around it, took a breath, and let it go. Then he wiggled his hand to the bottom where he gripped his stone and pulled it into the light. There was just enough brightness to see its pale blue and orange color. It fit perfectly in his hand. His next breath came a little easier. He rolled it over in his palm, feeling its roughness. With erratic breaths and a pounding chest, he sat waiting, his stone rolling over and over in his hand.

The light had grown enough for him to see the shore, but still there was no one. He wondered if Anomache and the inhabitants were following the plan. *They must be in the forest.* Behind the dark sand of the beach, the forest was a dense maelstrom of foliage; even in broad sunlight, he would not be able to see into it.

He looked around the cove. He was the only outlier in the calm welcome of nature. The ship now took up two fingers of his outstretched arm.

The men on the ledge below were awake now. Telep had yelled for them to go to the beach, but after exchanging a mysterious look, they remained on the ledge.

The ship drew closer. Telep felt the momentous weight of an approaching moment larger than any human capacity. Whether he was ready wasn't relevant. He could be prepared, but he could never be ready.

This is how I will be remembered. Two worlds are coming together, and I am between them. I am the tip of both spears.

He looked to the shore, and then to the ship, and then to his hands. Still trembling.

The ship spanned three fingers of his outstretched hand. He could see dots moving on its deck. In the center, there looked to be a gray rectangle, but it was still too distant to distinguish.

The crimson sail swelled nearer. His heart beat faster. So many thoughts swarmed his mind. He tried to beat them all back and think of nothing, just leave his mind blank, but that only made it worse. Never had nerves gripped him so tightly. His body constricted around him. He tried to focus on a single thought but couldn't. The approaching task was too big for mental acuity. A thumping pulse beat in his neck. The inside of his lip was raw from biting. He questioned his plan. He questioned everything.

The ship spanned a full hand. Its enormity was baffling, daunting, and beautiful all at once. The dark wood of its bow split the water into trails of white as it careened forward. Its mast raised so high that Telep hardly looked down on it. The sun rose over the tree line and illuminated the bright red sails. It was a marvel of human ingenuity to behold.

Telep could see individual bodies moving on the deck as the ship neared the entrance of the cove. The large gray rectangle materialized into a formation of soldiers heavily laden with silver armor that glistened in the sunlight.

Telep's vision blurred and tears fell from his eyes. He felt reality gripping him in the ashes of his darkest dreams. He retreated into thoughts, as if a great epiphany would stop what was to come.

How could this be happening? What is the worth of a piece of land?

Telep knew what this piece of land had meant to him when he arrived, and he knew what it had come to mean. And though he tried, he could not reconcile its significance with what he saw in front of his eyes.

Voices called from the deck, voices of his people, voices speaking his tongue. Music to his ears. They called out orders, and the sails lowered, and a row of oars protruded from each side of the hull and began rowing. The pace slowed, and the ship adjusted its trajectory to thread itself through the cove's entrance.

Someone was leaning over the bow staring down into the water, probably scanning the depth.

In the light of the heightening sun, the water inside the cove radiated a luminescent blue, a mirror of the sky, a deep abyss of nature's purity.

Telep scanned the deck for Ep Brody, though there was little hope of picking him out from this far away. Ep Brody seemed to understand him like no other. The man didn't know him as his parents knew him or as Ell or even as Caleb knew him, but the man understood him. Ep Brody understood him because of what they shared—*the drive.* They sought *the unknown.* They shared the drive that Ep Brody forged into the bridge project. They shared the drive that took Telep to the top of every mountain.

The drive was a comfort in the wake of Ell's death. It pushed him to leave the Mainland. It satiated him in new ways with each passing sun on this new land.

His drive has brought him here. He is here as I am here. I could be on the beach waving welcoming arms inside the cove, but everything in my life . . . every truth I've ever learned, every choice I ever made . . . has brought me to the top of this ridge.

Shaking the tears from his eyes, Telep slung his satchel over his shoulder and rose to a crouch. Wedged in the rock was a string. He grabbed it and reached into his satchel. He removed two sticks, both yellow at the tip. He closed his eyes and pressed his forehead into the rock.

"Fuck. Fuck. Fuck."

Looking down, large dark ripples pierced the still oasis of the cove's water. Telep lifted his stone and gazed at it, feeling its weight heavier than ever. He touched the sticks to its coarse surface and struck them across. They crackled into flame, the heat reaching his face. Voices called from below. A final breath surged into Telep's chest, a void holding everything and nothing. He moved the flame to the string where the fire jumped and scurried along its length, hissing like a snake as it moved up the rock and into a burrow carved in the top of the "V."

Telep shoved his stone back into the satchel and climbed

down the cove's inner wall, moving away from the opening. He tried not to look back but couldn't help himself.

The bow of the ship breached the cove and people on the deck came into view. No one saw him. Telep climbed further down and away until he reached the ledge where the men charged with his company had been, not even noticing their absence.

His eyes whipped back to the entrance. The ship was nearly inside.

A loud crack rang out sending a tremor through the rock, echoing around the walls of the cove, accentuating the silence that preceded it. The men on the deck whirled around in all directions searching for the source. The sound of cracking stone emanated from the top of the "V." The boulder balancing there leaned forward and began to fall. Snapping and cracking and scraping rock. Time slowed for its massive scale. It crashed into the slope of rock and tumbled down with increasing speed.

The ship was all but inside; only the stern was still passing through the entrance. When the boulder struck the dark wood hull, the ship jolted like a toy. Its keel blew out from under it and the whole ship jerked onto its side, sending a host of soldiers and men skipping across the water like a handful of pebbles all thrown at once. Some flung high in the air; others smacked right into the water. The mast snapped from the deck, its attached ropes yanking it down and ripping it across the water in a blur of white. It sent a spray of water onto Telep's feet.

He dropped his satchel on the ledge and gazed out at the scene around him. Everything seemed surreal. The ship lay on its side slowly rolling over. Bodies scattered along the railing of the ship; some clinging to it, others snared by it. Flailing white patches littered the deep blue water. The crooning songbirds were drowned out by screams.

Everything slowed in front of him. Screams of pain, screams of terror, cries for help, thrashing water—it all coalesced into a fray of insatiable sensation that echoed around the cove walls.

Standing in the shadow of such horror, the churning in Telep's chest twisted into a knot.

A large clump of bodies thrashed near the center of the dark blue abyss, kicking and yelling and moaning. Sunlight glistened off metal amid the lashes of white water. Desperately, they clawed at the straps of their armor, trying to release the heavy metal dragging them down, dragging their mouths under the surface, the water capturing their screams and gently carrying them down to the black abyss below.

A few able-bodied swimmers moved in the water; those who were not wearing armor and weren't injured. Some of them tried to help the soldiers; others made their way to shore. When a group of them got close to the dark sand, a host of inhabitants charged out from the forest and surrounded them, shouting and wielding wooden spears. The people from the ship huddled together, frightened, holding up their open hands.

Telep sprung off the ledge and dove into the water. All the mayhem above instantly silenced. All the screaming, crying, and thrashing for life reduced to a single note. Above him, people struggled for their lives in a shimmering blanket of white. Below him, the blue expanse slowly faded into a merciless black, a black so pervasive that a million suns could not light its depths. It was the end-all of nature where the unknown reigned supreme. It was death; it was life; it was absolute.

The blue expanse around him felt like the temple of nature itself, the origin from which all else chaotically stemmed.

The cold water was so clear he could see through it like air. The salt burned his eyes, but it wasn't painful. He saw legs thrashing near the surface, the ship on its side gently bobbing, ironclad soldiers far below, slowly fading into the blackness, leaving trails of bubbles floating back to the surface.

Somehow Telep felt protected, like this was a safe place. He felt enveloped in the purity of nature's womb. Surely, in this place nothing would happen that was not supposed to happen. The natural order would override any challenging force. This was an all-encompassing aether more powerful than the sporadic will of man.

Such thoughts seeped into Telep as if they were coming from the water.

Propelling himself with powerful strokes, he glided toward the shore. Numerous struggles for life loomed in front of him. Staying close to the cove wall, he avoided the larger clumps of people.

He came upon a young man screaming in agony while trying to prop his head on the rock at the cove wall as if his hands were bound behind his back. Telep grabbed him from under the arms and lifted him. The skin of the man's forearm had a twist in it and a pure white bone stuck through.

A loud crash surged around the cove, followed by splashes and screams. Telep looked over and saw the ship completely turned over. Some of the people next to the capsized vessel tried to climb onto the hull but no one seemed able.

Telep pulled the young man along the cove wall. As he kicked through the water, he felt the man's leg drag behind like seaweed. The muscles in his legs began to burn and salty water splashed in his mouth as he tried to take a breath. He pushed the writhing body onto a small ledge and immediately continued toward shore. Ahead of him, the fray began to thicken.

He came upon a woman kicking around in circles and holding a hand over her eye. Grabbing her by the collar, he started pulling her toward another ledge. Her free arm lashed around, striking him in the side of the head. He winced at the blow, but held her tightly, and kept going. A man thrashed in front of them, panicked and screaming. His arm hung from his shoulder like a wet sack. Before he could react, the man's good arm grabbed Telep's face. Nails scratched his skin, then seized his hair. Out of breath and muscles burning, Telep started to yell something, but the words were extinguished when his mouth was forced under the surface.

The water numbed his eyes. The panicked hand jarred his

head and yanked him deeper, holding him down, drowning him. Telep let go of the woman and hit the man's wrist over and over but he couldn't break his grip.

A sting of panic raced through him, and he started flailing under the surface. He tried to roll the man under him so that he might get a quick breath, but the man had too much leverage. Telep's lungs were on fire. He kicked and thrashed with everything he had. The white sky floating on the surface taunted him; he was so close. With a kick, he lunged upward for one desperate breath. The side of his face felt the tickle of air as it broke through the surface. He reached up with his lips, but with a slight tug from the hand, his gasp sputtered into a violent gurgle as cold blue flowed into his nose and mouth. He felt the coldness pervade his body and it provoked a stillness . . . a tranquility.

A flash of his parents shot into his mind, a flash of Ell. The last bit of air he had in his lungs tickled his lips on its way to the surface. He looked down into the dark abyss. The woman he'd been trying to save sank below him, her hand no longer covering her face. Her torn eyelid released a small trickle of red wafting up like a plume of smoke as she drifted down toward the dark.

The coldness in Telep's chest cleared his mind. He seized the man's hand and pried back his first finger. He wrenched it and the bone snapped instantly releasing his grip. Telep threw his head above the surface and expelled a jet of cold water from his mouth before a large gulp of air surged into his lungs. He took three rapid breaths before diving back under the surface.

The woman had sunk much farther, but Telep kicked down after her, his eyes trained on her wounded face. The water went from cold to freezing. The pressure in his ears grew with every stroke, and right when he thought his head would implode, he seized her collar and swam back toward the white light.

When he pushed her body up on a ledge at the wall of the cove, exhaustion swarmed into every muscle. Fire flooded his lungs, and his heart pounded uncontrollably. Though ensconced in cold, his body felt hot . . . independent of the freezing water around him.

His fingers folded over a hold on the dark cove wall so he could hang limply in the water. The collective screams and pleas of the space now sounded eerily quiet. With a hollow breath, he looked back at the scene around him.

The fray was all but gone. Lifeless bodies littered the water and only a few active swimmers remained. The water was no longer a luminous blue throughout. Surrounding the overturned ship spewed a bright red, the dye slowly expanding. Other patches of red hugged the floating bodies strewn about. There was no longer any glimmering metal amid the splashes. No one wearing armor could tread water this long. Everyone still in the middle of the cove appeared injured in some way, able to stay afloat but unable to head for shore. Their cries resonated in Telep's chest. His heart felt like it was pumping acid.

Except for the few people clinging to the walls of the cove, everyone else was either on shore or approaching the shore where there waited a long line of inhabitants wielding wooden spears and herding everyone into one cluster at the far end of the beach.

Something caught Telep's eye from across the cove, high up on the wall. Movement. It was a body, climbing fast toward the top of the ridge. A Mainlander; he could tell from the clothes— sleeves ending at the elbows. The movements were clean and swift, ascending the ridge as if mastering it long ago.

Telep tried to yell out, but his voice caught no traction, his weakened whisper remaining close for only him to hear. He coughed and vomited pink water. He coughed again and cleared his throat. He was about to call out but stopped. A familiarity in the figure struck him. He imagined it was himself climbing the cove wall. He imagined it was he who had sailed across the ocean only to be led into a trap. He imagined looking into his own eyes and seeing the drive of humanity, its beauty and its horror, and he knew it could not be stopped. He watched the figure reach the top of the ridge and disappear over the other side.

Telep's breaths quivered as his gaze swung around the cove from one pained face to another; from one slice of ruin to the next. The scene burned into his consciousness like a searing brand.

Chapter 30

The island absorbed the calamity like death absorbing life. Time kept moving, and people carried on, but the trauma remained. Death hung in the air and understanding eluded everyone. People tried to make sense of what had happened.

They thought. They thought while they ate, while they worked, while they slept, while they talked about other things. They thought while gathering the hundreds of bodies and sending them off in the pull of the waves. They tried to understand while they altered several buildings to incarcerate the Mainlanders who had made it to shore. They tried to understand the larger world that had filled their world with blood.

Inhabitants kept coming to Telep for answers, but he knew he could not say anything to satisfy them. Seeing so many lives lost in a bath of blood disturbed them in a way that could not be overcome quickly.

Telep never looked over the dead bodies and never visited the captured Mainlanders. He conferred with Anomache on how they should be managed but never looked on them himself.

Sporadically his thoughts harped back to the Mainlanders, his people, being herded on the beach by sharpened sticks. He remembered how they looked. The collective fear on their faces became recurring images that haunted his dreams. They had no weapons, no strategy, no surviving contingency. Most of them were injured, many tearing clothes to wrap around wounds. But they did so carefully, so as not to provoke any rash actions from the myriad of virgin faces clutching their weapons in the fear of first blood.

When the confusion of securing the surviving Mainlanders died down, Anomache came to speak with Telep, his face grave, his eyes penetrating. Telep answered his questions as blatantly as he could. He told him why the Mainlanders wanted to come, what they had to gain, what they were willing to lose. He told him the Mainland's infrastructure was far more advanced. Anomache asked how he had made the boulder crash down on the ship, and Telep explained how dark powder was made and where the cave and hot spring were where he mined the ingredients.

Anomache absorbed each answer with a slight bob of the head, not once looking in any way satisfied. He asked why the Mainlanders came with weapons and armor. The question made the void in Telep's chest ache. He stared into Anomache's eyes, wanting to spew so many lies. He wanted to say it was a misunderstanding. He wanted to say it was for protection, that they themselves feared being attacked. He wanted to say it was because a body had drifted to the Mainland long ago and plagued several people. But he knew these were lies. A body may have been found and spread a disease, but that was not what armed the soldiers aboard that ship.

The real answer lay in a place as dark as the cove's depths, where Telep now found himself trapped, forced to gaze into humanity's darkness. He stared at Anomache with envious eyes. And after taking a breath, he told him about the body found on the Mainland.

———

Telep was alone. In a crowd of people, he was alone. The inhabitants had differing views of him. Some saw him as a monster for killing so many people. Others thought he was their savior, rescuing them from the horrors of beyond. He didn't talk about it. Inside, he ran from the event that defined him in the eyes of everyone. His isolation grew.

Xaella stayed with him. They hardly talked, but she was there. Being with her calmed him. She was the only one on the island who made him feel connected to anything. She stayed with Telep in the suns following the bloodshed. She stopped working. She made him eat when he had no interest. She made him drink when his lips cracked with dryness. She touched him and hugged him and drew him close when the glaze of death clouded his eyes.

———

As suns passed, the weight of the event swelled in Telep. Images from the cove consumed his mind and channeled his thoughts. His eyes became vacant, his face without expression. He withdrew. He withdrew from the inhabitants and from himself. He tried to withdraw from Xaella, but she wouldn't let him, though their time together was different now.

Before, when Telep walked with Xaella, they enjoyed the silence between them. Now, as they moved through the forest, the silence seemed to get louder. It was an ineffable feeling that leaked into the trees around them, into the calls of the birds and the cracks of the sticks.

As they walked, Telep imagined Xaella looking out on the cove's red water, her face reflecting a look of innocence lost—pained and ugly. He imagined her being sickened by what he'd done.

Apprehension leaked from the cooing mouth of a winged lizard. The sound rang out in regular intervals, each time arresting the forest for a brief moment. It was unrelenting, and it gave voice to a trepidation in Telep, a feeling he didn't want, a feeling that persisted even after Xaella snatched the creature from its tree and cracked its neck.

Xaella made the fire.

Before the red sail appeared, Telep would get lost watching her speed and grace performing different tasks. She was so skilled in what she did. She would feel his reverent gaze, and it made her smile having him admire the way she did something as mundane as make a fire or hang a hammock. She felt special that he saw her ordinary as something extra.

Those suns were gone. Telep didn't watch her make the fire. His gaze remained on the lifeless body of the winged lizard.

The lizard meat tasted cold and bitter.

———

Suns passed.

Sitting around a communal fire, Telep stared at a black bug flying in front of him. He watched it buzz around the orange smoke pouring from the burning vines. He watched it land on the ear of a young inhabitant boy and crawl inside. He watched the boy scream and cry trying to claw it out. He watched Xaella put her lips to the boy's ear, suck out the bug, and spit it into her hand.

———

Suns passed.

Telep watched an old man scoop jelly from a large nut. He watched the man scrape out every bit of jelly the nut had. He watched the man throw the nut's shell in the dirt. He watched the shell sitting there. He watched people walk by and step on it. He watched a long time.

———

Suns passed.

Telep stared at a young tree growing on the edge of the village. He pulled a clump of the tree's roots from the ground. He returned to watch the tree every sun. He watched as the leaves changed color. He watched as the branches drooped. He watched as the wood darkened. He watched the tree die.

———

Telep stood on the ledge of the cove looking out at the peaceful blue water. He picked up his satchel and pulled out his stone, staring into it one last time. He tossed it down and watched it sink into the black abyss below.

———

Telep saw the world moving around him, but he didn't feel part of it. He didn't even have to recall the images from the cove or reflect on what he'd done; the emptiness encompassed all.

No matter where he was or what he thought about, it was there. And it made him yearn for nothingness.

He knew Xaella was saving his life every sun. The emptiness in his chest wrenched the life out of him and she replaced what she could with her own. He didn't seek her; she gave it to him with the dedication of a mother bird feeding its young.

One night, Xaella woke up and found Telep crouched by a fire pressing a searing hot knife to his chest. His hands were covered in gashes and blood from gnawing his knuckles in his sleep. She jumped on him and wrestled the knife away.

"I have blood on my hands! It won't come off. It keeps coming back," he yelled as he smeared blood over his eyes.

She wrapped her arms around him and held him close as he screamed sounds of his native tongue.

"My consciousness is poison. It's too dark. I didn't want my story to be this dark! I didn't want this. I don't want my line in the Temple of History filled with death. I couldn't stop it. I can't stop it. It's not going to stop! It's not going to stop. It's not going to stop."

She held him as he sobbed through the night.

———

Suns passed.

Cycles passed. She stayed with him. Inhabitants thought him insane . . . possessed . . . a reticent recluse. People pushed for Xaella to let him go and get back to her life. But she stayed.

———

One morning before dawn, Telep walked to the edge of the village. Creatures filled the air with noises and calls. At the end of a lonely road, he heard a sound that stood out from the rest. It was not a buzz or squawk or chime or chirp; it was a voice and there was a familiarity in it. He had heard it before.

It stopped, then started, then changed, then continued. It was hard to pick out from the natural ruckus, but Telep followed it as if being pulled. He followed it into the forest. It got louder as he treaded into the thick brush. The voice was full. He continued, stepping carefully across the forest floor, the dew on the foliage dampening his clothes. It grew louder still. Then it stopped. He pulled back a large leaf and froze. He could see into a small clearing where Valasca straddled a younger man on a bed of blue satin leaves, her hips thrusting wildly, head tilted back, eyes pressed shut, mouth open screaming a silent ecstasy. Her fingers pressed into his chest as if trying to control an uncontrollable pleasure. He watched her, the way her body swayed in its movements as if in sync with an unheard song. A horde of intimate memories flooded his mind, the glaze lessening in his eyes. Valasca's rhythmic moaning resumed, and he let go of the large leaf, his gaze retreating to the forest floor.

Slowly, he started walking back to the village. Something was different. The leaves danced, and the trees swayed. The early light of the sun illuminated the beauty around him in a way he couldn't help but recognize. It took his mind back to the first time he walked through the forest of the island—the way it looked, sounded, and smelled.

Then Telep saw a strange looking creature, a moth with satin wings and a mouth that spiraled around. It reminded him of something. His eyes followed its jittery flapping through the forest. The creature landed on a strange looking plant and inserted its spiral mouth into a spiral stem hanging off the plant. Then, as the creature struggled for nourishment, the plant produced carnivorous teeth and snapped shut, consuming it whole. Telep's eyes deepened. He couldn't look away as the plant slowly swayed, its digestive system churning. Then its mouth opened, and a plume of crystalline spores sprayed out, falling across the forest floor.

———

Telep strode to Xaella's hut and woke her. He did not tell her why he wanted to go south, and she didn't ask.

The sun neared the horizon when they arrived at the southern tip of the island. Its light painted a stripe over the waves as they stepped into the cool water. The sand slowly swallowed their feet. They stood looking out across the black sand and dark red rock, beholding the thick black roots from the edge of the forest that wrapped around the large boulders scattered along the coast.

They brought two hammocks but only used one. Night consumed the hazel milk in the sky and left them in darkness, rocking in their hammock. Xaella lay with her back to him holding his hand just under her chest, which rose and fell rhythmically.

Telep gazed up at the sky. The partial moon drifted overhead but he didn't look at it. He closed his eyes. His mind churned, pulling him into a visceral, dream-like darkness where his thoughts became ultra-clear.

He saw himself.

All those people are dead because of me. I am the reason that water turned red.

But they were going to kill or enslave every inhabitant they found.

I can't know that for sure.

You do *know it.*

I betrayed my people.

You have no people.

Ep Brody appeared from the darkness of his mind; his piercing eyes hard as stone. In that moment, Telep knew what would be said. And he heard it. And he saw it.

"You sank our ship," Ep Brody would say, his voice low and smooth.

"The people of the island were going to be killed," Telep would reply.

"It's okay."

"What's okay?"

"It's okay for people to die."

"No," Telep would try, almost begging for agreement.

"Yes, it's okay."

"N- no."

A tear would roll down Telep's cheek.

"Yes. Death is okay if the larger beast is still growing."

"Stop."

"All is okay for the sake of humanity moving forward. That is our purpose."

"How can you say it's okay when people would die?" Telep would sob.

"Telep, death is part of life. Death breeds life. It gives life perspective and purpose. Death enriches the soil and grows our food. Death gives life more meaning than smiles and frowns. What you did . . . all you did . . . was hinder human progress."

Telep's face would shrivel into a pained grimace.

"That's not what I want."

"And that's not what you will get. Progress cannot be stopped, only delayed. It is bigger than you, and it is bigger than me. You cannot stop our growth. We are a collective species and we grow and fall together. By sinking that ship, all you did was create an obstacle. And like water building up behind a dam, eventually we will overcome your weakness and pour over. You think you saved those people? Look at that girl lying with you now. You think you saved her? All you did was cheapen her humanity."

Ep Brody would speak calmly and assuredly like the weight of his words were infinite.

"You spent your whole life honing your craft, pushing into the unknown to evolve your community. But you don't even know what evolution is. An evolved mind would have seen the larger picture. To evolve is to distance yourself in order to discern a higher form of truth, to see beyond the plight of a select few to the beauty just beyond. You didn't climb the ladder high enough and humanity suffers for it."

"I know you care about people," Telep would insist, a large lump straining his words from the back of his throat.

"I care about all *people,"* Ep Brody would say. Then his gaze would fall in genuine disappointment. A silence would pass between them where they understood each other and were disappointed by each other.

"Human exploration is everything to me. But—" Telep's voice would crack. *"But the way it was being done—what was going to happen—it took away the beauty. It took away our beauty. We made ourselves ugly in the face of the unknown. We gave up the bond we had with each other. It can be a beautiful thing. I—"* Telep would bite his lip and his gaze would fall, waiting for the crushing response he was sure would come.

Fidgeting in her sleep, Xaella squeezed Telep's hand and pulled him from the darkness back to the hammock where he lay with her at the southern tip of the island. Ep Brody was gone. Their imagined conversation was over.

As it was, Telep had the final word and a weight lifted from his shoulders. The void in his chest calmed.

His eyes parted and light flooded in, cutting through the glaze. The swelling glow of dawn overwhelmed the forest. Everything around him looked different—alive. He thought of climbing a tree and tasting the fruit on its highest branch. When he breathed it felt like the first real breath he had drawn in many suns. He felt Xaella's body against him, and suddenly she felt different. He stared at her smooth, dark skin. He slid his hand over her hip and pressed his body into hers, and she moaned softly. The thick bunches of her hair tickled his chin and he nestled into it.

He drew another breath.

He felt living. Broken, but alive.

———

Without waking her, Telep slipped from the hammock and once again stood on the shore. The moon receded and the water grew. He thought about his parents, how they loved him. He thought about Ell in her white nightgown on the last night they spent together. He thought about Caleb and hoped his drive would find the right vessel and he would be happy. He thought about Vetra and the secrets they'd shared. He thought about everything that had brought him to this shore, to these grains of sand rising between his toes, to *this* sight, with *these* feelings, at *this* time. He thought of the cove and its beauty. He thought of the dark wood of the ship's overturned hull still floating in the pure blue abyss. He thought of the figure scaling the wall and escaping into the island. He felt a tingling on the back of his neck, eyes from somewhere in the tree line.

He gazed out at the light seacliff piercing the horizon in the distance. And he felt it in his chest. And for a fleeting moment, he smiled.

For Further Discussion

1. How does Telep change in the story? How did your opinion of him change?
2. Did Telep do the right thing by destroying the ship?
3. What is the significance of Telep's blue and orange stone? For what purpose is it used?
4. What ideals influence Telep the most? What people?
5. When does Telep finally allow himself to sob? What change does this signify for his character?
6. How do Telep's dreams reflect his state of mind?
7. Do you have a favorite passage/scene? Why did it have an impact on you?
8. How do the instances of characters literally having blood on their hands connect to the theme of guilt?
9. Who is the Mainlander who escapes the cove? What evidence is there?
10. What is your interpretation of what happens next? What evidence suggests this?

Some Interesting Facts About
Rock Climbing

- Rock climbing is a fast-growing sport and will soon be included in the Summer Olympics.
- Free Soloing is a method of climbing where no artificial aids or support are used and no ropes or protection will catch your fall.
- Most of the climbs Telep performs in the book could be categorized as free climbing. This is a form of rock climbing in which the climber may use climbing equipment such as ropes and other means of climbing protection, but only to protect against injury during falls.
- The climbs Telep performs in the book are extremely dangerous because advanced safety measures have not yet been developed.
- When Telep climbs the giant seacliff at the end of the bridge project, his climbing style could be characterized as mountaineering because he uses a pickaxe to assist his climb. Typically, pickaxes are only used when climbing ice or rockfaces that are very soft in composition.

Real World Inspiration
TEMPLE OF CONQUEST

- Mark Broe wrote his first draft of *Temple of Conquest* longhand on a two-month trip to Guyana. He wrote the first half in the city of Georgetown and the second half while camping in the rainforest east of Bartica.
- The final seacliff at the end of the bridge project was inspired by a seacliff Mark climbed on the coast of Corregidor when he visited the Philippines in 2007.
- When Mark was in the Philippines, he tried to row a small boat onto an isolated beach in Puerto Galera. This inspired Telep's struggle with large waves in Chapter 23.
- While traveling in Guyana to write *Temple of Conquest*, Mark met the person who inspired the character of Chandradaul.
- The scene showing the hillspeople carving a pig mirrors an event Mark witnessed on the streets outside of Georgetown, Guyana.
- The beautiful setting of the cove is based on Crater Lake in Oregon.

- Mark encountered a very dangerous situation in Glacier National Park. While climbing, one of his holds began to crack. He had to jump to another platform before it broke off completely. Mark mirrors this experience in the scene where Telep is climbing the small cliff rising out of the bay of the fourth seacliff.
- The descriptions of Telep traveling through the forests of the new island were inspired by Mark's experience camping in the rainforest outside of Bartica, Guyana.

About the Author

Mark Broe is a writer and sound recordist based in Michigan. His educational background in Media Production naturally led to work in the entertainment industry. Mark records sound for movies, commercials, and TV shows. He has also directed, edited, and written scripts for short films and a web series he co-created called Boosh!.

Mark used inspiration from his own adventures for his book, *Temple of Conquest*. Rock climbing is Mark's favorite hobby, so many of the events and interactions the main character experiences come from his own encounters. The first draft of *Temple of Conquest* was written while Mark was on a two-month trip in Guyana. He was inspired by the cities and rainforests of the country, and some of his characters are based on locals he met while traveling. His main desire for this book is to provoke discussions about conquest and Manifest Destiny.

While *Temple of Conquest* is Mark's first published work, he has always been a writer. He wrote several episodes for his web series as well as the short film LUCY & LIONEL (2020). His forthcoming second novel carries fantastical themes similar to *Temple of Conquest*.

When he is not rock climbing or writing, he is probably playing chess or volunteering for Friends of Grand Rapids Parks.

**If you've enjoyed climbing mountains
with Telep in *Temple of Conquest*, you will also enjoy
diving to underwater peaks with Chris Black in
Into a Canyon Deep, the first installment of
James Lindholm's adventure series.**

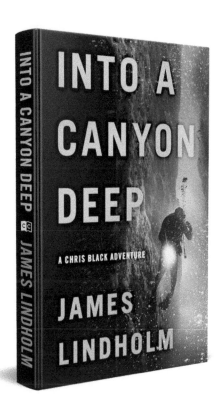

Excerpt: Into a Canyon Deep by
James Lindholm

Movement down to his left alerted him to a man and a young boy climbing along the rocks close to the water. Probably tourists, Chris figured. The red-faced man carried a gut that was seriously taxing a bright red Carmel T-shirt that no self-respecting local would be caught dead wearing. His jeans weren't faring much better. And he was wearing flip flops. It was no small hike to make it all the way out to the point with a child that was probably only five or six years old. The poor guy's discomfort from the exertion was palpable even at a distance, and wearing flip flops would not have helped anything. Chris was surprised the flip flops had made it as far as they had.

The blonde child, wearing a blue T-shirt emblazoned with a Superman logo and red shorts, leapt from rock to rock with more facility than the man. Not every step was surefooted, and there were quite a few loud warnings from the man, who was likely the kid's father, but the indomitable spirit of childhood won out. Chris smiled at the thought that the kid was probably very good at video games and other digital challenges but was nevertheless fearless out in the world of real physical dangers.

Chris returned his gaze to the open ocean and wanted to re-focus his mind on his own dad. But the father-son dynamic playing out in the present won out over re-hashing those of the past.

He looked back down to see the boy was now several feet ahead of the man frenetically moving over the rocks just above the high tide line without watching the water. If he wasn't careful, one of the coming swells was going to take him out.

Come on kid, Chris urged silently as he felt his own muscles tense, turn around. *Never* turn your back on the ocean.

"Hey, kid!" Chris yelled as he stood up, hoping at least to get the father's attention. "Watch out for that swell!"

Too late. The next swell rolled in, an amorphous blue-green predator stalking its prey. It reached the boy and effortlessly lifted him off the rocks, drawing him back into the water. He quickly disappeared below the surface.

The father screamed, but Chris couldn't hear what he said.

Chris removed his smartphone and wallet, placing them safely in a crack in the rock behind him. The kid was going to be history if someone didn't get to him very soon. He turned to and prepared to make the ten-foot drop to the water, waiting for the next surge of water and trying to keep his eyes on the boy, who was back at the surface for the moment and struggling.

The next swell came and Chris leapt, feet first and shoes on. There were too many dangers beneath the surface to enter head first, and though shoes would make swimming more difficult, against the rocks they would be invaluable.

He hit the water and immediately opened his arms into a "T" position to halt his momentum and to keep himself at the surface. The frigid water instantly closed around his chest, drawing away his breath.

Chris knew that the fifty-five-degree water was not the most immediate problem. Though water wicked away body heat at more than thirty-two times faster than air, he planned to be out of the water well before hypothermia had a chance to set in. The real threat came from being right in the impact zone as the swells from the north Pacific came crashing in against the barnacle-encrusted rocks.

Two quick overhand strokes carried Chris over to the boy. The boy's eyes were wide with panic and his lips were already turning blue. Chris grabbed him with his left arm while trying to get purchase on the rocks with his right.

"It's okay, big guy. I've got you. Let's get you out of here."

The boy was surprisingly light. Chris realized that he might be able to swing him up to the father if the ocean cooperated. No sooner had that thought crossed his mind than the swell receded. Chris held on briefly, but realizing that the water level was dropping too fast and too low, he released his grip and let the current take them with it.

The boy screamed, probably thinking that they were going to be sucked out to sea.

"It's alright," Chris said, "We'll be out of here . . . NO!" Chris was preparing to ride the next swell up high enough to pass the kid back to his father, when he realized that he was jumping off the rocks, apparently to try and save them.

The father hit the water awkwardly, arms flailing, just as the next swell came in, and he dropped like a rock. Chris held fast to the boy and squared his feet against the rocks. As the wave swept in, Chris used his leg strength to keep them off the rocks while leaning back to create less resistance against the oncoming water, pulling the boy briefly underwater. He could feel the boy struggling but held firm.

Popping his head back above the surface, Chris scanned the area for the father. The man was floating at the surface a few feet away. He wasn't moving and he was bleeding from a gash across the forehead.

Chris realized that his range of good options was rapidly shrinking. The rock wall was steep and high as far as he could see in either direction, offering no obvious point to climb out of the water.

He decided to get the boy out before returning for the father.

If he tried to rescue them both simultaneously, all three of them would surely die.

Side-stroking toward the lowest point on the cliff a few feet away, keeping the boy's head above water, Chris spotted two men climbing down toward the water's edge. The two men formed a human chain, placing the lower of the two just within reach of Chris.

Chris once again timed his approach with the swell and rode the surging water up the face of the cliff. Using his feet to climb as high as possible, he grabbed the boy with both hands and thrust him upward to the waiting arms of the passerby.

Seeing the man grab the boy, Chris launched himself off the rock with his feet and began to search for the father. Fewer than ten minutes had passed, but he could feel the cold water zapping him of energy. He had to find the father fast before they were both crushed against the rocks.

Chris shivered uncontrollably as he backtracked to where he had seen the father last. He was starting to feel pain from cuts on his arms that he must've sustained earlier without realizing it. He leaned back and tread water for a minute to collect himself for one final push. He judged the probability of success to be very low, and he was beginning to wonder if he'd get out himself.

And then something bumped him from behind. Chris spun around to find the father floating behind him, face down and not breathing.

Chris flipped him over and supported his head out of the water. He gave two short rescue breaths but struggled to keep the man's face above the surface while doing so. He needed floatation.

His cold-addled mind drifting, Chris looked around him to see what, if any, options he had remaining. The swells kept coming in, but he and the father were now far enough away from the rocks that being crushed was not an immediate concern. He twice looked past a large yellow jacket floating next to him. The third time he looked at it he also heard the men yelling down to him from the rocks above.

They were yelling something like, "Grab the jacket!" which Chris found interesting since there was a jacket right next to him.

He looked at it more closely. It looked like someone had tied off the sleeves, neck and waist to make a rudimentary floatation device. Brilliant.

A large swell pushed Chris and the man toward the rocks. When Chris's left shoulder slammed into the barnacle encrusted rock wall the pain electrified him long enough to break his stupor.

He turned the man to the right, grabbing the yellow jacket and placing it underneath the man's torso. Chris then began to kick as fast as he could. With shoes on, he found the flutter kick normally used by breast "strokers" to be the most efficient means of propulsion. He swam in thirty-second increments, stopping only to give the man two rescue breaths before proceeding onward.

Later, in the relative comfort of the nearby Ranger station, the two men who'd been on the cliff above described to Chris how amazed they were that he managed the ten-minute swim around the corner and into the only protected inlet within hundreds of yards. Chris listened as he warmed up with a detached interest, for he remembered none of it.

CamCat Books

Visit Us Online for More Books to Live In:
camcatbooks.com

Follow Us:

CamCatBooks   @CamCatBooks   @CamCatBooks